CAST A LONG SHADOW

CAST A LONG SHADOW

LEENA LANDER

TRANSLATED BY SEIJA PADDON

SECOND STORY Press

CANADIAN CATALOGUING IN PUBLICATION DATA

Lander, Leena, 1955–
Cast a long shadow

Translation of: Lankeaa pitka varjo.
ISBN 0-929005-66-X

1. Trials (Witchcraft) – Finland – History –
17th century – Fiction. I. Title.

PH355.L26L313 1995   894'.54133   C95–931761-9

Originally published as *Lankeaa pitkä varjo*
by Kirjayhtymä Oy (Helsinki, Finland)

Cover illustration by Laurie Lafrance

*Second Story Press gratefully acknowledges the assistance of
The Canada Council, the Ontario Arts Council,
the Translation program of the Ontario Arts Council
and the Finnish Literature Information Centre*

Printed and bound in Canada

Published by
SECOND STORY PRESS
*720 Bathurst Street Suite 301
Toronto, Canada
M5S 2R4*

PREFACE

CURRENT INTEREST in what is often labelled "new historicism," or, for that matter, aspects of the chronicle, has given birth to many contemporary novels. Leena Lander's *Cast a Long Shadow* is one of them. Lander is a writer in whom — in her own words — a particularly shattering historical chain of events, especially from the woman's point of view, "rang some sort of a bell." *Cast a Long Shadow* is a novel about the seventeenth century witch hunt on the Åland islands during which seven innocent women were condemned to die. Lander's fictionalization of the events is based on actual transcripts of the court proceedings. Macabre as it may seem to a contemporary reader, court proceedings dealing with witchcraft and magic were perhaps the best known cross-cultural events in sixteenth and seventeenth century Europe. Familiarity with the legal proceedings involving witch trials not only spread far and wide in Europe but, as we know, to the colonies as well.

The Åland islands, the setting of Lander's novel, lie off the southwest coast of Finland. Although not remarkable in terms of size (the area encompasses only about 1500 square kilometres), Åland has had an extraordinarily colourful history. The wars that spread over centuries and were fought over territorial claims along the Baltic trade routes invariably involved Åland. Although place names such as Åland show that Swedish colonists had settled along what is now part of the southern coast of Finland as early as the tenth century, it was during the high middle ages that Sweden's conquest of Finland became the most notable Swedish achievement in the battles for strategically important territory. The political impact of the conquest lasted until 1809, while its social and cultural effects have lasted to the present day. After Finland was annexed to Sweden, Swedish governmental, judicial and class structures, tempered by Finnish custom, became the accepted modes of social order in Åland and the inhabited southern coastal areas of Finland. Swedish was the official language of the entire domain and continues to be the official language of Åland within the independent and bilingual Finland of today.

During most of the middle ages, Åland was the investiture of aristocracy who, from Kastelholm castle, watched over their own interests as well as the interests of the Swedish Crown. The castle saw both the splendours of magnificent court life and the horrors of destruction and pillaging during various wars. Eventually, because of a fire in 1620, the castle lost its importance and the counties of Finström, along with Jomala and Sund (mentioned in the novel), became independent judicial districts looking after, among other things, their own taxation.

The witch hunts of the 1660s brought about a horrific and now infamous twist to the otherwise rather uneventful judicial life on the islands. It is fitting, perhaps, to illustrate the historical context in which the witch trials and the subsequent beheadings and burnings at the stake took place. Only forty years earlier, King Gustav Adolph II of Sweden had decreed that since hunting for deer on the islands was the privilege of the king and those of his guests who had been given special permission, hunting by others was punishable by death. No death penalties were ever carried out, however. Instead, those found guilty were driven out of the country.

In Lander's novel the realistic narrative terrain is complemented by her lyrical language, which blends the workings of her imagination and historical research in a way that gives the novel a fascinating and haunting voice. As readers we are faced — once again — with the rather unsettling thought that neither logic nor sanity can be put to definitive or lasting terms. We are reminded of the fact that when we see the present differently, we cannot but also see the past differently, and the shifting and changing of our responses become the sources from and ways in which literature such as *Cast a Long Shadow* is born.

— SEIJA PADDON

ÅLAND ISLANDS

SUND
FINSTROM
JOMALA

Arctic Circle

TORNIO

LULEÅ

S W E D E N

KRAMFORS

Gulf of Bothnia

F I N L A N D

TAMPERE

ÅLAND ISLANDS

TURKU

HELSINKI

UPSALA

STOCKHOLM

Gulf of Finland

*When a dwarf casts a long shadow
the time for the sun to set is near.*

— GIOSUÈ CARDUCCI

*I*MAGINE BEFORE YOU a semi-cloudy inlet of the sea. It is neither stormy nor calm. This is not one of those days when the sea is on the attack, but neither is it one when it timidly approaches the shore. No, scenery is a state of the soul, and this view must be grey and somewhat gloomy, but not entirely without hope.

A man with badly fitting clothes and laced-up shoes plods along, his feet sinking into the sand. The shirt is bluish and wouldn't look too bad on someone else; the trousers are brown and hopelessly old-fashioned.

The picture is not yet complete, not without the straw hat which, at this moment, lies on the crest of a dune and the man goes back for it, realizing he left it on the ground when he got up.

A straw hat? When a man wears a straw hat these days he has to be a little odd, or else he is a dandy. Perhaps he imagines himself Vincent van Gogh, pretends to be an artist.

You yourself stand on the terrace of a summer residence, and it is from there that you have watched the man struggle in the soft sand. You think it a nuisance that he is coming directly towards you just now when you had thought of spending a peaceful week with your own people. The last thing you'd want right at the moment is to be obliged to make conversation with a stranger.

"I'm the man you've been looking for!" he says brazenly before you've had a chance to exchange a greeting. You try to think whether you have been looking for someone, but you can't remember. He sits down on the nearest chair and wipes his face with a monogrammed handkerchief. With a cloth handkerchief! In these days of disposable, thin, soft paper ones!

"I was expecting you, and yet you broke the continuum!" he says. You must now consider the possibility that perhaps he is the landlord you haven't met because you signed the lease with an agent.

"What did I break?" you ask.

"The scraping of the clamshell against a rock on the shore!" he says, serious. "And the cry of gulls in the fog!"

You burst into laughter, relieved, and because of the inadvertent humour inherent in his dignity.

"Is that all?" you ask amicably.

The man pulls a pair of glasses out of his pocket, wipes sand off the lenses and puts them on. They're not sunglasses but reading glasses. What does he need them for?

"And the slow erosion of the granite mountain!" he continues obstinately.

You're getting irritated.

"Anything I now say can be used against me and, in fact, must be, because that is precisely the reason I am here!" he says.

At this point you finally wake up. He must be crazy! You're civilized enough not to laugh right in his face, but neither will you remain sitting in his company.

Now you're afraid that your holiday will be ruined because of this man. You're worried he'll be a nuisance. You reason that he has chosen you, specifically, to be the recipient of his bothersome confessions.

You are right.

Even when it rains, you can see his middle-aged, medium-sized figure on the terrace. Again and again he settles down into a garden chair and doesn't care that there's water dripping from the outdoor light fixtures onto his shoulders.

Can you imagine this?

This is my nightmare.

And I shall be your nightmare. I have accepted my part in the chain of events because I have no other choice. But are you ready to grant me the right granted even the most wretched petty criminal: the chance to confess? Don't belittle my words. Confessing is very important. Having an opportunity to tell one's own view of a case, a criminal is able to free himself of guilt even if he cannot be free of the crime itself. Besides, it's part of healing the soul: while he speaks, he lets out all that is base and wrong; by rendering a judgement on himself, he redeems himself.

In order to have the confessions appear in the light their nature deserves, I need to undergo a metamorphosis. I read old books, browse through files, scan yellow manuscripts, and when I find a chilling enough plot, I disgorge my inner being into it. Just like into this one now. The Psilander case. Nils Psilander sentenced seven innocent women to death. The legal process contains a strange collection of distorted testimonies, lies obtained through torture, concealment, juridical inconsistencies.

"This story is not for me," I said, though I knew it already had a grip on me.

Against my better judgement, I drag the mouldered body of the provincial judge, Nils Psilander, from the ground of Åland, and I begin to shape him anew. There's no reason for him to rest another day because I do not rest either. There are several documents about his life and I use every one of them: make him do it all again, make him repeat everything he did while he was still among the living. But, nevertheless, it would be silly to argue that my Nils Psilander is that same Nils Psilander, subject of those documents.

It is possible that mass murderers don't even know how to feel remorse, how to suffer from a guilty conscience. We ordinary people who slap our children, hurt the feelings of our fellow human beings, ignore our elders, quarrel, connive, envy, drink to excess, we know how the feeling of regret and self-loathing gnaws at us. But the real monsters don't know. If you think you saw tears in the eyes of the general who ordered the execution of Ayacucho's children, you are mistaken. They showed films about the concentration camps to Nazi leaders at the Nüremberg trials. Rudolph Hess sat in his seat openly disinterested, at times falling asleep, at times reading a novel. He even burst out laughing when there was something funny in the novel he was reading. What he was accused of couldn't have interested him less.

But my judge looks for a chance to make a confession. His thoughts whimper fretfully like foxes in a cage. Just like mine. The difference is that in the end I intend to skin mine, once I've had a chance first to imagine what they look like running free.

There's the reason why the man walks on the beach and the day is as cloudy as his mind. The man walks along the beach and wears a straw hat that doesn't suit him. The weather is neither stormy nor calm. The man holds onto the straw hat that he almost left lying on the ground.

He wants to confide in you, because that way he gains something which to him is as important as life.

Why wouldn't you give him that chance?

☙

PART ONE

The shadow cast by the conscious mind contains hidden, repressed, often nefarious aspects of the personality, the extreme branches of which extend into the lower reaches of uncontrolled emotions and primitive behaviour, reaches which encompass the entire historical point of view of the subconscious.

— C.G. JUNG

ONE

Chapter One, in which the Judge admits to being guilty of the murders and gives some interesting clues about human nature.

𝓘'M THE MAN YOU were looking for. I expected you, but still you broke the continuum: the cry of gulls in the midst of the salty fog, the slow erosion of a granite mountain, the scraping of the clamshell against the sand on the beach. Anything I'm saying now can be used against me and so you should, because that is precisely why I am here. You made me wait a long time; I managed to get used to my painless state of being; the years have smoothed my restlessness the way they've smoothed those dark red rock surfaces.

You must have your reasons for the delay. And what would make you hurry? My crimes will never grow old. Actually, I have reason to be grateful for having had a chance to listen to the muffled sounds of steps and the roar of the sea above me this long before my name is sullied so that everyone will despise it. But, as I said, I've become used to waiting, to mild self-loathing, and I've learned to enjoy the mystery of disintegration. When now I must pull myself together, gather stature for the sake of a full confession, it pains me and tears me apart.

I have caused the unnecessary deaths of seven women. That is true. But are you sure it wouldn't be in your own best interest, after all, to let them be? If you drag them too back from the material void which has given them complete freedom and peace, you take up quite a burden to bear. You become a participant, an accomplice.

I don't doubt your ability to endure watching the torture. You are familiar enough with it; you've been an onlooker before, heard the cries, seen the shattered expressions, the body's helpless, comical convulsions, the playful patterns saliva and blood make on perspiring skin. But what then when you realize you have awakened the others as well to endure their hell all over again; when Anna B. begs you to let her visit her child just once; when you see her rage against the unfeeling stone walls; when you hear her repeat again and again the same impossible request, and you know that within her there's an invisible finger pointing directly at you!

Do consider that you are then her God, her maker, but she doesn't care a whit about your sympathy, your righteousness, but accuses you of having given her her life only to take it away from her.

And if you do endure Anna's accusations, shrill female hysteria, then Margreta H.'s timid plea is all the more unbearable. She is taken prisoner soon after giving birth; besides the newborn, she must leave four other poor little ones at home alone.

And how does your sense of justice endure witnessing Kjellinus' triumph? I can't give you the satisfaction of telling you he came to a sorry end. I could comfort you with a small fabrication which wouldn't necessarily hold true. I could — to please you — decorate his parson's behind with burning hemorrhoids, with tender, bloody growths resembling pea-pods.

But all that brings meagre joy when one knows what ought to have happened, how evil ought to have had its due. Some do get their just desserts, but not everyone, and that will be a bitter pill for you to swallow. You begin to hope I would change the course of events, make them more pleasing to you; for some reason you see it as your right to expect that. But that is precisely what I cannot do. You have to understand that even I have my Great Notes from which one doesn't deviate, the score, like any orchestra conductor. My score is the truth, knowledge, life itself — that one cannot touch! The great themes won't bow to my will. If life feels pity for Ingeborg, then I'm glad to be the first one to set her free, but if it doesn't, I'm powerless.

You want to hear how I propelled seven women to their deaths. You know that the question concerns a crime, and the traces lead to me, Nils Psilander, Assize Court Judge of Åland county. You have found the court records, but for a few torn-out pages at the end, and you think you know, more or less, the whole truth. You just want to hear it from my mouth, demand that I finally confess my guilt and lay bare my motives.

And yet the court records cannot tell you the most essential part of the events. Not in any way. Just imagine you find a church organist's file from the same period, the first page of which tells that it contains the notes of a Passion. Thrilled, you take the folder to musicians and ask them to perform the main themes of the piece. They look at the papers for a moment and then tell you that — based on the notes you have given — they can't, as if by magic, produce the compo-sition for you the way it was performed in its time. You hold in your hand a kind of musical shorthand; the composer has noted on paper only the lowest tone flow, the *basso continuum*, the part intended to accompany solo voices. It is the solo voices that are missing. And in addition to everything else, the composer is expected to create independent, in-between notes within the note frame of the main bass, imitating the principal themes of the solo voices, and to create a suitable background for them.

You think I'm talking nonsense. You suspect I'm scheming to win time to plan an escape route, or at least a proper defence. That's a needless fear. After all these long years that covered my hair with the dust of wind-blown Silurian limestone, it feels strange to return to a state of being where one blushes, feels passion, cries, rages, feels regret and is horrified.

But I intend to come back to that. I'll tell you about those women who — in the years of mercy 1666-1670 — languished under the roof of Kastelholm castle waiting for the court's verdict. You demand that I tell you about the women, which means I have to tell you about the men. If men are the main characters of an event, then the matter mostly concerns only them, but when one tells of women, the true principal characters are still men. This belongs to those aspects of the world order which I cannot change.

So: it all began with an old woman who wouldn't admit she was old....

CHAPTER

TWO

✺

*Another very short chapter in which the Judge tells
old Karin P.'s sad but deserved fate.*

*I*T ALL BEGAN with old Karin P. who was tired of being just
an old woman.

She had left her cottage because it had nothing to offer
her but death by starvation. She had tried to support herself
by begging, but even that didn't seem enough to sustain life.
That is why, in the end, she had made a pact with the Devil;
Satan gave her the powers of a seer-woman, and Karin P.
began to wander from house to house telling fortunes and
practising magic.

Whenever anyone became a victim of wrongdoings, they
sent for her. If a lamb was stolen, Karin P. asked to hear the
names of the suspected thieves. When the right name was
mentioned, Satan appeared at her feet in the shape of a
hound with black spots, a hound that barked and made a hell-
ish sound although it was inaudible to human ears.

In November of 1665 a group of neighbours marched to

· 21 ·

my office to report a theft. Eight sheaves of rye had been taken from the field of the farmer Mats Pålsson. They knew who the guilty party was, thanks to the beggar-woman.

Karin P. understood that she was an important witness in solving the crime. She was proud of her art, and the fact that a real gentleman, the Judge, questioned her while a crowd of peasants was present made a great impression on her. At the sitting of Finström's Winter Assizes, Karin, her chest puffed up with pride, admitted everything they wanted to know about her and much more which no one even asked besides.

When she noticed we were particularly interested in the hound of Hell, after a moment's hesitation she eagerly explained the very root of the matter. The examiner didn't say an unkind word to her during the whole sitting of the Assizes; torture was never even mentioned.

Karin didn't need much encouragement to admit that she had visited Blue Mountain, the Devil's mountain where sinners crawled on all fours pursued by hairy devils. At times the devils were on the sinners' backs, at times they hung onto their stomachs, and they had the women screaming from some unnatural sensual fervour, not from fear, as one might easily have imagined.

Afterwards, having experienced old age as I have now, I believed that Karin P. fed into her story all her longing for pleasures that had left her before she was ready to relinquish them; it's only after the waters dry up that we know the well.

Being aware of the inherent danger in certain confessions, she was amazingly exact about details. Because another woman had had to suffer the Church's punishment after coming by a fortune in butter through sorcery, Karin stubbornly denied taking part in that sin. In some way they probably even felt meaningless to her, the spells about churns and butter which every peasant woman knew; it was altogether different to participate in what was going on in the Blue

Mountain fêtes where Beelzebub himself worked his fiery dasher.

My astonished expression, the jurors' unsettled movements, and the court recorder's wildly flying hand blew Karin's imagination into full sail; she told how a dark man had taken her late aunt to the Blue Mountain orgies. When Karin was at her most excited describing the delicious details of this Witches' Sabbath, I interrupted her by clearing my throat because the confession was obvious nonsense.

"Based on the words of God, one knows exactly how those who suffer because of their inability to repent and mend their ways do not end up in the situation that she (Karin P.) was now describing, and without a doubt Satan had described to her, but that they end up in a torture-chamber otherwise known as Hell ..." was written into the court records.

It wasn't wise to interfere with Karin's voluntary confession, but I was a man of principle and couldn't accept an obvious lie. Not only did the entire jury, robbed of a juicy tale, get irritated now, but so too did Karin P. herself. She would be very much offended unless her confessions were good enough for His Mercy the Judge, so perhaps His Mercy the Judge and the impertinent jurors would make up more suitable reports themselves! Why would ordinary peasant women as well as hairy devils be accepted at Blue Mountain, but not her own late aunt? Family pride threatened to cause Karin to deny even her earlier stories.

The Parson was clever enough to understand that the successful continuation of the trial required humouring Karin P. He explained to the woman why her claim caused offence; no one wanted to belittle Karin's confessions any more than the importance of her late aunt, who would be quite acceptable at Blue Mountain, true enough, but for the fact that the aunt was dead. When time takes leave of a human being and she ends up in Hell, according to God's laws she stays there. In other words, it wasn't at all possible that Karin's deceased aunt, whatever kind of a person she had been, could be an exception!

Karin was appeased. But she was clearly beginning to sense there was something behind the matter at hand, something other than just the sentencing of a thief who had stolen rye. She told the court of having seen how a clergyman had driven the Devil from an epileptic, and she announced that she herself was sick. "Satan comes into me and I can't do anything about it," she said. I realized from her words that Karin P. believed we considered her case to be some unusual malady. She didn't understand that she was already sitting in the seat of the accused.

Still, at the stage when she was taken prisoner and the matter was referred to a higher court, Karin P. lived in the belief that it didn't concern a truly serious crime. I believe she didn't understand the seriousness of the matter until the day of her sentencing.

After Karin P.'s confessions, there was no doubt that she fulfilled about all the conditions of a person who employs *magiam divinatoriam*. Only one sentence was possible: God's Holy Law, the Law of Moses, Exodus 22:18, dictated that a witch shall not be allowed to live. Karin P. had to be beheaded with an axe and her body destroyed by fire. When the sentence was read, the woman began to wail and cry; she begged us to show mercy to an old, foolish woman. She asked to be forgiven in case she had offended me or the jurors; she reproached her loose tongue; she beseeched people to remember how she, without any sorcery, had saved a little girl from drowning when the girl fell through the ice. She spat on the guards; her legs gave out; she cursed me.

Perhaps at that moment she evoked pity in me. It is difficult to tell after all these years, but I didn't lose any sleep over her. I was thoroughly repelled by the fact that she had sold her body and soul to the Devil, though no one else would have wanted the latter any longer. Her lewdness horrified me; how could such strong sap still swell in an old wrinkled body! Her ugliness was depressing; from the bent frame peered a sunken face with a red scar. What was there about her that could have touched anyone?

On the sixth of August, the year 1666, she was beheaded and her body burnt. And during those four months while she was lying on sour-smelling straw in her cell, she had the opportunity for revenge. It didn't occur to me that I ought to have disallowed visits to Kastelholm castle. I didn't do that, nor did the prison guard keep a list of the visitors.

It so happened then that before her sentence was carried out, Karin P. had named thirteen other women guilty of the same crime as she.

THREE

ↄ

Chapter Three, in which the Judge meets Maria N., a poor woman who was hooked because of her infant son; followed by a bothersome, but necessary demonstration of the basic function of thumbscrews.

*M*ARIA N. WAS THE FIRST woman to be taken prisoner because of Karin P.'s accusations. Maria had high cheekbones, large breasts and was halfway through her thirties.

A couple of days before Karin P.'s execution all those she had denounced were questioned together with her. The event brought to mind the frenzy of a market day, rather than any sitting of a court of law. I let the others go, but I couldn't dismiss Maria N. because in addition to the witch woman's testimony, there were other charges against her.

Three weeks later Maria N.'s case was brought up during an extra session of the Assizes, which was held at the home of the Emkarby village Police Chief. The accused travelled there with me in my carriage.

The woman wouldn't say anything at first. I saw that she tried secretly to sniff at her underarms. "Were you not

allowed to wash yourself?" I asked, and she answered "No."
After a moment she added that she had been allowed to wash,
but only once, and even then she hadn't been allowed to
change into the clean clothes her husband had brought her.

For the most part of the journey she was staring out at
the sea. It shimmered blue between chalk stone boulders and
the sun dappled its surface. A man wearing a hat made of
straw passed us on the road. He raised a cloud of dust with
every step as if his bare feet were looking for something in
the sand. "I wonder what the man is looking for?" I said just
to say something, and the woman answered "probably nothing," and went on to say how good it must feel to be free to
raise dust like that. She looked out to the sea and her face
became tense and wrinkled, but not the faintest sound came
from her throat. An iron manacle had chafed small red
moonslivers on her wrist.

She had no shoes. When she climbed onto the carriage, I
saw that her leg muscles were tanned up to the knees, and
from there up the legs were white. During the journey she
wiggled her toes the way small children do.

There were a lot of people in front of the Emkarby Police
Chief's house. As the prisoner stepped down from the carriage, an old man with blood-shot eyes and yellow tooth
stumps sticking from his mouth forced himself in front of her.

"Slow down, witch bitch, sweating won't help matters
any!" the old man said, squatting and peering all around.

I pushed the man aside and led the frightened-looking
woman indoors as swiftly as possible.

The doors were closed, but the faces of the jurors, twelve
Finström farmers, were as curious, taciturn and sweaty as
those of the people waiting outside.

Elias Hasselgren, the Chaplain at Getha and brother to
Finström's parson, who suspected Maria N. of profiting from
his brother's cattle by sorcery, introduced me to the Provost.

Hasselgren was very interested in the thumbscrews, the functions of which the torturer had already demonstrated to him before our arrival.

"Even the papists have managed to produce something permanent," the Provost said, showing the thumbscrews to me.

"It's very simple; a finger in here and then one begins to turn the screw!" Hasselgren, already an expert, explained.

The Provost insisted that for all its humble appearance, it was an unbelievably effective apparatus. I replied that I entertained no doubts concerning the device.

There were serious accusations against Maria N. Karin P. had seen Maria's mother at Blue Mountain and she had also seen Maria herself coming from there. In addition, some neighbours had told of seeing the woman throw silver into water and utter incantations. As if that wasn't enough, she had cured a boy by cursing the sickness away. When the testimonies were of this calibre, there was reason for the torturer to be present at the proceedings. If the suspect refused to cooperate, the thumbscrews would be the only means by which they could get at the truth.

As was expected, Maria N. didn't admit to anything at first. She claimed the information was a lie, and with tears in her eyes refused to speak ill of her dead mother.

"How can you believe that Karin from Emkarby village would have gone to her death with a lie on her conscience?" I asked.

"I don't know," she answered.

"What about the child, whom five people saw you save?" I insisted.

The accused looked at me with a crafty piety.

"God healed the child," she said.

"But you have thrown silver into water?" I asked.

"By mistake, perhaps," she admitted.

"Not on purpose?" I wanted to know.

"No, not on purpose," she insisted.

Elias Hasselgren's questions about his brother's cattle received equally off-hand answers. The accused denied or evaded everything else as well. It was quite clear she didn't take us seriously. We didn't know who was making fun of us, she herself or the demon lurking within her, but luckily we had the means of finding out.

When the accused saw the thumbscrews she started to cry, though she didn't even know their use. She tried to push the Provost away, but he spoke to her in a friendly voice and said she had no reason for worry if she was telling the truth.

At first the screws were tightened lightly. The woman moaned, writhed and shouted, stammering that they must undo the screws, that she would tell everything. But when the device was loosened, the prisoner began to cry and worry about not being able to mend fish nets any longer because her fingers were crushed. The Provost calmed her by saying that the fingers were not so badly damaged they wouldn't heal almost to their former shape. The woman blew her nose with her free hand, between the thumb and forefinger, as was the peasant women's custom. A shiny trail of mucus remained on her finger which the torturer, with great care, cleaned immediately with his red handkerchief. Apparently the man considered it a matter of pride that his device remain impeccably clean.

Now Maria N. admitted to healing a boy called Jacob with sorcery. She told of having dropped silver in water and afterwards having read spells.

"If someone makes water in a sauna, the water spirits could be offended and they have to be appeased," she said.

But when she was asked further about Carolus Hasselgren's cattle, or about meeting the Devil, she denied knowing anything about it. For those reasons she had to be tortured further.

After an unpleasant half hour, a full confession was extracted from her. When the Provost loosened her fingers from the bloody device, she told of having met Satan in the form of a dark sailor and having made love to him.

"You admit, then, that you met the Devil face to face?" "Yes, yes." "And you fornicated with him?" "Yes, God help me!" "You're not lying to escape torture?" "No, I'm not lying." "How was he dressed? Explain!" "I can't remember." "In that case we cannot believe you." "No, yes I do remember: in black trousers and in a black homespun coat." "Was he, for sure?" "Yes, they smelled of chewing tobacco, liquor and the sea." "What did?" "The clothes, Jöns' smells, the smells of my late husband, and he even wore the same hat." "What same hat?" "Jöns' hat, the one he put on the morning he drowned. The boys later found it stuck on the branch of a waterlogged pine." "How would Satan have had your late husband's clothes?" "I don't know, that way he got me to agree. I thought he was Jöns." "The Devil's intrigues? ..." "I made the coat for Jöns during our first summer together, for his journey to the city." "We believe it, but it sounds strange." "When he came back he had a tear in the sleeve, and the collar, where it's turned down, had vomit on it." "The Devil?" "No, Jöns, when he was still alive."

We were not interested in her late husband's drinking trips, but we understood that torture could confuse her mind. Therefore it was important to cross-examine her as thoroughly as possible in order that we have an admission of truth, not some stories made up in haste.

"Where did you meet Satan?" "On the beach, didn't I say that already? On the beach." "You had gone, then, specifically to meet him?" "No, but to clean nets. When I had carried them into the boat shed, I sat on the rocks and ..." "You knew, then, to wait for him?" "No, no, I just wanted to sit there for a while and look out to sea." "Strange. Well, did he appear then?" "Yes, I didn't dare look at the face, because I was afraid the scar the dragging hook had left would still be visible." "The dragging hook?" "It tore out his other eye. Poor Jöns! As handsome as he was alive!" "You made a pact with him?" "He stood there and stood there, the shadow was on my feet, I didn't dare to look up, but I knew him from the smell." "You knew him to be the Devil? Was it the smell of putrid smoke?" "No, the smell of the sea, chewing tobacco and liquor!" "The Devil took your dead husband's shape and made a pact with you?" "He didn't say anything, I took hold of his pant leg when I couldn't stand it any longer ... he fell on his knees like a horse that had been shot!" "He had to say something!" "No, nothing, but I felt so sorry for him although I knew he wasn't Jöns...." "You felt pity for Satan, woman!?"

She was no woman. A mere girl, although she had already been married for the second time, although she was a mother, although she was going on forty. A woman is a girl who has become conscious of herself, but this one was not like that. She had seen that men were filled with desire, but she didn't know why. We had wanted to smash her fingers, and when she had understood that, accepted it. She was tormented to the end, but she didn't hate us. We were men, justice was ours. If Jöns had come back from the dead, justice would also have been his. And whoever else went to so much trouble on her account. She hadn't been born to hurt anyone's feelings, she had been born to be eternally a girl.

Later on in the dungeon she told a different story. The one dressed in black, the one in Jöns' clothing had been her husband Axel. Axel had been Jöns' friend when Jöns was still alive. Axel had sat at the table when Jöns drank, when Jöns had gone to void water and left his fly unbuttoned, when Jöns threw up and passed out by the puddle, when Jöns came to and wanted to wake up his wife to make love to her, when Jöns burst into tears after his wife, with his child, had left for the in-laws' place. And Axel had watched Maria, who upon her return had taken care of her husband and said that sober he was the best man on the island. Axel had watched Maria, who felt like crying, felt like a frog in the teeth of a rake! That is what Axel had said after watching Maria, the wife of a good friend.

"When Jöns drowned and Axel came for visits, people started to talk," Maria said.

"What did they say, then?" I asked.

Maria fingered her naked toes. She looked at me, her chin against a knee. "A dog on a fence, tail between the fence-rails!" she answered.

"And it meant that you ... ?"

"They said that how could there be honourable goings-on when a man keeps visiting a widow's house!"

"Well, were they then?" I was curious.

"Yes, they were; we didn't sleep together until we were married!"

The girl had been badly treated. How could it have been avoided; the situation had evoked nasty thoughts; conveniently the husband dies, the admirer cannot keep away, their visit to the Parson's immediately after the period of mourning is over! People whispered; a window was broken in the middle of a night; the mother-in-law yelled and screamed all over the village that, together, the whoring couple had thrust her son aside. The girl was sensitive, she believed others knew better, she believed that mere wishing might have caused the death to happen, and she had begun to feel horror towards the man who had been so ready to take Jöns' place.

"When he visited us while Jöns was alive, I liked him so, liked him so much, because he didn't drink, nor was he nasty; I thought that if only I had got that kind of a man ... ," Maria explained.

"You wanted him then?" I asked.

Maria put her hand in front of her mouth. "A strange feeling came over me when he smiled ... but it's because of the child that I was hooked, so the child would have a father...."

"And afterwards, when you had him?" I led her on.

Maria turned away from me. "He cursed me at nights. Beat me and called me a cow and said I wanted him to die too, that I wished Jöns were back."

"Well, did you?"

"No. One cannot have back the dead. I would have been with Axel, but he always got angry."

And once, in the middle of the night, the mother-in-law had come and tried to take the child away so her son's son wouldn't have to watch the whoring his murderer-mother was carrying on! And how the criminal without a conscience, the one who had called himself her son's friend, despoiled the bed of the dead man. In addition to everything else, someone had destroyed Axel's new boat with an axe, the boat he had spent so much time and care in building.

Men have their own ways of taking revenge. A man is straightforward by nature, but when he doesn't know who his enemies are, he chooses the weakest person around. Axel had taken her to see the seals.

"Don't worry, we'll bag this one alive!" Axel had said while Maria watched a seal pup struggle in his arms. Poor pup! It had tried every possible way to slip back into the sea; frightened, it looked around, a baby's cry rose from its throat. "Let it go! Let it go into the hole in the ice!" the wife had begged, this girl who felt little ones shouldn't be tortured. "I will, I'll let it go; may I ask the missus to have a little patience!" Axel had answered, while he slipped the animal into a harness.

Axel's beard had been covered in white hoarfrost. It made him appear different, frightening, in Maria's mind. The rope ran between his bluish fingers and at its other end was the pup. When the animal had disappeared into the hole in the ice, Axel had quizzed: "What does a mother do when a child is frightened?" And he answered himself: "Comes to comfort it, hugs it tightly against her breast — do you understand — really tightly." And Maria had understood. The seal would come to the aid of her pup, hold it between her flippers and then the hook in the harness would puncture its stomach.

After Axel had pulled the seals up on the ice stuck together and still alive, he had laughed at Maria while looking for the club. "Was it because of your pup you got caught on the hook?" Axel had asked. He had taken his time finishing the animals off as they writhed in pain. "Did you think your little son would have me for a father? Did you think I would become a father to Jöns' son?" the man had asked. Maria hadn't known what kind of an answer the man expected from her. "Why don't you kill them?" she had cried into her gloves. "Why don't I kill you two?" Axel had asked and killed the seals. First the mother, then the pup.

Maria confided in me openly. She didn't understand that she ought to have feared me. Her role should have been to sulk angrily, mine to extract the truth by whatever means from a hardened criminal. But I had to tangle with this girl. I was forced to answer sincerity with cunning, friendliness with curtness, ignorance with shrewdness, and hopefulness without pity. Of course my meanness was not meant for her, but for the demon within that found clever ways to foil my investigation.

The worst stumbling block was her second story about meeting the Devil. That it might have been Axel and not Satan. That Axel's desperation had gone so far he might have dressed himself in his dead rival's clothes in order to get what he wanted from Maria.

A crazy story! We men wouldn't disgrace ourselves that

way, not for the sake of a woman, and particularly not because of such an expressionless, insignificant girl! Not any one of us, not even Axel N. in another man's clothes would make his way to the beach where men were fishing in order to sleep with his own wife.

The ultimate disgrace for Axel had been the fact that the trick hadn't even succeeded. When it didn't work at night, how could it then at any other time? If a dead man remained between them, how could he be done away with? There was nothing one could do to the dead; only the living could be dealt with.

"And then?" I asked.

"He walked into the water, threw away the clothes and said he wouldn't come back," Maria said. That too; self-pity and suicide! No, that was just too much!

"He said he wouldn't come back any more," Maria explained.

"And what did you do?" I asked.

"What could I do? I said, go if you want me to be a widow for a second time."

A marital drama that became as usual a farce! Because there are women like her who are not women but girls. Girls don't understand that when a man says he is drowning, he is begging for love, begs for it as much as a human being can, on his knees. The right woman follows her man into the water and begs him to return, gives him a chance to get up and stand again, because it's so hard to walk on one's knees.

Honesty is girls' virtue; a woman knows that with it you break a man's back. And of what use is a crushed man? This creature made her man return on his knees, wet, naked and torn inside although she thought she cared for him!

"And then?" I asked.

Maria was looking at her crushed fingers, looked at them amazed. "I think it was he who denounced me."

Oh, is that what she thought? Why not? First one kills the mother, then one clubs the cub.

I didn't tell her, the prisoner, my thoughts. I wasn't that stupidly honest. Besides, I was interested, first and foremost, in her relationship with demons, devils and other spiritual beings from the other side, not in an unfortunate husband. I could have hauled Axel before the court, inserted sticks under his nails and let him hang on the torture rack until the truth about the dress-up theatrics and the swimming trip could be thoroughly examined, but that wouldn't have changed the fact that Maria might be a witch.

Henricus Institoris and Jacobus Sprenger write in their book, *The Hammer of Witchcraft*, that a witch aims at destroying a person's spirit. "They destroy a person's spirit, lead him into madness, hate, or unorthodox lovemaking."

Let me quote books to you so you'll understand. "The witches' families are despicable folk, particularly the female members who, with the help of evil spirits or magic potions, cause the male sex unimagined losses. For the most part, they bewitch people and allow demons to torture them with unbearable pain. And they even have intercourse with demons." This is what Abbot Trithemius Antipalus wrote in his *Maleficarum*.

A girl or a witch? I asked myself. A demon or an honest person? And which one is the worst choice for us men, even that I didn't know. The only thing I could be sure about was the fact that there had always been witches. Books testified to that.

St. Augustine, the Church Father, speaks in *De civitate Dei* about evil spirits which cause destruction in the world. According to him, all the miracles ordinary people make happen come about as a result of the teachings of demons and with their help. St. Augustine tells of sylvans and fauns who bother women especially, ask for their favours and sleep with them.

The revered St. Thomas Aquinas emphasizes that it is possible for a demon and a human being to have a sexual relationship; demons have the ability to transfer male semen into a woman. He also writes that, with the Devil's help, witches are able to fly, to create the illusion of a person transforming herself into an animal, and to raise storms.

History proved all this theorizing to be true when the Inquisition first created a proper context for the examination of witches. Pope Gregorius IX decreed that specific people were to question and punish heretics. Almost by accident, witches became part of the expanded scrutiny of heretics when originally the focus was only on the Jews.

Witches were pursued in the regions of the Alps and Pyrenees mountains; in Spain they searched for Jews. Because it was considerably easier to recognize Jews than witches, Jews soon everywhere gave the Inquisition enough to do, and the number of witches continued to increase. That is how, at the onset of our century, learned men could state that the situation had gotten out of control; clearly it was still the Jews who had brought about the Black Death, but the religious wars could already be seen as disasters conjured up by witches.

As much as Martin Luther rejected the Pope's dogma, he had to admit that where witchcraft was concerned, Rome was in the right. A human being was but a rotten limb and could only desire to do wrong. There was a legion of demons on the move in the world taking advantage of human weaknesses.

Witchcraft struck right to the core of the matter. We are not the masters of our deeds, but their slaves. Nature is necessarily evil. Goodness and beauty emanate only from God.

Sprenger and Institoris' *The Hammer of Witchcraft* is, without a doubt, a horrific book. More than anything else, it is a manual for torture, but it has a scientific base. The authors prove that woman has more aptitude for witchcraft than man because of her insatiable carnality and vulnerability to falling in love. These Brothers argue that love is a form of sickness which must be compared with madness. According to them, the etymology of the word "femina" (woman), due to the fact that it is made up of the terms "faith" (fe) and "less" (minus) already, in itself, testifies to women's weakness. It is easier, then, for a woman than a man to relinquish faith.

I didn't of course believe the claim in *The Hammer of Witchcraft* that had there been no women, men would have socialized with each other like gods. After all, I could see that Sprenger and Institoris' religious vows had plunged them into orgies of misplaced hunger for love, which made them think the very worst of women. And when one Inquisitor had decided, based on the doctrines of *The Hammer of Witchcraft*, that female body hairs carry demonic powers, and shaved forty-seven women bare of all hair before burning them, I realized it was a question of madness, not of protecting the world.

But there are other more matter-of-fact propositions which confirm the witch theory. There is Balduin's pointed philosophy of law, Carpzow's radical, exhaustive survey, Loccenius' doubting conclusions, and many others.

When I left Maria N.'s cell in the dungeon, I threw myself into the study of these books in search of answers.

Ever since the day on Schöps' military campaign, I had managed to convince His Majesty of the fact that I wasn't worth being dragged along as regimental ballast in the secretarial post I held, and I had received from His beloved hand the position of Assize Court Judge of Åland county, I had made a vow that my life would be a hymn of praise to the Goddess of Justice. Someone else might have considered a position on an outlying island an exile of sorts, but to me it was a release; I hadn't liked being in the secretarial post even when the King had had the patience to stay away from the-atres of war. The ladies of the Court had birthmarks in the right places, but they weren't genuine, and although the pastries were delicious, they turned one's teeth yellow.

No, I loved books and the sacredness of the law I had learned as a student at Tartu. While still young, I had vowed that for every judgement I made I would first search its basis in a written text, however difficult the search.

I had seen bad judges. I had seen judges who employed deputies or law-readers, I had seen judges who accepted bribes. I didn't want to be one of them. Gustaf Idman, a friend from my student days, had a very cynical attitude towards dispensing justice. His letters contained mainly tidbits about jurors' recorded statements: "The County Police Chief was sentenced to hang, but because he didn't want to hang from the gallows, and those cavalry men who were supposed to come with us to the border did not have proper clothing, we agreed in the name of the merciful King to grant the Police Chief the right to buy his freedom from the gallows by paying ninety-five rubles for it, although his son wanted to talk him into letting himself be hanged so that the son could keep the money. But the father argued: 'If I'm to be hanged, you have to follow me to the gallows, because you were my accomplice in the theft!' After that, it didn't take long for the son to come up with the money for the cavalry men's clothing and other expenses, as the receipts will show...."

I didn't intend to dispense Maria N. anything less than justice, the way I had dispensed justice all these years to child murderers, whoring maid servants, crazy field-hands, people who slandered their neighbours, those who tupped cows, and rye thieves.

Never mind the fact that I had understood long ago that the people of Åland didn't consider my efforts worth a horse's fart. If I gave a light sentence, they viewed me with contempt; if I was severe, they began to hate me. The essence of justice remained basically foreign to them. They could — in anger — denounce a good friend, but when next day they regretted it, they thought I ought to have freed the accused without so much as a glance at the nature of the crime.

They didn't appreciate the fact that I searched through all the existing records for the foundation of every sentence. No one put any value on that. Gustaf Idman thought it funny. My wife thought it at times endearing, at times an infuriating waste of time. Even the accused didn't appreciate it. When I freed a man imprisoned for tupping a cow, he didn't even bother to thank me, although I had spent three days going through books before I found in Arnold Mengering's *Informatorium Conscientiae Evangelicum*, page 286, a precedent which indicated the matter to be an aberration caused by Satan. To the very end, the thought that the man was guilty after all bothered me, but I couldn't find any support for that point of view.

Now I had Maria N., a married woman accused of witchcraft, and I had a pile of books which knew all about the likes of her. I couldn't go ahead and interpret the case from my own point of view, because for a judge, self-centredness is too constricting and much too limited a peephole.

FOUR

⸹

*Chapter Four, a somewhat ticklish chapter in which the
Judge interviews his woman-hater field-hand and,
so help me, rapes his own wife.*

WHEN I RETURNED from questioning Maria N., my field-hand, Torsten, sat shirtless on the steps leading to the barn and, judging by the expression of concentration on his face, he had drunk quite a lot. I sat beside him and he shoved a bottle of spirits into my hand.

"If you're being offered a horse, buy it," he said, without meaning me specifically. "If you notice it limps, you can shoot it," he continued without smiling. "What about a boat, what about that?" the field-hand asked and stuck a straw in his mouth.

I didn't answer because I knew no answer was expected of me. Instead, I took a mouthful of the liquor.

"Buy that too! Burn it if it leaks!" Torsten carried on.

A long silence ensued. The bottle travelled from me to him and back.

"A woman appears, offers to be a wife!" the man said. "What do you do?" he asked. The straw flew, along with his spit, onto the sand. "That you cannot escape unless disease kills her or bad luck," he answered.

"What if she is a good wife?" I asked.

The field-hand studied me. "The wife? She is always a man's grave, half a fiend, she is!"

I understood his bitterness. He had had a wife, but she had left him for a sailor. "You are just jealous because you yourself have had bad luck!" I said, irritated.

"And you've had good luck then?" Torsten was pestering me. Drunk, he didn't respect anyone, didn't understand that for that I could very well have thrown him out. "Anyone can tell by looking at you that you know what I know," he said.

"What, then?" I asked.

"That when a wife is cold, she's made of ice, and when she is hot, she's a burning coal from Hell; either way you don't dare touch her!"

I burst into unabashed laughter. Torsten didn't feel like laughing.

"Some job you have!" the field-hand said. "You go and stare at naked women, feel their tits, whether the Devil has been biting them or not, measure their behinds!"

I pondered whether I should get angry, establish my authority as the master. "We're not fondling them; it's part of a matter-of-fact examination, part of a search for the proof of *magiam divinatoriam*," I answered.

"Watch out that they don't manage your downfall; when a female is distressed, she begins to ooze the smell of rut," he said.

"Better concentrate on taking care of the horses; you don't understand anything about my job!" I said.

"Sure, I'll clean your horses' shit, don't worry!" Torsten was offended and took the bottle to his side. I poked him teasingly: "Shitphilosopher!"

"What?" He was dumbfounded.

"Shitphilosopher," I said and began to laugh again. Torsten sat quietly, drank and brooded about revenge. It was his habit to think about what he was going to say. In that sense he was truly an exception to the rest of the peasants I had come to know in court.

"You are forty-six years old and you long for a woman, am I not right?" he asked. The voice was friendly and conciliatory.

"You're right in that I'm forty-six years old, otherwise you're talking about yourself," I answered.

"You are forty-six years old and you long for a woman because your wife has given birth to five children and doesn't want any more, particularly since the last time was so difficult," he continued.

A field-hand doesn't talk to his master like that. A man doesn't talk to a man like that. I ought not to have allowed it to happen, and yet I did.

Perhaps what hurt the most was the fact that my wife, Elsa, didn't appear to suffer from the situation. When our friend Captain Berg visited us, Elsa got her amusement from flirting with him. But there was something pathetic in a past beauty carrying on with the mannerisms of a young girl. The mother of five children! Luckily the Captain was a gentleman and answered politely to Elsa's playfulness, or else he really did see something in Elsa, something which no longer touched me.

"Do you envy every man who has a wife, or am I a particular target for your bitterness?" I asked.

He no longer offered the bottle; jealously he hid it and when he drank from it, he turned his back to me.

"You are my master, go ahead, kick me in the head!" Torsten answered.

If I asked him to cut the hay, he was busy at something

else; if I asked him to clean the cattle shed, he was in the middle of making a fence. He worked like a foreman, not like a field-hand. Once Captain Berg had overheard Torsten and I exchanging words and had asked, "Why don't you beat him? If my hired help were like him, they wouldn't have a single whole bone in them. Not a single one!"

"Are you saying that seeing that woman naked doesn't stir lust in you?" Torsten asked.

I didn't understand what he meant.

"The witch woman, the wife of Markusböle's Axel doesn't stir anything in you?" he insisted.

"Of course, she stirs something. Thoughts."

"Well, of course, she has breasts like wine casks, but you, boy, only think of sorcerers and demons!"

"You, poor man, don't understand the nature of jurisprudence; under your stinking head of hair revolves only one and the same thought! Do get yourself a new wife, for God's sake, so we'll be able to talk more sense!"

"Do you know what?" Torsten asked.

I didn't bother to answer. I was ready to leave in any case because the conversation was turning into an open quarrel.

"Once our division was stuck in one place for four months. It was cold as hell, no women, they didn't want to freeze with us. When I went into the woods on a scouting trip, I found a woman's footprint in the snow. I brought it back to camp, laid it on the snow under a cloth cover and charged a fee for showing it. I charged the officers a thaler. Guess what happened?" He looked at me with a sarcastic expression on his face.

"I'm no officer, I was along in wartime only in the capacity of secretary," I answered.

"Go ahead and guess anyway!"

"They laughed and trampled your footprint into smithereens!"

"No, they stole the footprint and ordered me caned for profiteering!" he said and started to laugh at my amazement. "Never does a man sink so low that he wouldn't sink even lower because of a woman!"

In Germany, Captain Berg said, a field-hand like that would have been tied between four horses and quartered so that the tendons and bones would have flown all over the place. He thought it a pity there was no serfage under Swedish rule.

"What is it then, the jurisprudence I don't understand?" Torsten asked. A handsome man who had gone on living his life without a wife.

"When I put on my judge's robe, I am no longer your master, Nils Psilander, but the instrument of the spirit which tries to make this world a better and more just place!"

"Why is the world such a bad place, then, since a good and perfect God has made it?" he asked.

I smiled apprehensively. "In order to be whole, there also has to be evil in the world. Without it, many degrees of perfection would be undone."

"Well, why are you picking at it then, changing the order God created?" the field-hand insisted.

"A human being has to strive for goodness. There's the eternal conflict in our lives!" I said.

"I don't understand. First we are made a certain way, then we must try to be different," Torsten complained, speaking out of spite.

"That's what I just said. You wouldn't understand it!" I answered.

There was another side to this about which I didn't talk to him. People needed, thirsted, called for a judge when they had done something wrong. No one could endure guilt. One mother was brought before me because she had — in her carelessness — left a pot of boiling water on a rock and gone to talk with a neighbour woman. A toddler had got hold of the pot's handle and the boiling water spilled all over her. I judged the matter to be an accident, but the woman refused to leave the courtroom without a sentence. She was thrown out; she went to a clergyman who agreed to administer the church's punishment. On Sunday during the church service, before the eyes of the congregation, the woman was absolved of her wrongdoing. The other women lavished their shock-filled pity on her; how could the poor woman be punished for a deed which was clearly an accident? Was it not punishment enough that the woman had lost her child? The important thing was that the woman didn't have to become embittered about herself; she had a new target for her loathing, the clergyman who had executed the judgement.

I left the field-hand on the barn steps and went indoors to bury myself in the world of books. Elsa met me with a different plan.

"We promised to visit the Bergs today, don't you remember?" she challenged me.

"I have work to do; there's an important interrogation tomorrow!" I answered.

"We can't cancel the visit at this late stage; what are you thinking of?" she yelled.

I assured Elsa that the Captain would accept my explanation and wouldn't be offended, so that she could just as well consider calming down.

"Of course what was wrong with this plan was that it would have given me a chance to have some fun!" Elsa raged, throwing her sewing on the floor. "What do you care about me as long as you can run around and fondle naked women and talk with them about much more interesting subjects than you do with me!"

She dashed into the kitchen where the children were enjoying their evening meal. She blamed them for being wicked, ordered the servants about, took a toy away from the youngest child, and ordered Märta to empty her plate and not give any food to the cat. Coming back with a brown and white wooden horse under her arm, she carried on her fury. I noticed her maroon taffeta dress was as tight as a sock on her, not loose as it was intended to be, and I felt sorry for her.

"I have to waste hours on a boring board-game just to keep you satisfied?" I asked.

"But you like playing games!" Elsa answered.

"No, I don't, but I don't know what else to do with your Captain!" I said.

"He is not my Captain, and yes you do like playing games. Why do you have to lie to me?"

I told Elsa that I would agree to the visit only on the condition that I needn't play games with the master of the house.

"Of course you don't have to," Elsa protested. "I think perhaps he doesn't like to play them either."

"Then why does he suggest we have a round?" I asked.

Elsa fixed the loose strands of her hair with a comb and smiled. "To please you. He is a soldier, after all, and soldiers cannot seriously be interested in such childish amusements."

"That's funny, because I have only agreed to play in order to please him!" I said.

"You are the worst judge of human character I know," Elsa retorted.

The visit was as painful as I had expected. The more often Elsa placed herself so that the hem of her red skirt rested on the Captain's boots, the more ill his sickly wife looked.

We talked about witchcraft. Unavoidably, it was the topic of the day's conversation. I explained that in my view every witch was a flame that could spread and become a forest fire, ignite the peasants' vulnerable souls into a raging inferno. I had once witnessed how a fire got out of hand because of carelessness, and the horror of the situation had made a lasting impression on me. At first some men and women are having a friendly chat out in the field, they're not careful enough in controlling the direction of the flames with their rakes; in the latter stages they cry and shout and the burning cattle trample everything that gets in their way in their agony.

The wives were horrified as befit the situation; the Captain nodded and told about a case in the Baltic countries where he had seen a witch's face cut out and the skin peeled off her back. Elsa suggested we forget all the miserable things and cheer ourselves with the little duets she and the Captain could perform, since their voices were so well matched. Kristina, the Captain's wife, announced she was sick and in need of rest, but we could, by all means, continue enjoying a pleasant evening.

On the way home Elsa was bursting with irritation. The Captain's wife had only pretended sickness and had offended us by going to bed early. I didn't argue and after a while Elsa blamed herself for being nasty-minded and silly. She leaned against me and said she was annoyed a pleasant evening had to end that way, so abruptly, and I patted her, assuring her I thought the same, although it wasn't true.

"The Captain was very disappointed at our leaving," I said.

"Really?" Elsa asked, interested. I noticed that she was smiling. She allowed me to put my arm around her. We watched the hills and valleys meander in the moon's milky light, unreal shadows and mystical hollows, and I felt the night to be special somehow. "Look at the stars," I implored her. "They're very beautiful!" Elsa answered.

At the front door I gathered my courage and asked Elsa what she would say if I came to her room for a visit. She withdrew from me and in a sharp voice asked whether I was crazy; did every beautiful moment only stir in me a desire to make her suffer! And once inside, she ran to the nursery to enlist the innocent sleeping creatures as her guardians.

I'm embarrassed to admit that somehow I was out of my head after the promises the journey home seemed to have held. I made up a shameless plan and executed it a while later, after I had heard her withdraw into her own room and change into her nightgown.

I went to the door and watched her brush her hair.

"I haven't come to seduce you, I would only like to talk about my work," I said.

She put the brush in her lap and pointed to an empty chair. Without taking note of her gesture, I went to sit on the edge of her bed. I knew Elsa was interested in the prisoners, particularly in Maria N.

Through the years it had become clear to me that a woman whose husband sees her only in the daytime has barely any connection with the creature who blossoms at night. The day-Elsa was a puritanical and self-sacrificing saint, the night-Elsa a two-faced bitch.

I told her how burdensome the interrogation of witches was, the loathsome forms it could assume, how Karin P. had lifted her dough-like breasts before of my eyes, boastful of the fact that the Devil had left his bites on them. I said there were times when I hated this work because of all the repulsive aspects that could be part of it.

Elsa watched me under her brows. What about Maria N.? What was her interrogation like? This witch bitch was reasonably young, almost her own age and the mother of only one child? Was her questioning also boring and unpleasant? She had earthy, ruddy features, high cheekbones, large feet and hands. Perhaps in the eyes of clodhoppers she was lovely, but in the eyes of a civilized person ... no, surely not, not under any circumstances!

Elsa came to sit next to me. I felt her breath on my cheek. "What about the shape of her body? What about her midriff and her breasts? And where were the Devil's marks on her; did the accused say how they had come about?"

I answered evasively and tried at the same time to slip my foot against Elsa's leg and lift, as if unaware, the hem of her nightgown. I soon detected that Elsa was not satisfied with the way I downplayed Maria N.'s charms. She wanted to feed her jealousy. I thought it strange that she wished to dwell on her own feelings of inferiority that way, but without a moment's hesitation I gave in to her. I gave her a description of Maria, and Elsa's cheeks reddened with annoyance.

"You are an unnatural and horrible husband; you admire hardened prisoners more than your own wife!" she accused me.

"Good heavens, I don't admire them, the witches!" I answered horrified.

"Yes, you do admire them!" she said. "You don't see anything beautiful in me!"

"She doesn't have breasts as lovely as these!" I said as I bared one of hers and put my mouth on it as a sign of my keen admiration. Elsa tried at first to protest, but not with a great deal of spirit. I pulled the nightgown higher now at the back so that she didn't notice it, and at an opportune moment I searched my way hopefully through the tangled web of fingers and hair to the final destination.

That is how I got Elsa to give in because even though she moaned and called me a monster, she wanted to have me.

After half an hour I woke her up and said I had forgotten to tell her something she might find interesting.

"I'm tired of hearing about your lewdness," Elsa answered in a sleepy voice.

"Without a doubt this is a matter one ought not to talk about outside the courtroom, perhaps not even inside it," I whispered into her ear.

"All right, tell me then, if you want to!"

"You asked once how Beelzebub makes love to a witch. Can you stand to hear it?" I asked.

Elsa turned her head on the pillow. I heard her swallow. "How then?" she whispered.

I acted before she could sense anything was wrong. I turned her around and for a short moment the protesting behind was a prisoner and lay conquered. A deeply shocked Elsa tore herself loose and hit my face with all her strength.

"Animal!" she shouted. Her voice was full of loathing.

"Forgive me, I thought you wanted it," I answered.

She hit me again, now in the stomach.

A few weeks later she announced she was pregnant. We never had any luck in these matters.

CHAPTER

FIVE

ᴄᴐ

Chapter Five, a moving chapter in which the Judge reminisces
about his childhood. The chapter's important character is
the headmaster-father who at night wears a guard
over his moustache and his hair in a ponytail.

WHEN I WAS A CHILD we lived in Växjö. Father was the
school's headmaster. At night he came into my room to make
sure I remembered my prayers. "Surely such a big boy isn't
afraid of the dark!" Father said. Because he was headmaster
and taught school, he knew what was right and wrong. A person with an unblemished conscience had no need to fear the
dark. He had a moustache-guard made of white linen. It bore
his initials.

Sometimes Mother also came in. She smelled of yews and
didn't talk much. "Tomorrow is a new day!" she would say.

On Thanksgiving Eve, the servant-boy cut his foot on
some wood splinters and the foot began to swell. "I can't walk
to church," he said. Father let him come with us in the carriage. After two weeks the boy died. I wasn't allowed to look

at him, but no one thought to tell me to go away. We saw how his back became twisted like a crossbow. It snapped and his face turned ugly. That is why I shouldn't have been allowed to be there.

Father stroked my neck at night when I cried. I asked if it was God who killed the field-hand and Father answered that yes, it was God. "Did he do it because Torsten swore?" I asked. Father said it was partly for that reason, but no one could know for sure what went on in God's head. When I thought of God's head, I thought he had a ponytail and a moustache-guard like Father. Father laughed and denied it; no, of course not. Then he became serious. "Surely not, not under any circumstances!" he said. "That is mockery, but perhaps you don't understand that."

After he left I cried for a long time. I prayed that I wouldn't die, although I too had used swear-words. I felt my backbone; to God's strength it would be as brittle as a fish bone.

Then came the pox which took Ambrosia from us. People called it the smallpox because it didn't take too many people, mostly only children, but it took Ambrosia from us. She was a servant, but she wore a barley-yellow skirt while all the other servants had dark skirts. Her clothes were burnt with her straw bedding that someone had carried to the middle of the yard. "A pity to lose the beautiful skirt!" lamented one of the servants. "That a person doesn't even get a proper coffin, but is shoved into a grain bin," people commented. But the clergyman said our Maker doesn't judge the size or look of a coffin, and those who died from the pox had to be buried quickly so the disease wouldn't spread.

"All right!" the servants said, "but even her head had to be flattened so it fit into the bin!" And I remembered how I had ridden on Ambrosia's neck with my hands around her forehead. She had laughed a lot. "You're suffocating me," she'd say. "Who's Ambrosia's little baby squirrel?" she'd ask and hold me in her arms.

When I was a child and went to Latin school, my father wanted me to become a choirboy. Father took me to a black-haired man who had a blue velvet vest and a small dog. The dog slept rolled up on a cushion; there were feathers sticking out from its corners. The dog didn't move a muscle when we came in. Father put his hand on my shoulder. Father said I would like to learn to sing. He called the man *Director Cantus*.

I learned later on that the man's name was Nicolaus Marci, and that he was a very friendly person. Still, I wouldn't have wanted to belong to his choir. The truth of it was that I managed to get accepted by deceit. *Director Cantus* was in the habit of choosing new singers by allowing the boy candidate to sing with the choir. If the new voice didn't disturb the harmony the others had managed to attain, he was allowed to stay. When I went to be tested, I only moved my lips along with the others without making a sound.

Nicolaus Marci taught us both simple choral singing and the more demanding harmonic singing. Before rehearsals he always asked the same three questions in Latin which we had to answer in unison.

"*Quid est Musica?*" The dog turned around and around on the pillow looking for a more comfortable position. Nicolaus Marci sat on a chair and stretched one leg over the other. "What is music?" He had thin ankles, but very long feet. "*Est ars bene canendi.*" A boy's voice echoed the last syllable later than the others. I wasn't the one, but was the teacher looking specifically at me? Ability to sing well. And correctly! Nicolaus Marci looked at his ankles and smiled to himself. Because of me perhaps?

"*Quid est Choralis?*" He took hold of his black hair as if he had wanted to take someone else by the hair, but did it to himself instead. *"Est que aequalem servat mensuram."* I wasn't able to stay in tune with the others; is that what he wanted me to admit? Perhaps he made us answer these questions just to see how thick-skinned I was?

"Quid est Musica Figuralis?" I moved my sweaty hands behind my back. I felt like crying. The little dog had fallen asleep. It had no worries. Nicolaus Marci was fond of it even though it couldn't sing. What is harmonic music? My weakest point. He knew I wasn't up to it. They all knew. Samuel Busander poked me. It was obvious. *"Est quae mensuram servat inaequalem."* How could I have changed the rhythm when I didn't even properly understand what rhythm was? Why didn't he say straight out that I had no place here? Was it because my father was headmaster of the school?

In the evening I decided to tell Father. He came to sit by my bed and laid his cool hand on my cheek. I said I wasn't a good enough singer, that it wasn't worth my while to sing in a choir. Father drew back. He sat looking at me and the dark hairs in his nose quivered from his breathing. Had *Director Cantus* said so? Father asked. "No," I answered, "I just sense it." Father's rough, cool hand returned to my cheek. I was a good boy, he said, but much too tough on myself.

Father went away and I hadn't even had time to burst into tears of disappointment when — surprisingly — he returned. He himself was sometimes dissatisfied with himself, he assured me, but one had to just go on. I nodded, sniffed, and put a hand to my mouth. "You take after me!" Father said. He considered that a good thing. I could tell from the way he smiled as he left. Later on I heard him say to Mother, "the boy is taking after me in many ways!" Mother concurred.

When I was a child Father took me along on a business trip to Kalmar. It was then I saw the sea for the first time. I had fallen asleep listening to the monotonous sighing and squeaking of the carriage when Father shook me. "Wake up, boy!" he said. "You can see it now. The sea!"

The sea rippled like a grey field of wheat. In the damp weather it was at its most gloomy, and I didn't know then that the sea could also be different. Father had often talked about the sea because he had spent his childhood on the coast. He spoke about it with pride, possessively, as if it were, in part, his own creation. I had expected something truly great. "What do you say, son?" he asked. "It's a lot of water," I answered. "Yes, isn't it!" Father said. It sounded as if he himself had filled the sea with it. "What do you say about the sea, Nils?" he asked many times. And every time I had the same answer. "Such a lot of water!" I said.

As we drove along the beach road, a crowd of shouting people stopped us. "Do you have a gun?" they asked. Of course Father had a gun, but it wasn't his habit to admit anything without first knowing more about the matter. Women wearing strange wide-brimmed hats told us there was a rabid dog on the beach. They wanted Father to shoot it.

Father thought for a moment. Perhaps he was afraid? He might have driven on had he not had me with him. I didn't think about it then, I just believed him to be pondering the best way to approach it, perhaps wondering whether the people were telling the truth.

He asked me to stay near the carriage. I leaned against the wheels and watched as an agitated crowd of people surrounded his receding figure. Suddenly I was afraid something would happen to him, afraid that I was seeing him for the last time. I began to shout, but at that instant he looked towards me from the middle of the crowd. His eyes looked straight at me and he threw an invisible rope to me. I knew he wouldn't let go of his end. I saw him disappear behind the sand dunes, but I had my rope.

I had to wait a long time. I crouched and drew pictures

with a stick in the sand; the lines immediately filled up with new sand. The sea was turning blue and more beautiful. I was glad for Father's sake it was no longer colourless and gloomy.

That's when I saw the dog. He came from a thicket of birches. Between their white and black trunks one could see a reddish spot which appeared and disappeared in the tall grass. He left the woods, swaying and limping, and came towards me and the carriage. Saliva was dripping from his jowls and he stared straight ahead as if chasing some animal.

I didn't shout. I knew it wouldn't help, because there was no one nearby. The door to the carriage was locked. Father had taken the key with him so that bandits couldn't take our luggage. I didn't dare crawl under the carriage, because I was afraid of frightening the horses and being trampled by them. So I stood there squeezing the rope, at the other end of which was Father's comforting strength.

The dog came closer. He looked at me with a yellow, vacant look. He came closer still. I held my breath and squeezed the rope with all my strength. He stopped. His reddish fur was tangled, and here and there were hairless blotches where you could see flaking skin. Strings of drool ran into the sand where a moment ago I had tried to write my name.

The dog crouched low. At first I thought he would attack. Then I understood. He saw my rope in front of him and crawled under it. Once past the obstacle, he got to his feet and continued his solitary, crooked walk along the sand. Finally he disappeared behind a boulder.

When Father came back I didn't talk about the dog, but about the sea which had turned blue. Father was delighted. He said if we ever moved to the coast he would get me a boat of my very own.

SIX

Chapter Six, in which the Judge tells — sometimes in a confused manner — about the chorale notes he brought from Germany and at other times about the sitting of the Assizes during which he had a bothersome cold.

How could I send Maria to the gallows, when to the very end I was unsure about her relationship with the Devil? How could I go to see her, when the purpose of the meetings grew dim as other motives began to shape my interest?

I couldn't. When I realized that my own interpretations were inadequate, I began to look for a church authority to share the responsibility. I remembered the parson at Sund, Bryniel Kjellinus, whom I knew slightly. Some time ago I had tried to organize and bring about some musical life in Mariehamn, and I procured a portable organ from Stockholm. Kjellinus had seemed interested in getting one for his church then and had tried to instill the same desire in his cantor. I had bought chorales and a manuscript for a Passion in Tartu, and I was nurturing the fragile hope of one day hearing part of it performed on our backward island. Of course I understood that I could never experience what had bedazzled me during my student days in the ancient church of Jaani, where the vaults were filled with the solemn canon of violins above the *basso ostinato*. It was a Passion in which every instrument made its own specific impression, and the arias were — in their pathos — the most beautiful I had ever heard; in them the emotion of the recitation was deep and real. And what of the choir? I couldn't understand how boys whose voices hadn't changed yet, and who hadn't experienced life otherwise either, how they were able to express pain and empathy in such a moving way.

My musical plans came to naught because no one knew how to read notes properly, and even if they had, there was a lack of good singers. Bryniel Kjellinus vowed to school suitable singers himself, but for some reason the matter ran aground and was forgotten. We did, however, have time to conduct some interesting conversations about the theory of music, and based on that I had formed an opinion of him as an intelligent and reasonable man.

I explained the background of my problem. Bryniel Kjellinus demonstrated his familiarity with Carpzow's *praeses* by saying that from the point of view of sentencing, there wasn't an essential difference between whether the witch's agreement with the Devil was imagined or real. Even in the former case a witch had to be in agreement with the Devil, because she believed her imaginings to be real. "Satan gives birth to imaginings," Kjellinus said, quoting Carpzow, but the witch is responsible for them because she longs for the very things she experiences in her delusions.

Kjellinus' confident opinions stirred in me both a sense of relief and worry. I had wished that somehow I could have helped Maria, but these words took her closer to the axe and pyre. I told Kjellinus I suspected Maria's confessions were lies brought about by her torture. The Parson said he would be able to clarify the matter by discussing the salvation of her soul with her. He added that witchcraft is the most horrific crime one can imagine and so well hidden that only one witch in a thousand is caught, hence too much leniency in this case wouldn't be appropriate.

I felt he was right. He behaved in a polite and sensitive manner, and that influenced my decision.

Maria's interrogation had begun in August and was carried to its conclusion at the end of December. Bryniel Kjellinus' help came at an opportune time, because I fell ill with a bad chill and fever in the second week of December. The illness left me physically weak all through the holidays. The idea that I should take part in yet another court case concerning a witch, a case which I had announced would begin on the thirteenth of December, 1666, seemed almost overwhelming. The indictment had to do with Lisbeta S. who also had been denounced by the Karin woman. Based on additional testimony, she had been taken prisoner some time ago. I had questioned her because of the testimony, but she had denied everything, and I didn't think the accusations against her were serious enough to warrant starting a regime of torture. That was why I had written the Court of Appeals asking first of all how much weight one should give the testimony of witch wives on their way to the gallows and, secondly, to get an approval for the use of a reasonable amount of force in order to get at the truth in cases where the accused were strongly suspect.

All this is a matter of official record, so you'll note that I don't at all try to lie about my own part in all this. I was of two minds anticipating the Court of Appeals' reply. If their attitude towards Karin P.'s denouncements was negative, it would mean that Maria's case would have to be reconsidered regardless of what decisions had been taken, and that Lisbeta S.

would immediately be set free. The whole matter would dry up, and I would no longer lose sleep crawling through the jungle of defensive and offensive arguments. I did understand, of course, that afterwards I wouldn't be able to be altogether certain whether or not I had contributed to the spread of demons on this poor island. If a wave of plague, or a hurricane, should sweep over it, destroy the cattle, kill our children, tear up our houses, I would end up with my conscience in turmoil.

Perhaps you now laugh with scorn, pretend to know my true motivations. You may ask why I can't admit that I wanted a feather in my cap out of this rapidly growing process, credit for a judge who had been banished here, behind God's back, whose battles on the side of justice couldn't be ignored after this? You may ask why I can't admit that in my daring application of witch doctrine I saw an opportunity to get people's attention, because, as I said a short time ago, I wasn't respected here, no one recognized the fact that I applied science as well as art to my cases, though I could have — without anyone questioning it — thrown sentences like cakes of dung at the ignorant sod-turners and fishermen.

No, I especially cannot admit that, because it's not true. After a life in His Majesty's court, neither fame nor honour tempted me, they made no impression on me. Of course I hoped that the people among whom I lived would value me, but their thanks were not important. The most important thing was that I myself was satisfied with the work I produced.

The answer from the Court of Appeals came at the end of October. It confirmed the importance of the witness' denouncements and considered the use of thumbscrews quite proper. Turku's Court of Appeals became my partner in crime, the first but not the only one.

Because of the trivial nature of the testimony against Lisbeta S., I had reason to assume that in her case it wasn't a question of witchcraft, but the malice of gossiping neighbours. I decided not to postpone the sitting of the Assizes because of my illness. I believed the sitting would be short, and the thought filled me with a sense of relief. After all, the woman had been imprisoned for several months already, and it was getting close to Christmas.

When on the thirteenth of December I stepped into the house of Tossarby's Police Chief, blowing yellow mucus into the folds of Elsa's skillfully embroidered handkerchief, I was sure that from the point of view of the accused, the matter would be brought to a positive conclusion. The jurors at Sund were clearly more alert and forthright by nature than jurors at Finström, where I was frustrated by the extent of their lack of enterprise. That in turn meant that I practically took care of the whole matter myself. I assumed that the jurors, like me, would settle for a punishment dispensed by the church.

Bryniel Kjellinus, whom I had empowered only a few days earlier to represent Maria's case, came to the sessions somewhat late because of church duties. As a man of a quick intelligence he soon understood in which direction the case was headed. I saw that a couple of times he wrinkled his brow and shook his head as if to suggest I was lost.

His strange behaviour upset my concentration. When I had to follow, simultaneously, the legal processes, his ambiguous messages, and be mindful of the fact that my fingers didn't touch the used part of my handkerchief, I got irritated to the point where I ordered a recess.

After the gavel had struck, Kjellinus approached me limping. Despite fifty-four years of age, his figure was slim, youthful, but his walk betrayed the fact that he wasn't in as sound a condition as he looked. He was the son of a farmer from Värmland, and I wasn't surprised the father had in his time sent his son to study to become a clergyman. The son didn't have the necessary stamina for work on a farm.

I sensed him looking with disgust at the mound of handkerchiefs in my hand, and I put them in my vest pocket with a smile on my face which begged that I be forgiven.

"Miserable cold, the skin is broken under my nose and my ears are blocked," I tried to defend myself.

He didn't appear interested. He leaned over the table and said in a low voice that the case was headed in the wrong direction, that serious questioning had to begin again from the beginning. "Maria has denounced Lisbeta!"

"Maria?" I asked, shaking my head.

"Yes," said Bryniel Kjellinus. "Maria has admitted to having seen Lisbeta S. at the Witches' Sabbath. Lisbeta too is a witch; there's no doubt about it."

The news took me by surprise. I wasn't satisfied with what I heard. "Why didn't she let me know?" I asked. Kjellinus answered that I had been sick and the admission had been made only recently. That meant we would begin the whole legal process all over again and in an altogether different spirit. The thought didn't please me.

"It goes without saying that in a case as serious as this one we can't bluff to get a confession!" I said to be sure.

"Of course not," Kjellinus said, "that much is obvious!"

SEVEN

*Chapter Seven, in which the Judge tries to pry facts from
the formidable Lisbeta S., but realizes that he fails
where Parson Kjellinus reaps a bountiful harvest.*

LISBETA S. WAS FIVE years younger than me. A blond, skinny,
tough woman. Her long hair was done up in tight braids which
were bound closely around her head, but when she let her hair
loose so that her head could be shaved just before her beheading, she looked like both an ageing angel and a prostitute.

When she saw the court was not working to set her free,
she announced in a calm voice that no one was going to get a
confession out of her. I said the truth will always come out
sooner or later. She argued that even if she were beaten to
pulp, it would make no difference. Still, she said, her blood
was going to be avenged, and the truth about her innocence
would come out if anyone tried to force her to say anything. I
warned her that threats in a court of law were of no avail, but
rather a detriment. Lisbeta said she was making not threats
but promises. I smiled and said we would see.

Kjellinus demanded that Lisbeta undergo an examination

of her body again, since her arrogance suggested she was hiding magical tools which provided her with the Devil's protection. I was against it because nothing about Lisbeta's figure had given us reason to suspect the Devil had left his mark on her, and no one could claim the examination made by the Provost had been carelessly conducted.

"But has he taken into consideration the reference Carpzow made to the fact that the sign could also appear in secret places such as inside the lips, under the arms, under the eyelids, et cetera?" Kjellinus asked.

And since he referred to an authority I valued, I had to give in.

I wasn't present at the examination. Afterwards I heard from Lisbeta that Kjellinus had performed the examination in the most degrading manner, forced her into positions which exposed the body's every crevice, but even hearing that, I believed Kjellinus had acted in Carpzow's spirit. No mark was found, nor any secret tools either.

When they made an attempt to begin the torture of Lisbeta S., the thumbscrews, due to a technical fault, refused to work.

"Do you see, I've put a spell on them too!" the accused scoffed.

"We'll take that to be a confession!" I answered.

"Take it any way you want!" she snapped. The Provost, who was fighting with the contraption, looked miserable. This had never happened before. What if the prisoner had cast a spell on the device? There was something altogether unusual in this, because the very last thing the night before he had checked each part of it to make sure everything was in working order. Lisbeta S. was freezing, her lips were blue. I asked a servant to throw a blanket over her.

The thumbscrews were fixed. Lisbeta yelled, swore, twisted and turned, but didn't confess. The blanket fell from her shoulders, her feet shook as if she were in a trance. She didn't confess.

The Provost was amazed. He hadn't met this kind of opposition before, and he didn't know how far he would be able to go. That is when Bryniel Kjellinus suggested the interrogation be stopped and he try to talk sense to the woman alone, just the two of them. I agreed. The Police Chief's servant washed the blood off the floor, and a soldier led the white-faced Lisbeta out of the room.

Later on, after several weeks, Lisbeta told me she hadn't felt any pride in being able to withstand the pain. "Self-satisfaction is the worst sin!" she said. "It is the worst sin in the eyes of the people."

She told me she looked at the jurors' faces during her torture. As long as she was quiet, their faces remained cold and severe. Only when she burst into tears and begged for relief had there appeared a flash of understanding in them. In Lisbeta's mind that was her life's most important lesson. "Unfortunately it came too late," she whispered.

When Lisbeta was being interrogated for the second time at the special Assizes, she announced she wasn't going to stick to the truth because it was of no use in any case. "I'd rather speak nonsense than allow myself to be tortured!" she said. She offered a story similar to Maria's and received the death sentence. I didn't send the papers to the Court of Appeals right away because her answers before the torture gave reason for doubt. I needed additional proof.

I questioned the prisoner in the dungeon. Lisbeta looked bored and ran her finger along the edge where the wall's red granite turned into bricks. Moss and dried sod stuck out between the two, and she was grinding it between her fingers. She watched children outside balancing themselves on the walls.

"I don't actually like people!" she said. "So what reason is there to grieve so much?"

"Why don't you like people?" While I questioned her, I had a pen and paper on a small writing tray before me.

"They have never understood my attempts to have fun!" Lisbeta answered.

She told me that even as a child she had been a good swimmer. When she played with the village children on a bridge railing, she had let herself fall down, and she dived so far that everyone was sure she had drowned. They went and got her parents, men ran around with their dragging poles, grandmothers had heart attacks, and when Lisbeta stepped up soaking wet and trying not to laugh, everyone rushed towards her in anger, the grandmothers first in line.

"Cruel joke!" I said.

"But something unexpected!" Lisbeta sighed. "Although life is hard, it could still be magnificent!"

"Perhaps that is asking too much?" I asked.

She looked at the children playing on the wall. "At least sometimes!" she answered.

"Is that why you grasped at the Devil's temptations?" I was curious. Lisbeta started to laugh a cheerless, exaggerated laughter. "I would have grasped at anyone's offer had someone had the sense to make me one!" she said. She looked at me for a long time as if weighing things in her mind. The expression on her face tightened. "What the devil are you still struggling for? You already have a confession."

As a young girl, she said, she had, in the midst of her field chores, unhitched the plough and gone for a ride on the horse. "When father caught up to us, he beat both me and the horse, but the worst of it was that the hag had trotted along like an old dog and not at all like the stallion of my dreams!" Lisbeta said.

"But of course; it was a workhorse!" I corrected her and smiled.

"Yes, but I had imagined it also had dreamt of being free!" she lamented.

She told me about her first romantic adventure. "I was so terribly in love with that boy, I was ready to jump into fire for his sake! Then he took me to the woods and groaned and mauled me for a while. He asked me to marry him. When I watched him pulling up his trousers to cover his naked behind, I was crushed. Was this what it was all about!"

I put the pen aside because Lisbeta wasn't saying anything worth writing down. She was disappointed in life, in men, and people in general. She was like a hen who cackled loudly when it laid an egg, but only managed to produce a leather egg. And she blamed others for her misfortunes. If a girl wants to pretend to be a knight on a ploughhorse, whom should she blame if it doesn't turn out to be a success? However much one tries to fill up the cup of life, it's of no use if one only has water to pour from it!

The jailer said Lisbeta screamed at nights that her head had come off and was watching her from the corner of her cell. Or she cried and moaned like an infant. "Some of the ones who have been sentenced to death take things that way!" the jailer said. I was astonished that in daytime Lisbeta was so vulgar and defiant.

"Now, something unusual did happen to you!" I egged her on.

"Oh yeah, it isn't just any girl who gets to die twice, first by beheading and then on a pyre," she answered and looked me in the eye unswervingly.

During her entire stay in prison she kept her hair carefully braided. As we were talking about her death, she suddenly undid one of the braids and pulled loose a handful of hair.

"Keep this, or give it to someone!" she said. She didn't want all of her to burn." "You might give it to Peril, the thick numskull!" she said, meaning her husband.

As I was leaving the dungeon I threw the hair away. The jailer's wife told me later that Lisbeta saw me do it through the dungeon's peephole and went into a rage. To me Lisbeta said nothing.

Bryniel Kjellinus offered to officiate at the follow-up examination. Again his skills turned out to be nothing short of phenomenal. In four days unbelievable additional proof was drained out of Lisbeta, among which the decisive one was the witch ointment. The Parson got the prisoner to say that Satan had given her a tube of salve with which she had oiled herself, turned herself into an animal, and ridden to a Blue Mountain party. Kjellinus had burnt the witch ointment in the prison oven. Lisbeta had also informed on another witch.

I went to meet the prisoner three days before her death. Lisbeta said she longed to wake up at home.

"It was so nice when one didn't know what the day would bring," she said. Immediately afterwards she admitted, however, that each day had been the same as the one before.

"A human being ought not to know the time of her death, nor its place!" she reminded me, referring to the Bible. "I know mine!"

"That's your own fault!" I said.

"And shit," she said, "if it depended on me, I would open that door and walk out of here!"

"What would you do then?" I asked.

She shrugged her shoulders. "I would work away and wait for something nice to happen!"

She was quiet for a long while. "And I am certain one day something nice would too happen!"

EIGHT

Chapter Eight, in which the Judge becomes puzzled. Ebba K.
is so certain of her own guilt that the Judge begins to have
doubts. In addition, we'll make the acquaintance of a fine
character whose name is Rucksack-Mats, as well as
with some poor, less fortunate creatures.

*N*O ONE HAD ANYTHING disparaging to say about Ebba K. Besides Karin and Lisbeta's denouncements, it was very difficult to find any other proof. No one wanted to confirm the accusations about the widow's practice of witchcraft; on the contrary, neighbours insisted that a more decent person couldn't be found in the village.

I wouldn't have been as keen to examine her case had not the headsman sent word he wasn't going to make the trip for the sake of only one or two death sentences if it was probable that more victims could be found. He let us know that the journey between Turku and Åland was long and arduous enough; he had no intention of making it several times a year. We had to accept his word on it.

Elsa was angry because Ebba K.'s interrogation took so much time. She would have wanted to entertain guests during the Christmas holidays and in turn be visiting others.

What kind of a man was I that I allowed the dregs of society to dictate to me, Elsa asked. As far as she could remember, in her youth the executioner had been the filthiest man in the city and smelled of putrefaction because part of his duties was also the removal of dead animals from streets and people's houses. "This executioner is a foreign-educated fine gentleman!" I tried to explain, but to no avail. Pregnant women have sensitive nerves.

"Obviously you are ready to spoil the children's Christmas because of the wenches!" Elsa accused me. That is why I asked Kjellinus whether he could spare the time for interrogation. He promised to sacrifice his Christmas holidays and examine the witch wenches; he considered the situation serious. The Parson made me ashamed of the way I evaded my duties, but I didn't have the strength to do battle with Elsa.

You probably see me as uncaring. You consider it unreasonable that I gave more weight to my wife's caprices than to the pursuit of truth in this important matter. Those of you who are married understand me better, because you know how the gently biting teeth of marital life crumble society's passion and defiance.

And Ebba K.'s case demanded the tough hand of an expert. For the first time the common peasantry, that ignorant, malicious lot, was actually against someone's imprisonment. Finnby people showed their fists to the court officials and yelled profanities while the officials led the badly agitated widow between them. Women were crying.

The situation was altogether so troublesome that on several occasions I questioned Bryniel Kjellinus about the possibility of an error. What if Lisbeta had meant some other widow; what if she had lied? But the Parson was sure he knew what he had heard. He claimed he was soon going to get at the truth. The most surprising fact was that the saint of the Finnby folk made an immediate confession. There had barely been enough time to bring the widow before the Provost when she voluntarily gave a full confession.

The widow had wrapped herself in four or five thick woollen shawls from the middle of which her skinny chicken feet stuck out. Hands which she rubbed nervously against one another were covered with brown spots, and her finger-nails were thick and splitting. When I came to see her, she asked me to walk her around the dungeon so that her feet would stop aching. She leaned against my arm, and there was a sour smell of old woman about her which I didn't like.

There was no need to question her; she went on and on, endlessly telling everything possible about herself, right from her childhood onwards. She was like an old bottle from which — at long last — the cork had been pulled out, and the sour contents foamed out without anyone being able to stop the flow.

When she was eight years old she ended up as a servant in Warg's Manor. Her duty was to care for a deformed child who was kept hidden from others in a room without windows. Ebba's ward was a girl about her own age who didn't know how to speak or eat. Ebba gave her food, changed the rags on which the girl defecated, and tried to keep her company.

"Everyone was amazed how well I nursed Lisa," Ebba said.

"Really?" I asked.

"She didn't have any hair or eyebrows, and her eyes wandered in every direction," Ebba went on. "At first I was terrified of Lisa, I was so afraid I cried while I was handling her," Ebba explained.

I wished we could have moved away from the subject; I didn't think it was important in terms of the accusations made against Ebba.

"That is when I used witchcraft for the first time," the widow claimed.

"In what way?" I asked suspiciously. She had only been eight years old.

Ebba told me that after a while the child began to show affection towards her. Lisa always took hold of her when she came within reach. Ebba's ward brushed herself fondly and stubbornly against Ebba. Ebba had been able to stand her dullness and indifference; Ebba had calmed the animal-like wailing which accompanied Lisa's bouts of defiance; the daily defecating had not broken Ebba's will, but love had been too much.

"After a year they let me visit my home for two days, and I decided then and there I wouldn't go back," the widow said.

"And your wish was fulfilled?" I asked. She looked at me with an air of superiority and fussed with her mud-coloured hair.

"It wasn't a wish, I cursed her dead," Ebba answered.

She had held Lisa's milk jar in her hand, a jar in which she was supposed to carry beastings for the child, because at her home a cow had just had a calf. As Ebba went into the cow barn, she saw the jar shatter right in front of her eyes. "I called to Mother that Lisa had died, and I started to cry," Ebba went on. Her mother had cried with her. Soon a field-hand had come from the Wargs to tell them the girl had fallen from her bed and suffocated. They were all convinced the sick child had missed Ebba and tried to go and look for her. The strangest thing was that the jar that had broken into pieces right before Ebba's eyes now looked perfectly whole.

I wasn't happy about the story. All that had happened nearly sixty years ago. From our point of view it wasn't desirable that people here believed the Devil had already put down his roots so far back in the past.

Ebba wanted to hear what I thought of the fact that she had learned to play an instrument so quickly it was unheard of before. "Did the Devil teach you?" people sometimes asked her when she played for them during some major holiday. Even the instrument hadn't been just any old thing, but a violin, the kind no one on the island had seen before the old musician came. And when time had parted company with the old man, Ebba was given the violin as an inheritance.

"With its help I got myself a husband!" Ebba said.

"With a violin?" I asked, reluctantly. I had a feeling that this confession wasn't the kind we expected either.

"That's right; you see, my looks simply weren't pleasing to men," she answered.

The man was called Rucksack-Mats because he wandered all over the islands selling goods he had brought from Stockholm, goods which he carried in a large leather rucksack.

Rucksack-Mats had come to Warg's Manor where Ebba had stayed on as a kitchen maid. The pedlar had waited for the owners to return from the fields. While he was sitting in the livingroom, the man's eye happened to wander from the gun on the wall to where the violin was kept. "Who here knows how to play the violin?" an astonished Mats had asked the servant doing the cooking.

Ebba had downplayed the matter, laughed and said that what great skill is that now; didn't they know how to play the violin in Stockholm since it so amazed the traveller! "Your master has of course bought it to boast about a foreign invention and can't find any use for it but to have it hanging from a beam!" the pedlar had mocked. "What will you give me if I start playing it?" Ebba teased him, blushing. She had laughed after asking the question, and of course the man had misinterpreted it. "All the contents of my bag!" the man promised right then, also laughing. "You'd lose the bread from your mouth," Ebba answered.

The next spring when Rucksack-Mats had visited them again, he remembered the joke. "I don't suppose you're planning to take the bread from my mouth by playing the violin?" the man asked. Ebba said again she had enough pity for a travelling man not to cause him such misery. And Mats Henriksson had laughed and laughed.

The third time the man had appeared, in the fall during the harvesting festivities, he had scarves and combs for sale. Ebba hadn't bought anything. She gave as the reason the fact that no one would dance with a grey sparrow like her however many combs she had in her hair. In a good mood because of sales he had made, Mats had suggested he would twirl Ebba around if that were what her buying depended on. "No need; besides, I'll be playing the violin there."

In the evening before the dancing began Ebba had seen the pedlar with his hand around a girl at the festivities. Mats had been drinking too. That very moment Ebba had walked to the table where the violin waited for her. She was shaking and trembling and didn't even know why. Lifting the violin to her chin with her sweaty hands, she had watched Mats' loathsome sneering expression.

Ebba had started to play. She was sure Mats was looking at her. That was enough, and she played as if the Devil had taught her.

Afterwards she was annoyed. She had understood her trembling was caused by her anger and triumph; she trembled because of the joy of having a chance to humiliate a courting pedlar.

Next day the man had come in the house and thrown his rucksack on the floor in front of Ebba. "Look after what's yours!"

Ebba had asked what kind of betting that was where one had nothing to lose. After giving the matter some thought, Mats had admitted it was her right not to take the rucksack's contents, but that had humiliated him even more now that he came out second again.

When I watched Ebba speaking, I noticed she was touching an invisible violin with her hands, and I felt she heard music my ears didn't hear. But the matter itself, it had to be considered confusing and poor proof, because one couldn't entertain the thought that a person's special talent came from the Devil. I said it right out, and Ebba got annoyed.

"But how about the fact that I didn't agree to give Mats any children although he so wanted to have them?" Ebba asked.

"Did you not agree to live a wedded life?" I was astonished.

"In that sense, yes, but I decided I wouldn't have children because they could turn out like Lisa, so I didn't have any," Ebba boasted.

Besides, the widow admitted, Mats Henriksson, who in time had become a powerful trader, died in a peculiar way. The man had died while helping to move a church bell from a half-burnt bell tower. As the bearers' hold gave way, the enormous lip of the bell had crushed Mats' ribcage. "I'll make a bet that you won't get as large a crowd around you when it's time for you to go!" were the man's last words to his wife.

"I would so have wanted him to beat me in something just once!" Ebba said.

"Well, yes, I do understand." I answered.

Unreasonably, Ebba refused to assume direct responsibility for the accident.

"I didn't wish for his death, but no other woman's husband has taken leave from here like that," the widow said.

She had a great deal to ponder in that. "Go ahead, Judge, and think about it, yourself! A church bell! A church bell kills a man! It isn't something that happens just any day!"

Other times she told of the charges she had all over the county. She worried how they might manage now. Most of them were feeble old people or sick children whom their own parents mishandled. In the same breath she laughed about her reputation as a good Samaritan.

"I look after them for personal gain!" she insisted.

"How so?" I asked.

"Well, I'm thought of as a saint. Isn't that enough of an answer?" she snapped.

"Why do you worry about your wards then?" I wanted to know.

"It's just a habit," Ebba answered.

"Go ahead and forget them then!" I said, tired of the whole matter.

"I can't, and I don't want to," she argued, and began to cry.

I couldn't help but realize that her behaviour showed she cared for those wretched people. Ebba dried her eyes and asked why I didn't understand that her self-accusations were just an attempt to make others see her as a good person, something they wouldn't see if she spoke well of herself.

"Even the Judge fell into the trap of my malevolence!" Ebba was astonished. "It's terrible to think that I'll soon die, and I must still try to make a good impression on people," she said sadly.

I had to admit she was a special case. She stubbornly made herself look guilty. Using strange logic, she turned everything she had done against herself. She didn't even spare her good deeds; quite the contrary, she showed just how much weight in the end one could attach to the confession of the accused. This was true even if the confession hadn't been extracted by torture. I had learned there are people who prefer to be sick rather than healthy. Were there also human beings who preferred guilt to innocence?

The interrogations turned out to be comical. Ebba piled faults on her head, I made light of them. We needed confessions, but not that kind of confession.

Ebba told of an old man who lived in a hut which was about to fall down. She started to nurse the man because in some way he reminded her of Lisa, the deformed girl.

"How can an old man resemble a child?" I asked.

Ebba explained: The man was bald, and he was cross-eyed. The man's legs were abnormally short and he wasn't able to walk.

"His name is Otto and he hates me!" Ebba said.

"Surely not since you are helping him?" I was astonished.

"Otto says that whatever I do, he sees through me, that it's useless for me to deceive him with kind gestures!" Ebba said.

I was amazed at the arrogance of the cripple when I thought how dependent he had to be on his benefactor.

"Although the man is crippled and ugly, that doesn't necessarily make him stupid!" Ebba was seething.

"It shouldn't make him insolent either," I reminded her.

"It's better not to boast about a horse one hasn't ridden on!" Ebba answered.

I asked the widow whether she ever had enough of Otto's gruffness. Ebba admitted it had happened many times.

"But Otto knew I'd get over it and would understand he was right," she said. "Otto knew I fed my own pride by caring for him, and that is why he loathed me," Ebba insisted. She believed the man had denounced her to make her pay.

"How could that have happened; the man can't even move around?" I asked.

The widow was convinced a dammed-up grudge finds a way.

"But why would he have shot himself in the foot like that?" I asked.

"The Judge hasn't understood anything then!" Ebba said.

"What is so incomprehensible in all this?" I asked.

"The whole thing," was her answer.

NINE

☙

*Chapter Nine, in which the Judge admits his
perplexity in front of the children.*

*E*BBA'S CHILDLESSNESS WAS her misfortune and her blessing.
When I admonished Ebba about children's unruliness, she
answered bitterly with the proverb: whosoever has a wife has
a burden; whosoever has a child has two!

I haven't talked to you about my children. It isn't because
I don't consider them important. Children are a touchy subject for a man. During the witch trials they were still small;
only Hans and Ilia were in their teens. I worried about them
a lot. For summer I had them outfitted with leather shoes,
the kind we grown-ups wear, so that a snake couldn't sting
them, or they wouldn't step on anything sharp. But when I
watched their play from my study, I saw not one of them
wore shoes. I found the shoes under the steps where they
were hidden amongst wild lettuce and fireweed. Only Ilia,
her father's girl, kept hers with her. She was wearing them
around her neck as if they were a pagan amulet.

I worried a great deal about the children, but I didn't understand them. When they heard that Karin P. had been given a death sentence, they demanded permission to take biscuits and sweets to the old woman to console her. Despite all that, they were interested in the details of the beheading and kept asking when the executioner would arrive on the island. "We'll let the executioner sleep at our place, won't we?" "What does an executioner eat?" "Father will let the executioner eat at our place, won't he?" Karin P. was a pet to them whom, in spite of their great affection, they were ready to exchange for the creature who would end the pet's days.

I remember how little Märta sat on my lap on an August evening scratching the innumerable mosquito bites on her fat legs and leaning her mop of hair smelling of the sun's heat against my chin. "Which way would Father rather die, in the fire or head cut off?" she asked. "Neither, because I haven't done anything bad," I answered. "Well, but if you had to, if someone forced Father to make a choice?" she said. "No one will enforce such a thing if one has been good," I said instructively. Märta was not satisfied. "Karin also says that she hasn't done anything bad, and yet she has to choose them both," Märta said. "Karin is lying," I answered. Märta was quiet for a moment and had me scratch her mosquito bites. "Which way would Father rather die, then, in water or in fire?" she asked.

I was once at a funeral where all the family members of the deceased cried, with the exception of the four year old daughter. While the others lamented and blew their noses in their handkerchiefs, the girl threw pebbles on her mother's coffin and sang her ditties. Back at the house she cried for the first time and that was because she wasn't given freshly baked cake. The girl was the only child, the apple of her mother's eye, and everyone had always thought of her as a kind, tender-hearted child.

It's wrong to say that children don't know how to mourn, but they don't mourn death. They bear sorrow about strange things, but they don't understand great losses. That's why I sometimes found it difficult to socialize with children; their lack of logic made me confused and ... horrified. I let Elsa take care of them and comfort me by saying that they were good and funny children and I had reason to be proud of them.

I would have wanted to have a close relationship with my oldest son, Hans. I would have wanted to go into his room in the evenings like my father had come to mine, but Elsa was the one who made sure that Hans went to bed. Usually he had already fallen asleep when I went to his bedside. I'd put my hand on his cheek, but he used to push it aside and mumble in his sleep that he was hot. I felt my hand. I wondered why it wasn't cool like my father's hand used to be.

When those who were sentenced to die talked longingly about their children, I felt sympathy towards them. Their crimes didn't, by any means, close my eyes to the human side in them, but the scene I had witnessed at the funeral convinced me that the pain of parting was more real to mother than to offspring.

Anna B.'s case was different. The tragedy which began at the time of her imprisonment upset me thoroughly. With the widow Ebba I had, in spite of the problematic nature of her confessions, lulled myself into a kind of belief that things would take care of themselves as they should. Bryniel Kjellinus performed miracles again, which amazed me. When I asked Ebba about other witches, she said that she could, of course, name a group of other women, but how would I know that it wasn't a malicious wish on her part to see innocents suffer. I ordered her to make her knowledge known and not to examine the reasons, because that was our duty, but Ebba said that without lying she couldn't be a witness to anyone but her own unworthiness.

The Parson made her talk. Ebba named Anna B. from Högbolstad, saying she had seen her together with Maria and Lisbeta at the Witches' Sabbath. I told Bryniel Kjellinus about Ebba's statement, and we agreed that we wouldn't take any action with Anna without absolute, additional proof. During the very first examination the Parson found a clear *stigma diabolicum*, marks left by teeth between her ribs, marks which were not tender when the Provost, unbeknown to the accused, pricked them with a needle. That was reason enough for imprisonment. Up to this point we had considered it self-evident that finding a witch's mark was also reason enough to proceed with torture, but Ebba's words had made me doubtful.

I spent many days searching for confirmation in writing. By itself, the opinion of Turku Court of Appeals didn't convince me. To Anna's misfortune, for the first time I got thoroughly engrossed in Bernhard Waldschmidt's work *Pythonissa Endorea* and he, in agreement with Bodin, stated that the mark was indeed justification enough for torture. He argued the matter exhaustively and logically; after that I had no pretext for saving Anna.

When I had a conversation with Ebba H. after Anna was taken prisoner, Ebba swore we were crazy if we seriously believed evil of Anna. I reminded Ebba that she was the one who, without being tortured, had denounced Anna. She screamed we must not add more to her burden, but must let poor Anna go immediately. She argued it was at Sund's church she had seen Anna, not Blue Mountain, and that it was cruel to make an innocent woman pay for her mistakes. I said her statement didn't make much sense; a person couldn't possibly confuse Blue Mountain with the House of God. Ebba stood stubbornly by her word.

During the first week of Anna B.'s imprisonment Ebba's hair turned grey. When I went to see her one February morning, she tore the woollen hat off her head and showed it, pointed at her lifeless and drooping hair.

"I cannot stand her cries," she said. "Torture my orphans, disgrace Mat's grave, but don't do any harm to Anna," she said and cried.

"Anna has nothing to worry about if she is innocent!" I answered soothingly.

"Why do you all lie?" the widow asked. Her eyes were watery and bloodshot like a drunkard's, or like the eyes of someone who is sick. I realized she was becoming confused in her ranting.

She took me by my shoulders and shook hard for someone so small and weak.

"What have you done to me, what are you doing to all of us?" she screamed. She looked at me piercingly, mouth open, a bubble of saliva quivering on her gums.

"You better rest and calm down!" I said in a friendly manner. I decided right then that Anna would be moved further away; undoubtedly it would make Ebba's situation easier.

CHAPTER

TEN

ℭ

*Chapter Ten, a dark and tragic chapter in which Anna B.
is forced to taste the most bitter mead in a woman's life.
The Judge meets a servant girl whose cruelty shocks him deeply.*

I WAS PRESENT when Anna B. was taken prisoner. It wasn't
part of my duties; I had just happened to come along. I guess
I must have had some reason for it, but I can't for the life of
me remember what it might have been.

Anna B. was of medium complexion, an ordinary looking
woman. When we arrived at the yard she was at the well.
With a swing of her hand she took the pail from the pole and
the winch sprang upright. As she got hold of the poles, we
saw that she was wearing a pair of men's boots under her red
skirt. The sleeves of her sweater reached down to the tips of
her fingers and her cheeks were frost-bitten.

"Joseph isn't here," she said. She put the poles down and
came to stand by the sleigh. "Joseph is in Stockholm, but he
said he had taken the deed for the land to the Chief of Police
before he left," Anna explained. Light flakes of snow fell on

her hair and melted away immediately.

She reminded me of Ambrosia, my mother's servant. I don't know why. Perhaps Ambrosia had sometimes come to stand right in front of the fireplace with snow on her hair, and I had watched it melt as it was doing now. Or did it snow when Ambrosia was put to rest in her improbable coffin? I remember watching drops of water running along a wrinkled hand left hanging outside the feed box. One of the farm hands had picked up a long stick and moved the hand so it rested on her body. Was Ambrosia's hand now stretching towards me from the mist of my childhood and showing me how tiny patterns of snow could vary so?

Anna's fingers reached down towards the buckets, but didn't take hold of the handles because the Chief of Police hadn't answered her.

We got down from the sleigh. The driver walked towards the horses' heads, the Chief asked Anna to follow us indoors.

"Has something happened to Joseph?" the woman asked. Her voice didn't reflect any worry. "Do you have some information for me?" She followed us, then remembered the pails of water and went back to fetch them.

"Take some clothing with you; you must come with us to Kastelholm," the Police Chief said.

"Why?" Anna asked.

The Chief didn't answer. Anna went in and came back with a two year old child in her arms.

"I can't go anywhere; the boy is sick and Joseph isn't home," she said.

"Don't you have a servant?" I asked.

She answered that she did, but the boy couldn't be left in the servant's care. She smiled apologetically while saying it.

She didn't understand the seriousness of the situation. Or perhaps it was an act of self-deception; the fingers that rested on the child's thin shoulder told of something other than self-deception. The boy put his fingers in his mother's mouth while she talked. To me the child didn't look sick, just sleepy.

The encounter that followed was so repugnant I regretted I had come along. When Anna understood we wouldn't leave without her, she held onto her son and begged us to wait until the child got better, or Joseph, her husband, had returned. She and the child both cried. The Police Chief cursed and asked her to come voluntarily.

"You cannot take me now!" she screamed.

The Chief called to the driver and ordered him to separate Anna from her child and let the servant, who was peering from behind a pony, look after the boy. After he made a couple of listless efforts, the man shook his head; no, nothing would come of it! He didn't want to touch the mother any more than he wanted to touch the child. The Chief got angry. What in hell was this? Couldn't a full-grown man handle a woman? Why hadn't he brought blankets along! He poked the driver in the back, but the man only managed to take a couple of unwilling steps towards the woman, put out his hand in a gesture of begging. Then the Chief tore the child from Anna and thrust him into the servant's arms.

"These fool's games end right here, woman!"

One of Anna's boots was left lying in the snow as she vainly struggled to get free. I pointed it out to the Chief, but he didn't notice my gesture. I myself went to pick it up, the boot had swallowed a mouthful of feathery snow, and I beat it clean against my leg. One could hear the child's piercing cry from indoors.

As I got into the sleigh, I handed the boot to Anna, but to my surprise she flung it violently into a snowbank. The resistance continued for the entire duration of the journey. I had to drive the horses myself, while the driver and the Chief held the violently struggling woman down. I fervently hoped no one would see us.

Watching Anna I learned the innumerable forms female hysteria takes. It simply wasn't possible to carry on a sensible conversation with her; every time I went to her lockup she cried for me to let her go to her child before it was too late. Or she wailed quietly and shook her head in desperation, swaying her body monotonously from side to side. Nothing but the child at home interested her.

"What kind of a witch am I?" Anna yelled. "A little boy dies while you demand I talk nonsense!" she said.

"The servant will look after the child; he is in no trouble!" I comforted her, but she shook her head.

"Elin hates the boy; I've seen it right from the beginning!" she insisted.

"Surely not!" I argued. "Why would she hate a child?" I asked.

"Because she was Joseph's mistress before we got married and might still be!" she said.

I was silent. She had made a serious accusation; at its least serious, the matter would have demanded examination as possible slander, but pity overtook the judge in me.

"It is sad if that's the case!" I sympathized.

"That doesn't matter! If I can get to the boy, nothing else matters!" she answered.

"Truly not?" I asked.

Anna's answer was "No." "Not any longer!" she said. The Provost was also puzzled about Anna. "That woman is made of stone!" the torturer told me. He complained that he couldn't get anything out of Anna by ordinary methods. "That means she is innocent," I answered, relieved. "Not at all!" Parson Kjellinus interrupted our conversation. He explained he had heard that Anna refused to talk because if she did, she would lose her last chance to see her child. "But how can she stand the pain; that is what I cannot understand, unless she is, in fact, innocent," I argued. "Women will endure anything for their children," Kjellinus reminded us. "After all, they stand the pain of giving birth and often don't make a sound."

I noted in my report on the proceedings that Anna B. resisted torture as if her fingers were made of stone, but also that we wouldn't give up as yet.

"Can't anyone tell me how the boy is?" Anna cried when I, following the Provost, went in to interrogate her. "Is it too much to ask that someone would go and see how Thomas is?" she cried. She took hold of my sleeve and I, annoyed, tried to make her let go of it. The crushed fingertips left stains on the cloth. The jailer's wife advised me the blood would come off if the sleeve were first soaked in cold water and only after that soap and warm water were used to wash it away.

I told Bryniel Kjellinus I didn't believe in Anna B.'s guilt and that I was going to inform the jurors of my understanding of the matter. The Parson suggested we try one more method. We would promise to go and see the child on condition that Anna became more cooperative. We might also agree to arrange for some other woman to be the boy's nurse.

The suggestion made me apprehensive; Anna was so distraught she could even lie if she thought it would benefit the boy. Ordinary humanity demanded that the child of the accused be cared for while both parents were away. The Parson, for his part, didn't believe the child to be in any danger, but when Anna stubbornly claimed that to be so, the suggestion could be used as proof of good will on the part of the examiners.

"I feel that in this case we make more progress with the good than the bad," Bryniel Kjellinus said.

After consultation, we agreed that Kjellinus should promise Anna that her child would be visited, and that he would be taken care of, but on condition that Anna answer honestly the questions put to her.

I ought to have gone along. I had, after all, suspected Bryniel Kjellinus' unusual efficiency all along. But I had also harboured in my memory images of the Parson's sense of charity.

One January evening I had visited Kjellinus and found him in his study nursing a sick cat. When I arrived he had been on his knees on the floor washing up a smelly mess the cat had released from one or another orifice. "What is that — excrement?" I asked, repelled. And he answered that it was what it was; the cat no longer had control of his bowels, that's how sick the poor thing was. And I asked why he didn't finish the animal off, or at least call for a servant to clean up the mess, but he said the cat had been his friend for eleven years. He wouldn't even consider abandoning the animal in its time of suffering.

Kjellinus finally got Anna B. to open up. In the presence of the jurors, the accused confessed she had conducted cattle sorcery, or used magic words in various situations. She didn't admit to having slept with the Devil, but we were satisfied with such a promising beginning. Between confessions, Anna licked the tips of her fingers; they had started to ache now, she explained. I suggested we bandage the fingers, but Anna said blowing on them eased the pain enough. She swayed back and forth while she spoke; her body was no longer of stone. While we pondered how late the interrogation would continue, the prisoner leaned her head on the bench's back with her eyes closed. But she wasn't asleep.

"If only one could fall asleep," she said.

After the interrogation Kjellinus was sent for to attend a dying parishioner. Anna looked upset.

"What about me?" she asked after Kjellinus had gone. "The Parson was supposed to take me to see the boy!" she said.

"No, not at all!" I answered. "We promised that the boy

would be taken care of, nothing more!" I corrected her.

Anna's look shifted from me and the jurors to the smoke-blackened walls beside the hearth. What was so interesting there? A couple of stones had got loose. The flames visible in the opening between them reminded one of lightning. Behind the crevice shone a muted fire.

"Bring her some barley gruel!" I said to the Police Chief's aid.

Anna stared at the wall in deep concentration. A thin line appeared between her brows.

When the servant pushed the dish of hot gruel onto the prisoner's lap, she turned to look at it, examining it as intensely as she had examined the wall a moment ago. The jurors were silent. They expected the accused would spoon the gruel into her mouth. Or at least blow on it. And lap it up; yes, under these circumstances no one would consider devouring it wrong, for they knew that she hadn't enjoyed a decent meal in days.

I don't remember which happened first: did the plate fly, or did Anna scream? Suddenly the servant had the gruel all over him, and he also started to scream. The plate rolled along the floor and bumped against the boot of a farmer from Sund. The servant howled that he was burnt, a juror bent down to pick up the plate and dangled it between his thumb and forefinger, perplexed, while drops of gruel dripped slowly onto the floor. And above the whole commotion rang the powerful canon of Anna's changing screams. Once begun, it renewed itself untiringly at varying strengths and sounds.

After she had been taken away, the screams remained in the courtroom.

I understood that Anna had been deceived. I knew who the deceiver was: Bryniel Kjellinus was supposed to promise that the son of the accused would be cared for, but he had gone ahead and promised more. He had anticipated what would make the woman give in — the possibility of seeing the child, of taking him into her arms, of saying soothing words to him, of hugging him.

All that I had got out of Anna with one sentence. And the Parson had known that too.

Later on the jailer's wife told me Anna B. had promised her ten thalers and several sacks of grain if she fetched the child to the castle and let her see him now and then. When I admonished the wife for keeping it a secret at first, she said the only thing she regretted was that she didn't go and take the child to her own mother. Women are like that where children are concerned, nothing breaks their defiance. They are too suspicious of each other to be of one mind, but they don't forgive any interference with motherhood.

I didn't go straight home. I would keep my own part of the bargain, I thought. Personally. This time I wouldn't send either the Chief of Police or the Parson on the errand. The sky produced grey, thawing snow; the driver complained about the snowdrifts on Högbolstad road, he might get stuck. I told him the horse would be beaten into blood sausage if necessary, but we wouldn't change direction. And he kept beating it. The horse struggled in the snow as the blows fell on him; foam ran from the bridle. I didn't doubt for a moment the horse's ability to take us all the way to our destination.

I found Elin kneading dough. Seeing us, the servant began to smooth her hair with floury hands. The table shone as if newly washed, the benches gleamed.

"I'm making bread for Anna," she said.

I nodded.

"I don't suppose you have come to fetch the boy yet?" She sounded worried.

"What do you mean?" I asked.

"I thought they might as well take fresh bread to Anna

when they take the boy," the servant said. She explained in an apologetic voice that she had had difficulties sending anything to her mistress because the roads had been in such a miserable state, and no one had had any errands in that direction.

"What taking of the boy are you talking about?" I asked.

"The Parson visited here and promised to send someone to get him!" Elin answered.

Elin scraped the hardened dough from the edges of the bowl. "The Parson promised to take care of the boy since I'm alone here," she explained.

I kept nodding, vexed. Behind Elin was a cupboard-bed, the door of which was partly open. In each of the four decorative squares was a large, engraved flower, but the paint had faded and flaked off.

"Where is the boy; I want to see him," I said.

My question raised Elin's eyebrows. She quickly licked the dough off her fingers.

"In the barn. Yes, I certainly can't very well keep him indoors!" she said. She started to work the dough again to avoid meeting my stare.

"As far as I'm concerned, he can be taken away now; I can send the bread along later," she said.

I looked at the gleaming benches and the table which were scrubbed so that the grain shone as if it were a piece of freshly cut wood. I looked at Elin's clothes and the fresh boughs of spruce in the corner. The driver, who had followed me in, blew his nose and took off his fur hat.

"Did Bryniel Kjellinus know the child is out there?" I asked.

Elin stopped working the dough. "Of course he knew; he was the one who gave him the last rites."

She said the Parson had promised to take care of the funeral and even do it for nothing. Kjellinus had promised that as soon as he could take time from his other duties, he would send a man to arrange it.

"When did he say that?" I asked.

Elin moved her floury fingers. "Three, four days ago!" she said.

I left without saying goodbye, the driver at my heels. On the steps I turned around and marched back in.

"How did it happen?" I asked the servant, who was kneading the dough with all her strength, thinking she had got rid of me.

"The death?" she asked.

I nodded.

"I was alone here; somebody had to do the chores!" she said defensively.

"How did it happen?" I asked. I had not struck anyone for many years. In Tartu I had often fought, and at the beginning of our marriage I would return Elsa's blows. Now I knew I would strike Elin if she didn't answer.

"How did it happen?"

"The boy was sick; didn't the Judge know it?" she said in a loud voice.

"How did it happen?" I shouted. I didn't touch her. I slammed the open door of the cupboard-bed closed.

Elin burst into tears. "I wasn't here; I came in here and he was there, in the corner, in a heap!" she explained. "I had told him he was to stay in bed, but ... the boy cried for Anna the whole time!"

She had left him alone! Left a sick child alone, for who knows how long.

"You couldn't listen to the crying, and the chores had to be taken care of," Elin whined.

"How long were you away?" I insisted.

"Not very long; I had to go to the ship and sell butter!" she answered.

"Did you come home alone?" Holding onto her arm, I pushed her against the table. "Did you?"

She cried and couldn't manage an answer. I let her go. "Answer!" I ordered.

"I did, on my word of honour!" her voice was thick, as if she had a cold.

"Is that the truth?" I insisted.

"It is, but ..." She started to cry again.

"But what?" I asked.

She raised her hand to her mouth. "The weather was horrible, I was forced to wait ... you wouldn't have put a dog outdoors."

"Did you get back before dark?" I asked with so calm a voice I even surprised myself.

She took a few steps backwards. "No, I didn't," she answered. She looked at me, frightened; the skin under her eyes shone and her cheeks were streaked with flour.

"You won't tell the master!" the servant pleaded.

I turned around and left. The driver stood in the middle of the yard making a lot of noise clapping his hands together. Only then did I notice that my own hands were still squeezed into fists.

J AM NO LONGER completely convinced that the story makes any sense.

The man isn't sitting in the rain under a dripping porch light any longer; he is in my study. He wanted to tell a story and I needed one, but the collaboration isn't working the way I had imagined it would.

As my sympathy towards him has increased, so has his humility fallen off in equal measure. He is self-assured, even arrogant, when he sees that he is being listened to. He also takes notice of my irritation.

— People avoid a person with a guilty conscience. They're probably afraid that it is contagious, he comments sarcastically.

I don't answer him because I'm not yet confused enough to start talking to ghosts.

And what would I answer anyway? That the way he leads me on irritates me, the way he tells of things other than those he pretends to be telling. It seems to me he isn't telling the truth. In insignificant matters he is — to be sure — exhibitionistically honest (when he knows I'll verify things) perhaps in order to lie all the more outrageously about greater ones. For example, the way he presents the Parson as the guilty party is rather questionable. Is he thinking of making a confession as a matter of course, or is he plotting to compose his own detective story?

I leave him and go downstairs to make sandwiches and coffee. Into another world three hundred years hence in time. As if suggestive of something, there's a pile of laundry in front of the washing machine, toys and crayons on the floor, in the middle of the carpet a muddy pair of boots, size twenty-four, on the table a newspaper open at the foreign news pages: Iraq struck a tanker from Cyprus; Hindus killed in India; Israel fired at a mosque; Tourists died in Taiwan; Gale returned to the USSR; A violent skirmish in Spain; Columbia chose a new president; Tamils attacked again.

Perhaps my theory about novels is too constricting; I don't accept in a work of fiction the kind of insanity which in the course of ordinary living I swallow every day. A limited amount of suffering, surprises, happy or unhappy events are appropriate in a novel; life, on the other hand, can waste them all at will.

The phone rings. My friend sounds short of breath as she tells me what her jealous husband has done again. She is unhappy, even cries a little. What should one do? she asks. Tell me, for God's sake, what do I do with the man? Perhaps one ought to leave a man like that? But no. How would one live without a man now, tell me! And they're all the same, making a change won't help matters, and nothing would come of it anyway.... We must get together one of these days, she says, really talk about things.

We all have our nightmares. My collaborator, whom I have voluntarily chosen, is a mad murderer. Although history is full of good, heroic people! An old, misguided man with a sick mind is waiting upstairs, a man I let in. Why?

Why did Robert Koch struggle with the tubercle bacillus even though he had a nice, flourishing practice in a well-functioning small town? What was there in watching bleary-eyed, sick guinea pigs and unpleasant microbes for hours on end when he could have concentrated on collecting art or going to opera?

Postscripts speak about willingness to heal, a doctor's innermost calling. I think it's nonsense. We can't talk about ambition either; the chance of success is so remote. Koch wouldn't have wanted to hunt microbes at all, but rather big game in Lahore or Patagonia. While he struggled with tuberculosis-infected guinea pigs, he dreamed about heroic deeds among tigers or boars. The microscope was only a toy for him, a kind of compensation for adventures that had remained unadventured. And all that because the woman he loved had promised to marry him only on condition that there would be no more talk about foolish dreams and trips to foreign lands.

The discovery might have been very beneficial for humanity, but not for Koch. In his old age he took revenge on his wife by eloping to the ends of the earth with a ballet dancer.

No, no! Psilander's case is clearly beginning to affect everything I'm studying. I'm like some village Colombo who digs for underhanded reasons, hidden motives and wrong appetites under seemingly innocent deeds. Why did I begin this task? And why do I let him terrorize me? I made him up, after all, and he simply has to function in accordance with my plans for the world, give wrong judgements when I so dictate and grieve when I give him permission to grieve. It shouldn't be so difficult; you don't have to be a genius to be a character in a novel!

I go upstairs full of self-confidence and the will to do battle. I have proven the world needn't necessarily be evil, that a human being is not just a selfish beast....

I forget to turn the washing machine on. It's the only task I have to take care of during the day. It isn't asking for much. To put the washing in the machine and hang the previous load up to dry. Nothing else is expected of me.

I stand at the door arms full of damp clothes and outside it's snowing wet snow. It is ridiculous to confess these have been stressful times for me, stressful to sleep, and even more so to wake up and go with effort to the typewriter and pile of papers. The October scenery is bereft of joy; so is the subject in which I have, against my better judgement, immersed myself. How is it possible that someone could envy this role?

Before drowning in self-pity, I think of the alternative: having to get up two hours earlier, stand in a downpour on the side of a road by the edge of the woods waiting for a bus, force myself in front of unfriendly faces. *A poor mother searches for her child.* "Which word is the subject of the sentence?" "A mother, a poor mother!" "And the predicate?" "Searches." "And what kind of a verb is the predicate?" "The main linking verb." "It is particularly important to remember that the predicate is the most central element of the sentence and cannot be missing from a single complete sentence."

And not a word about what will happen to the child? What happens to the mother? Does she find the child before it's too late? And why has the child disappeared in the first place? What other human tragedies does the chain of events embrace? Why does such a heavy misfortune have to happen specifically to a poor mother? But no, only the fact that the predicate is the main linking verb is important. And at the same time one knows that it isn't at all important, not to me, and especially not to the bored students. It is least important of all to the anxious mother trying to find her child.

I'd rather endure the anxiety the Judge has awakened in me and accept the challenge of the empty page. There's just the necessity of finding a strong enough armour; with it on I could approach the one I'm describing without worry, without him aiming his invisible cupping horn at me to suck at my identity.

I mustn't fear him. Not even if he is the male shadow of my subconscious spilling forth. Jung conversed with his own feminine shadow many years; I guess I can stand it for a few months. If my personality is of lesser value, and the rejected part wants to speak through the secret language of fiction, it is merely a good sign. Not taking notice of the shadow, or its rejection, rather, can lead to dangerous conflicts, says Jung. On the other hand, becoming one with it is even more destructive.

But when I'm upstairs once again at the typewriter and study the Judge, I feel psychoanalysts alone aren't enough to explain his presence. Men live in every woman, women in every man. That surely is not nonsense, but there's something else in him. Something that doesn't originate in me, something which has nothing to do with me.

— Bryniel Kjellinus' study was gloomy and cold, quite different from your author's study....

I don't start writing but turn my back on him, and, scheming, study Jung's collected works.

— I describe here Parson Kjellinus' study; it was like ...

I let him speak, I make comparisons, ponder whom to believe, Dr. Jung, myself, or the old man.

Judge: — If you're having a bad day for writing, perhaps ...

(C.G. Jung: — The shadow cast by the conscious mind con-
tains hidden, repressed, often nefarious aspects of the personal-
ity, the extreme branches of which extend into the lower
reaches of uncontrolled emotions and primitive behaviour,
reaches which encompass the entire historical point of view of
the subconscious. If to date we have been of the opinion that
the shadow is at the core of all evil, now we can acknowledge
that the human subconscious doesn't contain only pursuits
rejected on moral grounds, but that it embraces also a lot of
good, that is normal instincts, meaningful reactions, realistic
perceptions, creative impulses and so forth....)

If the Judge is my shadow being, where is his hidden persona? Is the novel about to become a series of mirrors and hidden riddles?

— I'm not having a bad day. If that were the case, I wouldn't be sitting in front of the typewriter, I'd run around the house with a paintbrush in hand instead, and I would busy myself with every possible task like a little demon. Five weeks ago, for your sake, the innards of this house changed their colour to white, but when this task is finished, I believe I'll be your master!

— Bryniel Kjellinus' study was gloomy and cold....

☙

ELEVEN

Chapter Eleven, in which the Judge and the Parson chat about the old university days and a little about other matters as well.

BRYNIEL KJELLINUS' STUDY was gloomy and cold. The windows were streaked with dirt, and dead flies lay in the dust in front of the windows. "I don't allow women folk in here messing things up," he had said once. "Not even your own wife?" "Especially not her," the Parson answered. He had smiled, and so had I.

This time the atmosphere was different. Before, I had pretended to accept the disorder of his books and the soiled chair-covers as signs of a distinct personality; the fact that a person didn't care about his surroundings was a sign of a rich inner life, I had assured myself. Now his study brought to mind a barbarian's cave. I saw it as symbolizing the landscape of an uncaring soul.

"Of course I knew about the child's death; it was I, after all, who conducted the burial service," the Parson said.

I asked why he had insisted then that there was nothing

the matter with the boy.

"To get a confession," he answered.

"By telling a lie?" I asked.

"It wasn't a lie; the boy is in paradise already, is he not?" he said.

"You can't be serious?" I asked.

"Of course I am; how else could I conduct the duties of a clergyman," he asked.

He wanted to split hairs. Perhaps to embarrass me because he suspected I had come to relieve him of his duties. Why not, I thought. Let's talk in a way that placates him. There were moss-green goblets on the table. Some were empty, some still had a drop of wine in them. He obviously took a clean glass each time he sat down to write, but he couldn't be too greedy for wine since he didn't drain the glasses to the bottom.

"What, in your opinion, is the meaning of faith?" I asked.

He needed no time to think.

"To save souls for the eternal life," he answered.

"You are the sworn enemy of death, then," I said. He nodded.

"And it isn't the least bit strange to you that you show your animosity by destroying life?" I asked.

The Parson shrugged his shoulders. "If a grain of wheat perishes not ... ," he said. He offered me a chair covered with cat-hair. "Do not, dear friend, claim that I was the one who invented death," he added.

"Not death, not even killing," I admitted.

"Death was invented by murderers and judges."

"Sometimes one does ponder the difference between the two," I confessed. The Parson believed he knew what it was.

"The more people there are taking part in deciding about someone's death, the more it belongs in the realm of justice, not murder," he said.

"Or, the greater the number of people killed, the less one can talk about it as murder," I said.

It was said in irony, of course, but at the same time I felt I wasn't altogether wrong. People are not horrified when they hear the papists have killed ten thousand of us in a battle, but, spurred on by passion for revenge, they are ready to enlist when sailors tell of a monk who strangled a single girl he had raped. If someone tells them that soldiers shame and kill women and, depending on the soldiers' leanings, even small boys, people will merely say: but of course, they are soldiers, aren't they!

"The central idea here is one which, in the course of its protection, sometimes demands a killing!" Kjellinus said. He opened a cupboard behind him and took out a bottle. He raised it questioningly; I shook my head. He set up a glass before him, but at the same time he gave an embarrassed laugh when he noticed the bottle was empty. So it is then referred to as God's idea, the state's idea; we call it a punishment. But appealing to one's own personal view does not qualify as defence in an ordinary murder case. There wasn't a philosophy of murder for everyone; God's rights were not to be appropriated, they were given! And quite by accident I had got my own philosophy during the Schöps' campaign when the King had grown tired of dereliction and having disagreeable faces around him. Bryniel Kjellinus, in turn, had received his system of justice by being too delicately built to walk behind a horse and plough, or to lift and carry logs.

"How do you know that it is we, specifically, who know how to interpret the idea correctly?" I asked.

He was quiet for a moment. Then he wanted to know if I remembered the conferring of my own Master of Arts degree. I said I did, but couldn't understand what that had to do with all this. At the convocation they had played the very beautiful hymn *Veni Sancte Spiritus* which I sometimes tried to hum when I was alone. But the Parson had not been referring to music. He asked which of the symbols I had received was the first one.

"A book," I said.

"Exactly. A book. The storehouse of all knowledge and wisdom."

"Yes. It's from a book I too have set out to do what I'm doing."

"Quite so, but was it open or closed at first?"

"First open, then closed."

"Why was it open at first?"

"I can't remember; it was part of the ceremony, I think!"

"It did have a meaning, but what?"

"I really don't remember!"

Bryniel Kjellinus smiled. Triumphantly. How he enjoyed a brotherly opportunity to pull my hair because of my poor memory.

"The books had to be open so that those about to be conferred their degrees wouldn't be overtaken by the empty, false belief of being all-knowing!" he said. "Being all-knowing is not for human beings; only God is omniscient," he said.

"But of course, and in awkward matters clergymen were the interpreters of the All Powerful!"

Only later did I notice that Kjellinus hadn't said anything about the second part of the ceremony. Closing the books also had its symbolism. It suggested the graduates shouldn't merely trust books and therefore continually be led by the opinions of others.

That came to my mind only a few days later when I read Ludwig Dunte's work, *Decisiones mille et sex casuum conscientiae*, that had come out only a couple of years earlier in Ratzeburgh. An acquaintance of mine had forwarded it to me specifically with these witch trials in mind. The book disturbed me. Dunte had found out there were melancholic witches who were under Satan's influence to the degree that they believed they had made a pact with him and confessed things that were purely imaginary. According to Dunte, under no circumstances were they to be punished, because they were sick. Even generally speaking, the learned writers of the work warned officialdom in stern words not to sentence innocents as witches. Mayfarth especially argued against torture because it had been found to result in false confessions.

"The law is fascinating," I said.

"Yes, the symbol of sovereignty!" the Parson answered. It seemed he was very proud of his own.

"That is what they gave also to the freed slaves in Rome," I said.

He pretended he didn't notice my needling.

"We had freed ourselves from brutality and stupidity, with manly courage struggled to free ourselves from ignorance!" he said.

I had had enough. "I do not endorse what was done to Anna B.," I said.

He was moving books around in the midst of the flies and dust in front of the window as if he was looking for something specific. "Is not the fact that we got a confession the main thing?" he asked.

"First of all, it was only a partial confession, rather a flimsy one at that, and secondly, I do not accept the doubtful means by which it was secured," I answered.

"Well if that is where the fault lies, that the confession isn't substantial enough, I have an idea how to get a better one," he said.

"What do you mean?" I asked. I was barely able to believe he could be that arrogant. I had been utterly wrong about his character.

"I believe the case can be brought ahead so that she can be beheaded with the others," Kjellinus said. He turned to look for a book he wanted me to read. He was serious; all that searching didn't mean that he couldn't look me in the eye. I watched his bent back, its lack of strength, with loathing. He couldn't grasp the fact he had made a tragic mistake. He wasn't going to leave unless I specifically asked him.

The sun tried to peek into our cave of spider-webs; it was melting the icicles in front of it. One could see fingerprints on the windows, and for the first time I realized that the Parson too had children. Possibly they had peeked in the window while their father wrote his sermons or thought about different ways to torture women.

"What would you say if your children ... ," I began. He asked me to go on as I wondered where the book he was searching for had disappeared. No, I couldn't ask him that, after all.

I would be like five year old Märta: which way would you rather die, by water or by fire? One couldn't ask that kind of a question, either.

Bryniel Kjellinus was a worthless human being, but was he wrong in the legal sense? The child of the accused had died. That was a fact we could no longer change. It had to be in the power of the interrogator to decide when and how the prisoner would be told about the death. The Parson had chosen the cruel method of being silent this long so that the case wouldn't be affected by what had happened, but that couldn't be held against him.

No! I was a coward who had difficulty stating facts as they were. I went to the door, safely near the path of escape.

"As far as you are concerned, the investigation of this case ends here!" I said.

He turned around, surprised. The sun was in his eyes and he squinted as if he saw a strange animal before him.

"What?" he asked.

"You have made an unforgivable mistake," I said.

"You cannot be serious." He was astounded.

"Yes, I am," I answered.

The Parson flushed deeply. He said he couldn't accept my decision. I replied it didn't require his acceptance. He reminded me that in matters of witchcraft we always had to be guided by the authority of the Church, that he would make a complaint if he wasn't heard.

"Good," I said. "In the chapter on Anna B., I'll make note of your differing opinion; I'll write that you thought the case could be brought to a conclusion at the same beheading where the others suffer their punishment."

The Parson nodded. What was meant to be a sarcasm comforted him. As I was leaving, he even asked if I didn't want to know which book he had wished to lend me. I said I didn't.

But it was a lie. I noticed myself wondering about it many times that evening.

CHAPTER

TWELVE

ↂ

Chapter Twelve, in which a coffin is opened and other secrets are hinted at. The Judge finds out that he has been bitterly deceived.

ANNA WAS TOLD about the child's death in as gentle a way as possible. Not about how he cried after his mother, his hiding in a corner, having been left alone. Only about a sudden rise in fever and a quick, painless departure. But even that was too much. When a new interrogation was arranged, she confessed her guilt concerning every *magiam divinatoriam*.

I had to sentence her to death.

It was a loss as far as Kjellinus was concerned; by confessing voluntarily, Anna had slipped the hammer in the bells of death the Parson had been casting with such skill and zeal. And so I had to change our weighty disagreement to the weak agreement I now owed Kjellinus.

A couple of days later Anna recanted her confession. She said she had confessed because she was deranged by sorrow. Now she must get out of here because she wanted to bury the child herself. I said I couldn't under any pretext allow a witch who had been sentenced to death to leave the prison prior to the day of execution. She attacked me and tried to scratch me. The jailer barely managed to come in time to help me get away from her.

I looked at Anna through the peephole before I went in the next time. She didn't stay more than a moment in one place and walked, wailing and wringing her hands, around the cramped cell. "Is she in pain, or has she gone mad?" I asked the jailer, Erik Eriksson. He answered that Anna B. had been like that from the day she was taken prisoner. I said to him it would be good if he stayed close by when I went in.

"Has Joseph not come back yet?" Anna asked.

I said not to my knowledge at least.

"Is my son dead?" she asked.

"Yes," I answered, adding that she knew that.

She rubbed her hands against her clothes, up and down against the faded dress. "How do I know what is the truth, what are lies," she said in distress. She had woken up in the night feeling that despite everything, the child was still alive and she was told of his death only so that she would confess. "Why am I not allowed at least to see his body if he is dead?" Anna asked, thoroughly shaking my hand. "Why doesn't anyone tell me?" she shouted.

After a moment she asked why Elin didn't come and visit her.

"Don't you two feel hostility towards each other?" I reminded her.

Anna bit her nails, which no longer had anything left to bite. "People can feel hostility, but still, it is customary that a servant visits the people of the house," she said. "If Joseph or Elin says that Thomas is dead, then I believe it," Anna said.

I remembered that the servant had sent her a bundle. I knocked on the door and told Eriksson to go and fetch what had been brought to the prisoner. Anna didn't appear interested. She went to stand by the iron bars through which one could see a sliver of the sky and the bent crown of a leafless oak. She wore a woollen bonnet she was constantly adjusting. Matted, unwashed strings of hair pushed their way down from under it.

When the jailer pushed the bundle of food in, Anna asked if Elin had brought greetings from the boy. I closed the door and said only family members are allowed to come all the way inside the castle and she ought to have known the rules by now.

"To hell with the rules!" Anna screamed, "I would only have asked the whore whether Thomas is alive or not." Anna tore the bundle from my hands and trampled on it like a horse. I thought she behaved stupidly and I said so. As an answer she kicked the squashed, egg yolk-soaked mess of cloth into a corner. "I'm not hungry," she said.

Something about her bothered me. There was something that didn't belong to her.

Anna hadn't had a bonnet when she was taken prisoner and no one had visited her. Where had it come from?

She examined the egg-soaked bundle on her knees. Perhaps she hoped to find a sign that the boy was alive, a greeting sent by the child. Her hands groped through the slimy cloth, tore at the bread. Not even by accident did she put her finger in her mouth.

"Where did you get that headdress?" I asked. Anna didn't answer. She got up quickly and dried her hands.

"Will I be allowed out to bury the boy if I tell?" she suggested.

"No; you have to tell in any case," I said.

She smiled. "Are they going to sink hot irons into my breasts, are they going to break my joints, unless I tell?" Anna asked.

I raised my eyebrows. "What is that supposed to mean?"

"That is how the Parson threatens the others!" she answered.

Learning about Kjellinus' audacity wasn't the biggest shock, but that Anna had spoken with the others. And not only spoken, but one of the women had given her the bonnet, I was sure of it. But Anna wouldn't admit it. Whenever I confronted her, she turned her back to me.

I felt an impotent rage. I began to sense the kind of irritation that had driven the Parson to use questionable methods. One couldn't always fetch the Provost; legal pressure tactics didn't necessarily guarantee results. I had to get Anna to speak; this was too important a matter to remain in the folds of her stubborn dumbness. I had pushed Bryniel Kjellinus aside; now I might need his kind of persuasion.

A conspiracy! A calamitous conspiracy of witches, and I wasn't able to do a thing! Had I not sensed all along that something was being whispered and murmured inside these dreary granite walls, words and plans which travelled through the walls as though they were mere curtains waiting to move aside when the witch women arrived? The women were the Devil's hirelings; I had said so to myself, though I hadn't understood it.

Satan can turn into stone as easily as into a cloud, dung is honey to him and flames are drops of rain, rotting flesh means beauty to him and the cries of the innocents are music to his ears. And I had so pitied his allies while they were plotting revenge, scourge and destruction upon us!

How would I get Anna to speak? An officer of King Kaarle's had dug out the eye of an enemy spy with a spoon, and the effect had been instantaneous. At the point where the silver rim of the small bowl was being forced into the eye socket, the man swore he would tell everything. As the eye was flung away, the man died in the middle of his confession. Something had gone wrong. The head of the guards had cursed the blundering fools his men were nowadays. In the old days a one-eyed victim became a good example to be used in training men who got bored during long periods of inactivity.

Not for a minute did I contemplate doing anything like that to the women, although I believed the island to be in danger; I couldn't have handled them so barbarously. I imagined little Märta scratching smallpox abscesses instead of mosquito bites; Ilia with his violet-blue eyes sinking under surging waves; people with accusatory expressions standing outside the office building asking why I hadn't done anything while there still was time.

"You'll be allowed to see your son if you'll tell me everything," I said to Anna. Don't ask whether I even intended to keep that promise. I didn't think about it then. The bonnet had roused a beast the likes of an eagle in me.

Anna was doubtful. Perhaps she was weighing what the betrayal would cost her.

The Devil had forgiven her the confession; surely he would forgive this as well.

"Will I truly see him?" she asked. She had to trust me; it was her only chance.

"Yes," I answered.

"I got it from Lisbeta," she said. "Lisbeta offered shoe polish and the headdress; she had heard that I didn't have enough clothing," Anna went on.

"Shoe polish?" I asked. What did this mean? Did she mock me? She had only one boot, why should it ... ?

"Yes, for witch salve!" Anna said. "So that I wouldn't be tortured any longer."

Shoe polish as witch salve! Kjellinus had demanded she explain. Lisbeta had managed to steal some from the jailer and the Parson had immediately stopped the torture. She had given it to Ebba also, Lisbeta who was so brave. Anna hoped that Lisbeta wouldn't be tortured because of this, but if she was, then perhaps she might understand that she, Anna, had to do this for the child's sake.

"A woman cannot die without knowing how matters stand with her child," Anna said.

This couldn't be true! The conspiracy of witches was turning into a farce about shoe polish; a tragedy of fate whose hero I could have been — one sentence turned things into a farce in which I was a donkey-eared fool. Anna had to be deceiving me; she had cooked up this kind of an answer because she didn't dare tell the truth. That's how it had to be; that deceitful bitch was ready to come up with anything for a chance to see her child!

From that exact moment on I organized an extra interrogation at which the jailer and his wife came up with the answers.

Erik Eriksson stroked the yellowish hair he had combed to cover his bald crown. His wife nodded to him encouragingly. "It's been a hellishly cold winter," he said. "What has that got to do with this?" I asked. He explained: he had to let the prisoners out of their cells to warm themselves in the front hall. Eriksson's wife nodded. "The cells were ice cold during the worst spells; they would have died in there," the woman said.

"But the sentenced and the accused were there at different times," the jailer said. "That's true," the wife added.

I felt both tears and laughter shaking my insides. Unbelievable! Incredible, and without a doubt, true! And the shoe polish, had some of it disappeared? "Oh yes, there were fingerprints in it!" the jailer said. He himself used a piece of felt, so in using it he didn't leave any prints. The wife confirmed he had always used a piece of cloth!

"I already knew it at the time the Parson burnt the witch salve!" the wife said. "I recognized the smell." They were both astonished that Kjellinus didn't sense anything familiar in the smell. Nothing astonished me any longer.

"Was the door to the entrance hall open or closed when the prisoners were warming themselves there?" I asked.

"Closed," the jailer insisted. "Except when food was portioned out."

"Why didn't you tell me these things before?" I asked. My voice no longer had any strength; I wasn't even angry. A human being can stand only so much of his own stupidity.

"I would have, had the Judge asked," the jailer said.

That I hadn't done. And the Court of Appeals had upheld Maria, Lisbeta and Ebba's sentences. They had been sentenced to death on trumped-up evidence! Who knows how great a number of other confessions were equally false.

I went out. I couldn't stand the Kastelholm air, the smell of urine and excrement mixed with the smell of watery pea soup coming from the cells. Eriksson's children were playing in the yard; they had made snowmen, a whole army of snowmen with stick noses and stone eyes. Some of them were prisoners; the children were guards and hangmen and heads made of snow fell one after another to the ground. A little girl approached me and put her hand — blue with cold — into my hand. "Sir, you must pay for watching!" she said. I gave her something from my pocket. She was right; it was customary to pay for watching.

THIRTEEN

ᑲ

Chapter Thirteen, in which the Judge tries to dismiss past mistakes by searching for new offenders. The Judge learns the lesson of a sensible man: whom to accuse and whom not to accuse.

YOU WANT TO KNOW what I did? You read court records, put big red question marks next to court decisions, make sarcastic comments in the margins. You write an article in an historical journal proving I did nothing though I saw what was wrong. You offer different theories about how I was afraid to overturn my own sentencing and therefore have my credibility questioned, or that I was pressured from above, or even that I was as thoroughly hardened a villain as one might expect of a man of law.

You don't understand that entering the shoe polish farce into the records is indicative of taking a stand; I could easily have left it out, but I made a record of it because I wanted to show how matters stood. Doesn't that prove I intended to do something?

There were also facts you can't find in the books, but

ones you ought to know.

I arranged matters so that Anna B. was allowed to see her child. You wouldn't have believed that of me, correct? You guessed that I would not go against the rules by taking Anna out of prison, but that means you underestimated my resourcefulness.

I had the coffin brought to the prison.

First Anna looked at it through the hatch. She said it couldn't be her son's coffin because it was so small. I told her she could come out into the corridor and lift the lid.

Anna came out of her cell and stood by the coffin. She touched its light birch surface with her finger.

"Let's not open it. There's someone else in it, not my son," she said.

"So, it can be taken away, then?" I asked, but she shook her head.

"Perhaps it's a good thing to see how he looks," she answered. "Under the circumstances," she added.

A kerchief under the chin and tied at the top of his head had given the boy's face an expression you might find on the face of an old woman. His head rested on a dark pillow, making it look like a white chalk stone sculpture someone had accidentally dropped there. Anna picked up the hand that had fallen from the position of prayer. "Such a small hand!" Anna said. "It will never do anything any more," she said and laid it, folded with the other, on his chest.

"Well," I cleared my throat.

"He is not my son!" Anna stated. She smiled.

I didn't say anything. Anna kept looking at the child. Slowly a smile spread from inside her face like ashes thrown on water. She touched the lace frills of the shroud respectfully and let her hand slip under the boy's thin neck.

We didn't have time to do anything. The jailer's wife had been choking back tears for a long time now, as women will in these situations. When Anna snatched the body from the coffin and fled down the corridor with it in her arms, the shroud fluttering, Eriksson's wife started to laugh and applaud.

"Do something!" I shouted angrily. But Kirstin Eriksson pointed in helpless laughter at the linens on the floor and the fleeing prisoner and howled.

"Calm down!" the jailer yelled, embarrassed, but only after he had looked at me and understood what was expected of him did he start to run after Anna. She couldn't get far, of course. When she reached the end of the corridor, she looked in vain for another escape route. The jailer stood arms akimbo behind her as if playing tag, and his wife carried on her hysterical laughter. Anna crouched down and covered her child so we couldn't see him. She became a shield between us and the child, and pressed her head against the stone wall.

"Take the child away," I said.

"What?" Erik Eriksson asked. One could see he was upset; the situation came close to being a desecration of a body.

The jailer dragged Anna to the door and tried to tear the child away from her. When the prisoner realized she couldn't keep him, she let him go.

"Don't hurt him any more!" Anna said. Tears ran down both sides of her nose. She didn't have shoes on, only worn-out slippers and wool stockings. That's why she had managed to flee without making a sound, practically floating along the corridor. Now she walked with the heavy steps of a plough-horse back to her cell.

After this incident I wouldn't speak with Anna any more. The jailer swore she had become an exemplary prisoner. "You wouldn't believe she is the same person who caused such turmoil in the prison with her wailing."

Peace had been achieved in the prison, but my own mind was a battlefield of conflicting arguments. The discovery of the shoe polish farce was a serious matter, but from the legal point of view it wasn't significant enough to merit a new trial. The deception by itself didn't prove the women's innocence, only the fact that they'd go to any lengths to avoid torture. I needed more proof, but where would I get it? No, the sentences would be carried out unless I found clear enough grounds for overturning them.

I read up on foreign court cases, scanned records. I went back all the way to Karin P.'s case. I went through the accounts the jailer and his wife had given of the conversations they had overheard at Kastelholm. Finally I believed I had found something to focus on, another starting point.

While in prison, Karin P. had exposed Jomala's parson, Olof Beckius, as a fornicator. Karin had insisted that the Parson himself had fathered the child for whom his son had been judged responsible. At the time the matter had been brought to court and Beckius' son had then drowned himself, a fact considered to be a clear proof of his guilt. But during Karin P.'s stay in prison, the unwed mother had brought food to her and given her information which exposed the Parson as the guilty one. Karin P. told the interrogators the parson of Jomala, Olof Beckius, was a worse sinner than she was and was in alliance with the Devil because he had made his own son pay for his sins and in addition paid the poor disgraced woman to keep her mouth shut.

The matter hadn't been examined further at the time because it had been before the court of law once already, but now remembering Karin P.'s reference to the Parson's alliance with the Devil made me suspicious that the matter might, after all, have a link with witchcraft.

To my amazement the Prosecutor wasn't interested.

"Messy," he said. "Messy and insignificant gossip."

According to him it was better to forget the matter because Olof Beckius had sorrow enough already in the loss of his son. "And if he was to be interrogated, who would look after his duties at Jomala?"

"His chaplain, of course!" I answered.

"A sick man. At this point he's not good for anything. Shouldn't we think about the good of the parish at times like these?" the Prosecutor insisted.

Our conversation sounded to me like an argument. The Prosecutor didn't consider it wise to begin proceedings against a well-respected man based on some witch woman's vindictive prattle. I, on my part, reminded him that Karin P.'s remarks hadn't been thought mere prattle at the time the list of suspects was drawn up.

"The Judge ought to know witches; they're the first ones to throw mud on God's servants," the Prosecutor said.

I said I wasn't giving in. The matter was unclear and demanded investigation. The Prosecutor said in that case I ought first to send a summons to the unwed mother, not to the Parson. "He's been punished once already; no one can be imprisoned twice for the same crime," I reminded him.

"But if you suspect he's guilty of perjury, there's reason for a new trial," he answered.

"What about the child?" I asked. The woman was alone in supporting the child who would be abandoned if the mother was called in for questioning.

The Prosecutor had a smirk on his face. "A moment ago the Judge wasn't worried about the fate of a whole parish and now there's concern over a single child's well-being!"

I got angry. I reminded him that in any case the Prosecutor must see to it that a summons is delivered once I've made it. He admitted that to be a fact, but still didn't recommend I enter into such an uncertain endeavour by which a respected man might be unjustly smeared.

After I had dictated the summons, based on court records, and sent it to the Prosecutor, I heard Parson Olof

Beckius had gone on a voyage to Turku. In his absence the Chaplain was looking after things. The Prosecutor considered the fact the Chaplain had recovered from his illness at such an opportune time to be a sign from God. I asked the Prosecutor when he thought Olof Beckius might return. He answered he didn't know what business the Parson had on the mainland.

"I suppose it depends entirely on the circumstances," he said. Later on I realized what he meant by circumstances. Bishop Getzelius sent me a letter in which he hoped Church affairs on the island would soon return to normal. Parsons, he announced, should not be prosecuted without cause, particularly since the plough of justice had more appropriate fields to till.

At this point the summons no longer held the original meaning in any case. I tore it up. The Parson of Jomala returned to look after his duties without further ado.

FOURTEEN

ᘓ

*Chapter Fourteen, in which the Judge is present
at an execution and sees a live wolf.*

THE DAY THE WOMEN were executed, I saw a wolf. A large grey dog or a wolf. In retrospect, I can't be sure which.

You don't want to hear about it, you are more interested in the beheading itself and why I didn't prevent it from happening. The matter slipped from my hands, as I said.

Do you think I didn't visit the prison and try to make a coat out of a vest, a forest out of a sapling? But the women wouldn't give anything away. After upbraiding Kjellinus, I had taken him back, and he accompanied me as an interrogator. The results he got only supported the earlier sentences. The matter of the shoe polish was a moral irritant to him, but he didn't consider it decisive, nor could I. Besides, the Court of Appeals confirmed Anna's sentence although I had placed the details of the farce into evidence.

I heard Lisbeta sing. The song told of a man who for his love's sake was killed like a lamb and skinned like a fish.

Lisbeta had an especially beautiful voice. When I entered, she fell silent.

They were of one mind right to the end. First they had named each other; now their pride dictated that what they had talked about together was never to be divulged. Anna was forgiven; the others understood her suffering. "Don't you understand that I'm trying to help you?" I asked, but they didn't trust me.

I think they weren't able to submit to death, to the thought of it. One of Bryniel Kjellinus' duties was to expose a possible conspiracy, but I myself didn't believe in such a thing any longer. There was a great difference between a vain hope and a hope born of a plan for escape; the one who knows it is vain to hope for salvation is calm on the surface, the one planning an escape is restless as a caged animal. Ebba even tried to hang herself; she braided a rope out of torn strips of her coat, but it was too weak; it gave way. A couple of ribs were broken; her rebellion had no other results.

There's not much to tell about the execution. The only happening which remained clear in my mind was the fact that Maria slipped on the slushy snow and kept the whole lot of them standing and waiting while she brushed the snow off her skirt. It was a usual, womanly thing to do; the other prisoners didn't pay any attention to it. It upset me. Why did she clean her skirt? Generally one did that for aesthetic reasons, or so that wet clothing wouldn't cause a chill; in this situation the gesture was inane. How a person clings to habits right to the end! How she hangs onto her life through those habits, a life which inevitably is taken away from her.

Nearly the entire island populace was present. After all, a group execution was an event no one had seen before. Family members cried; others were either exaggeratedly horrified or interested in the details. I heard afterwards that they had made bets on which of the women would calmly suffer the beheading, in what order they would be killed, and what their last words would be. There were a great number of children; probably only the children of the condemned and my own were absent. No, not altogether. At least Lisbeta's boys were there; they called out encouraging goodbyes to their mother. "God will take revenge on your behalf!" they insisted.

I don't want to go into details. Your loss is that you were not living then and able to witness the execution *in concreto*. I swear, separating the head from the body isn't beautiful to watch, however skillful the executioner, and particularly not if one of the heads for some strange reason refuses to fall into the basket along with the other three and starts to roll like a bloody ball towards the audience. Or perhaps a sudden movement in the collective body of the onlookers manages to make a sudden start look as if the head were rolling, because in the end it's a question of a mere blink of an eye, after which the executioner catches the head with his gloved hand and puts it where it belongs.

Burning human flesh doesn't smell good, but the pyre was handsome and there were flying embers surging upward like fireflies towards the sky. When someone insisted one of the bodies moved and made gestures, people became hysterical. Those who understood these things better said the fire made it seem like the body moved, that's all.

On the way home I saw a wolf. In its grey fur frozen drops of water glistened, small icicles which rattled against each other when the animal moved. It sat by the edge of the forest, quite calm, though it saw me.

The wolf had come from some other island, or perhaps over the ice from the mainland, I thought. Perhaps it had fallen into a hole in the ice and pulled itself up with the help of its sharp nails and great strength. Now it was so tired it couldn't travel any farther.

The snow made small swirls between me and the wolf, but the animal was downwind and even my horse didn't sense its presence. The wolf turned its head lazily; the ice bells in its fur made up the first notes of a tune.

I wasn't afraid. I was filled with defiance: I would shoot it. After that, I'd throw the carcass at the feet of sceptics. The man who killed a wolf! Perhaps the news of the beast's arrival had already spread around. Who knows, perhaps parents at that very moment were keeping their children indoors behind closed doors in fear of it. What luck that I was alone, because this was a one-man job.

The wolf yawned when I turned to bend down and pull the gun from under the sleigh's blanket. That was mere bluffing, a typical wolf's gesture to frighten the opponent. A deep yawn made his jaw shake, stretched the grey neck far out, the icicles clattering against each other. It wasn't afraid of me. It looked at me with sleepy inquisitiveness: why don't you go on past while you still have the chance.

No, I thirsted for blood, I wanted to sink my bullet into its arrogant, silvery fur. The wolf was sitting down. It was as if the snow swirls had tied it to the ground. It doesn't have a chance, I thought.

My hand couldn't find the weapon; it must have been further back in the sleigh. The horse shied, not out of fright. It wanted to go on; it was cold, the closeness of home spurred it on. I would have had to turn further to get hold of the gun, but the beast's calm bothered me. A wolf isn't stupid; why did this one behave so foolishly?

The grey coat wasn't looking at me any longer, it had turned its head to gaze at something beyond us. More wolves? Was that possible? Of course it was, they moved in packs and all the while I had been the target of their observations. I wasn't the hunter, but the prey! I wouldn't have time to reach for the gun behind me, in the snow squall the animals invisible to me would jump at my neck the moment I made the first care-less movement.

My whip smacked on the horse's back. Quick, quick! We had a slight chance to get away. A vanishing chance, but if the horse didn't betray me, we'd be saved. They had come as a pack over the ice, a grey, hungry army in the middle of the night when no one saw them. The animal I saw was the leader; it had fallen into a hole in the ice, which meant it had travelled as the lead. What if the whole pack had fallen in and only this one had survived, but in that case no ... !

When I turned, snow swirled behind me; in the white sky a red dot like a single eye of a giant albino was barely visible. No sign of beasts' gaping maws, only the traces left by the horse's hooves and the sleigh in the snow. What a relief, what a shame!

When I slowed the horse down to its usual speed, I felt a twitching pain in my stomach. First I thought I would make it all the way home, but the cramps got steadily worse. Before I had gone past the woods I had to make a decision. Once on the road that led through the village, I would no longer be able to stop. The wind had died down; it was as if it wanted to lift the curtain of snow before the coming spectacle on purpose!

I stopped the horse. The scare a moment ago was a warn-ing to me not to tie it to a tree and go into the woods. Hanging onto the reins, I crouched down by the horse's hind legs. I shoved the cape made of otter skins under my arms. The only thing missing in this humiliation was someone standing in the woods seeing it all, I thought. I felt like laughing despite the pain. Luckily the field-hand wasn't along. "This was a one-man job!" I said to myself and laughed out loud into the empty evening.

Beyond the horse's legs I could see a snow-covered pond I had passed without noticing it. Frost covered the reeds and the sticks children had stuck there in the snow. They were cold blue and very beautiful. I stopped laughing in wonder. The sight of them had a calming effect on me. I didn't feel the cold at my back, and even the cramps in my stomach had eased off. I was pitiful. Even in a lifeless reed there was more dignity than in a human being.

The horse turned its head and kept lifting its hooves.

I felt ashamed; the mare didn't. A human being goes through a lot precisely because he is the slave of demeaning functions. If the wolf had appeared at that very moment, if he had, after all, followed me, I suppose I would have rather let it sink its teeth into my bare behind than dirtied my pants to save my life. I couldn't have gone home in that condition; there wouldn't have been any end to the laughter it would have caused.

I thought of the execution and the people witnessing it. This island led its own life despite me, and cleansed itself in its own way.

They had given me a group of women with whom they were dissatisfied and whom they wanted, for one reason or another, to remove from their midst. They simply wanted me to use the axe entrusted to me.

Ebba was an exception. People didn't give her up, she herself wanted to get rid of herself; she knew her own inability to fit in. Therefore even her sentencing was natural, dictated by the rules. A woman didn't leave these islands without a man except in a funeral boat.

The reeds were swaying, reddish-blue. I stood up and buttoned my trousers.

THE
LATTER
PART

Our consciousness doesn't indeed create itself,
but erupts from an unknown depth.
It awakens by stages from childhood on
and every morning it awakens from
the state of unawareness of dreams.

— C.G. JUNG

CHAPTER

FIFTEEN

Chapter Fifteen, in which the Judge's field-hand seeks honourable compensation. The Judge is puzzled because, according to his understanding and the laws of the land, a field-hand doesn't have honour.

J WORRIED ABOUT my field-hand Torsten. Every time the island steamer came into harbour, he began to drink to calm his nerves. He expected his wife to return, but when she didn't, he forced his way on board and picked a fight with some seaman.

One early spring morning I woke up when someone was hammering on the window.

"Judge, you are needed here," a voice said. I got up and looked out. Torsten stood swaying in the yard and waved his hand for me to come out. "It's a question of murder, Judge must come out!" he yelled. I put my dressing gown on and went out, swearing under my breath.

"Have you lost your mind?" I asked. "If you've done something, go and talk to the Police Chief, don't pester me."

Torsten stood in the middle of the yard legs apart and a look of daring on his face.

"You're the judge!" he answered, and for some reason he began to laugh out aloud.

"What's the matter with you? I'm beginning to have enough of you," I said.

Torsten took a bottle out of his pocket and came to stand by my side. "Let's first take a drop and after that we'll talk," he suggested. The morning was grey and cool, the first birds twittered in the grove at the back of the house.

"Have you killed someone?" I asked and pushed away the bottle he tried to force into my mouth. There was a bloody scratch on his cheek; his hands were mangled. He smelled of mud.

What did I think of myself, sitting with him on the steps in the morning dampness, letting him order me around. A field-hand! An arrogant field-hand, who in Russia would have been driven into the woods naked, and they would have let the hounds know he was a fox to be torn to bits alive.

What was wrong with me? A year ago I had sent four women to Eternity, now I couldn't keep one loud-mouthed man in line.

"What do you say, Judge; aren't we going to drink a bit first?" Torsten asked.

I took the bottle from his hand and raised it to my lips.

"You're my only friend, even though I hate you," Torsten said and put his arm on my shoulder.

I pushed it away. He was a man who had to go to extremes; I had sensed that in him right away. Judges' field-hands don't care about the law.

"Well, let's have it," I said.

He looked at me with protruding eyes. "Are you my friend?" he asked.

"No, I'm not!" I answered. After all, I was his master, the

master of a criminal! He got up and swayed in front of me.

"You're lying, but who cares!" he dared me. I was cold and took another gulp. Torsten started to talk. He had challenged a seaman to a fight. The same seaman who had taken his wife from him. This time he was sure. Absolutely sure he was the right man. You could see the man's guilt in his eyes and even his words showed it well enough. The knife was to be the weapon. And God knows, he knew how to use a knife. What he hadn't decided was whether to kill the pig or leave him an invalid for the rest of his days; he wouldn't come out of it easily whatever happened.

"But it's an honourable duel and I want you to see it out from the beginning to the end so you'll know how to judge me fairly," Torsten explained. "If it gets to the point where I have to kill him, he won't have a Christian burial, but the kind they give to criminals."

"Is that what is important in this? That he can't be forgiven even after his death?" I asked.

"Exactly, because he is not a victim of a crime, but the criminal himself," Torsten insisted.

"What if you die yourself; then you too are thrown into the earth without a blessing," I pointed out.

"I won't lose this battle!" he answered, showing his fist.

He was defiant, and touching. The most manly moment of his life separated only by a couple of words from its greatest humiliation. I had those words; all that was needed was an open mouth and I could tell him what a laughable mistake he had made.

He couldn't fight honourably against the man who had humiliated him, whether the man was guilty or not. The King's edict forbidding all duels didn't concern a man like him. The lawgivers of Kaarle XI didn't consider a common man to have honour. Only aristocrats and soldiers had the right to go against the royal edict. Field-hands were judged according to civil law, which meant the crime was interpreted to be murder or an assault and the victim would be buried in blessed ground, while the killer wouldn't avoid punishment through exile or fines, but most likely would end up being hanged, or in the case of a misdemeanor, shame would be his punishment.

"I see, those kinds of plans!" I said, while at the same time I handed the bottle back to him. I had no reason to pity him.

"That doesn't bring your woman back, you know," I added. He swung out his arm.

"About time she went; now it's a question of my honour."

"What if the man won't come?" I asked.

Torsten sank his fingers into his yellowish hair. "I make him come."

I shook my head and got up. "In any case your request is crazy; I can't, as a judge, come and watch someone commit a crime," I said.

He took hold of the hem of my angora-wool gown.

"Come as a friend, then," he asked.

"You really don't understand anything about justice, you boor!" I answered, and wrenched myself free.

What was I doing? How should a self-respecting Jurisdictional District Judge behave at the moment he hears his field-hand planning to kill a man? In no way at all. Or to put it better, I went back indoors and continued my sleep. And that's not all. At the moment I fell asleep, I felt strangely good. Reluctantly I admitted to myself I was already enjoying what he would do to the rascal. I thought it was a good thing there were still men like my field-hand in this world.

In the morning I heard from the servant that Torsten had come home in a sorry state. His face was swollen, he had some broken ribs and his body was badly beaten. Later on Torsten said the man hadn't shown up after all, and when he went on board, the sailors had beaten him up.

"If only he would finally calm down now," Elsa said. "He brings shame upon the whole house!"

I admitted I thought so too, but when the field-hand didn't just calm down, but turned into as humbled and meek a man as the sheep behind the wall of his sleeping quarters, I found no pleasure in the turn of events.

"If a woman humiliates a man, the man can still maintain he is a man, but it's useless to brag after one has brought about one's own humiliation," Torsten said on his way to feed the horses.

"It's not your fault it ended like that," I consoled him. "That man was a coward."

"They laughed at me, didn't even take me seriously, just kicked and punched me for fun," he answered and hid behind the horse's broad back.

It was difficult to say anything encouraging; I didn't know what it could have been. He had wanted to commit an honourable murder, but other men had kept him from carrying it out. Probably because he was mistaken; blinded by his jealousy, he had picked on the first opportune victim. And even if he had succeeded, the court, at the very least, would have made a fool of him. Wasn't an anticlimax without a body and a murderer by far the best conclusion to a senseless frenzy?

On the way to Kastelholm, where after a year's interval they had brought a woman accused of witchcraft, I pondered Torsten's behaviour. His utter humiliation didn't augur well; it was not like him to be that humble and therefore it couldn't be genuine. What if he was planning something? Some day perhaps I would call him to bring the horses in vain, and I would go into the barn and find his lifeless body hanging from the roof beam, face blue, tongue and eyes protruding. What would I say then; what would be my defence?

I used to scold him for kicking bales of hay that happened to be in his way when he was angry. Now it bothered me when I saw how he bent down to pick up something he had accidentally overturned. He held children in his arms like some grandfather, and the way his clothes hung on him, dishevelled, spoke of a man old before his time. How could one incident so alter a man's character? There was no sense in that.

But where was there sense, generally speaking? The road took a sharp turn to the right, exposing the castle's massive red granite east wing, at the side of which was the main entrance. The castle was used as a prison when it wasn't serving its main function, that of being the King's hunting lodge. All those rocks piled up on top of each other, only so that useless governing bodies would be comfortable enough, men who on some pretext had to be sent away from where the real decisions were made. So many days of sweat and work in case the King would take it into his head one day to go to Åland and hunt for elks, there the castle would stand. Who could — after seeing Kastelholm castle — believe that rationality ruled the world?

The jailer came to meet me at the gate and began to tell me how the prisoner had behaved during the four days she was locked in her cell.

"Rather a calm case, but she's complained about the food," he explained.

I hadn't met this Ingeborg O. yet. Actually, I didn't know anything about her, except that she was one of the women Karin P. had accused of witchcraft. The Parson's examination had revealed her to be a most suspicious character. I hadn't officially given Kjellinus the right to examine women who were suspects, but we had agreed that if necessary he could ask other members of the congregation questions. In Ingeborg's case so much incriminating material had piled up that the official indictment couldn't be postponed. She was not an islander but had come from elsewhere. She had openly spread heresies and I couldn't overlook the possibility that she, specifically, was the person who had brought demons to this island.

"Is the Judge going in alone, or do I ask a guard to come along?" Eriksson asked as we walked down the corridor. The suspects were not in irons since experience had shown they didn't try to escape.

"I'll go in alone since she is so calm," I said.

We stopped in front of the same cell where Anna B. had been kept in her day. The jailer opened the door.

The prisoner sat in the corner on some hay, but got up when I entered. After half an hour I no longer remembered I even had a field-hand.

J'M PUZZLED, and more than anything else, very tired. He woke me up in the middle of the night, stood at the foot of the bed and drummed on my shoulder. Fortunately I didn't wake my youngest one who had come, complete with his pillow, to sleep next to me.

Never before had he come downstairs, and that confused me.

I had my doubts about the importance of the matter, but he swore he wouldn't leave me in peace for the rest of the night unless I made my typewriter hum to the beat of his confession.

In the kitchen I was brave enough to turn on the light. It blinded me but not him, this astral being.

"I heard you fought about me today," the Judge said, self-satisfied.

"We didn't fight about you. I'm just tired of the whole story and one can't ask the family to put up indefinitely with ..."

(Perhaps we did fight. Perhaps I'm only becoming miserable because my main character is miserable. In any case, he sucks the joy and energy out of me so that I don't have the strength to take interest in anything the way I did before. This is a stressful time for the family; I, who hover day after day over sheets of paper like a spider in the process of making a web, am now content in my hole. Before, I used to stop writing even in the middle of a sentence when I saw a car turn into the yard and on its way in give a push to the gate I had left half open, but now I've begun stealing more and more of our time together and caring less about it. Minutes turn easily into hours although I know the shouts and thuds downstairs are triggered by impatience and longing for us to do things together.)

I gave in again, I made coffee and with my mug climbed back upstairs to witness an impossible story.

Wouldn't it be altogether natural to stay on these obvious rails I have, at long last, uncovered under all the trash?

"Why don't you want to describe the falling in love, what do you have against that?"

The Judge asks. That's not the question. I'm trying to write a work that is universally acceptable and the general idea underlying it is what a loveless life makes a person do. I have written enough already about happy pairs romping across spring meadows.

I talk like a parson, I preach and make speeches. Am I becoming the village idiot when I carry on these senseless conversations with a non-existent being? Walking past a mirror I see a pale, distant human being whose hair is untrimmed and whose eyes show the effects of strain.

And only a few weeks ago while reading a newspaper article I felt sorry for Donald, the local self-taught genius who had passed away; who had made perpetual-motion-machines; read the encyclopedia from A to Z, hunting for errors; harvested stars by whatever means in his head. He considered his studies generally valid, as I consider mine. He made up a master chart of indivisible sums. He had been working on it for years, decades, and always completely convinced of the validity of his task: "*The master chart is now calculated up to 221, 763, 122, 508. During the last 44 billions nothing new and interesting came up, but that could change any time, so that one continuously works under a certain amount of suspense....*"

I'm thinking of Donald, an ugly, strange, little man, whose optimism survived to the very end. Was it not made possible by the loss of all sense of proportion, a sick interest in a problem which for others didn't even exist? ...

— There is no loveless life; everyone snatches a little love for him or herself. In whatever shape, if no other way than in self-delusion, the Judge insists.

One has to be on guard with him. I can't get away from the thought that he mocks me and my plan for a novel. I read source materials till my eyes ache; I have experts verify the meaning of all archaic Swedish expressions; I make comparisons between varying sources of the same period; but in spite of the clear story line, everything is heading towards disintegration, escape from my hands, towards transformation into something singular and strange.

— This book describes a judicial process, mindless subversion of justice and an insane game which, in principle, is possible still today. The only necessary ingredient is an absurd enough accusation and the guilt emerges as if by itself. Love has no say in this matter.

I've allowed him erotic liberties, he's been able to peek at and touch the prisoners, rape his wife, trace perverse influences in his environment; why should he, in addition, be allowed to raise havoc in the sanctuary of Great Love.

"I want to confess a love which transcends even the threshold of death," he says.

I'm stunned and sorry.

For a moment I don't see him. I don't even see the writing properly, because the lamp above the table is too dim. Papers lie in disarray in a maroon-coloured glow;

they look unreal and unnecessary. Pages of a novel. Parts of an old story already damaged at birth. Am I the author of that maimed creation? Is there still spirit in me to pull it together? I'm horrified when I realize that my pages are not just my pages, but the dwelling of this stranger who came from a far, dim distance. An unplanned longing lives in the pages, and I'm scared. As if someone had given into my care a deformed child of whom it is said that he himself doesn't sense his misfortune, although I would see in his eyes the suffering that comes from the pain of understanding.

— Isn't faith in the improbable the only message that a work of art can convey?

Did he say that, or did I?

Faith in the improbable! I do believe, even in the impossible. I believe precisely because something is impossible. I saw it written on someone's face a couple of days ago: an old woman sat next to an ambulance driver clutching her purse but otherwise calm. The driver knew the man was already dead when they came and got him; the woman believed the man would still revive. And the expression on the woman's face made the driver sound the siren, drive fast through red lights so that all of us who stood by the curb would believe along with her.

Belief in the improbable doesn't save one from suffering, but it shortens it. Perhaps it makes the suffering endurable that way.

— Good. Let's agree then that you go on with your story and we'll see what comes of it. In any case the novel's structure is already tangled and mixed-up, and there's hardly anything left of the original notion of a Passion Play.

— Passion Play?

— It's laughable to return to it at this stage! I had in mind some kind of an ironic version of a medieval morality play, an anti-Christ explaining himself, the sorrow-filled trudging towards an allegorical nailing to a cross. The passion of this person, that is, my passion, would have been to dwell in suffering. In terms of technique, I thought of a narrative division in which, on the one hand, Protestantism would be reflected in its barren absolutism, awareness of sin in all its variety and, on the other hand, in its longing for purification....

I start to laugh. My explanation sounds crazy. Could my starting point have been so artificial and unreal? It was in this loftily far-reaching way, then, that I intended to have the heart run amok from futility into the world of imagination!

When I look at the Judge, do I look at myself? If so, it has to happen in a peculiar way and distort the truth as if seen through Professor Stratton's lenses. Stratton made the world's acquaintance upside down while experimenting on himself using lenses that turned left into right. He didn't recognize himself the first few times; later on the problem reversed itself and getting used to the former reality resulted in thoroughly strange experiences.

— Sounds great, all right ... the Judge agrees. It's clear that he now considers it important to maintain his hold on me.

— Life may be hard as long as it's magnificent, as one of my friends used to say. She left her well-paying job and followed her calling. In social terms, nowadays, they label her "functionally limited."

— This woman of whom I ...

— She too was a woman, a fine, strong-willed person who believed that a person's first duty towards herself was to live life to the fullest. And it's possible she'll never regret anything, although an outsider feels regret is an unavoidable result of that kind of rashness.

The Judge lets me speak, because he knows his turn will come. The dog that came in to lie at my feet yelps in his sleep. Perhaps he too hunts for an invisible prey.

My colleague, a seven-fold murderer of women, might be right: plans have the flaw that they don't leave room for choices. Has anyone written a book that would contain choices for resolution, parallel chapters and different endings depending on each turn? That would be a good life's work for an author to write; based on the same beginning, an unlimited number of novels, happy and unhappy, dark and light, passionate and bland, believable and unbelievable, ugly and beautiful, rational and absurd.

But no, I do have my notes; this is a documentary novel which has its basis in extant court records.

— The last pages of the records have been torn out. Researchers claim the pages were removed at the time the book was full. What do you know about that?

— May I tell things in chronological order; we'll see then where there ...

— Not a detective story with suspense about the last pages!

— I have woken you up to tell you about myself and a woman.

I take a stack of paper from the desk drawer. It too takes on a reddish hue. The dog whimpers in his sleep and shifts his position. Jung's book lies open before me. *Sleep is the tiny door hidden in the innermost part of the soul,*

a door that opens into the cosmic primal night that was the
soul long before there existed consciousness of the self.

The Judge runs his fingers impatiently through his
hair. No, it's useless to imagine that this would be a
dream, that I would be sleeping with a child in my arms
in my bed. In dreams the unreal doesn't feel like unreal.

But I am dreaming.

In the dream I'm Jung's faithful disciple. I want to
change the world for the better, end wars and aggres-
sion. *An individual's psychology reflects the psychology of
nations. Only change in the attitude of individuals can begin
to change the attitudes of nations.*

In the dream Jung doesn't look at me with sadness
through his round Herman Hesse-lenses (teachers
always sense when a disciple is about to become a rene-
gade), but smiles, satisfied. *If ever there was a time when
introspection was absolutely necessary, it is our present, deca-
dent period.*

I fight in my sleep like an exhausted soldier in the
labyrinthine corridors of the subconscious. I conjure up
the monster I'm supposed to meet there, I shout until
I'm hoarse. I'm tired, but basically brave and defiant.
And the mundane worries of reality are far away, worry
whether I find socks in pairs for the children in the
morning, whether the publishers of my stories pay
enough, whether I have aged. The uneventful mail is far
in the distance, as is lashing out at incidental things.

— In a way I envy you because you still have all that
to live through, he says again.

— All what?

— Life, that's the only thing that actually separates us,
isn't that so?

All that's missing now is that he turn pathetic, poetic

about the wonder of spring; that he remind me how it feels to be squeezed in the arms of children; paint a misty morning landscape with its buttercups and lemon butterflies; speak of the bliss of love; glorify the joyous dawn of dreams. No, I heard him wrong, a guide in the dark realm of sleep doesn't speak like that. And why would he want to wrench my angst away from me?

— You were going to tell something....

The paper is already in the machine. The clock on the wall is on the hour. In four hours the sun will rise.

CHAPTER

SIXTEEN

*Chapter Sixteen, in which the Judge meets Ingeborg O.
and gets to know what Hanswurst is.*

$\mathcal{S}$HE WAS DIFFERENT.

I don't mean she was particularly beautiful. She had an animated face, and depending on the expression, or her position, she was more often enchanting than ordinary. When I stepped into the cell, she greeted me with a smile that was difficult to interpret. She spoke, and her low voice with its warm tone made a deep impression on me. I felt as if she wasn't a prisoner I had come to interrogate.

She was sure there had been some stupid mistake and I was the man who had come to correct the error. She demonstrated she was not carrying a grudge about the four days she had spent without cause in this unpleasant and humiliating place.

When she spoke I found myself nodding and agreeing with her, and it wasn't deceitful manipulation on my part; my attitude was genuine, one her self-assurance projected onto me.

I couldn't make myself say there were an extraordinary number of accusations against her. After visiting Bengt Olsson's deathly ill child, she had announced the child would recover; to Lars Thomansson she had said the heifer he was looking for was dead; while Anna Eriksdotter mourned her husband who was lost in the stormy seas, Ingeborg O. had gone and said the man was alive; she had comforted Agnes Markusdotter, a sailor's wife, with the same reassurance, although a man in the next boat had seen her husband at the mercy of the waves. And all her soothsaying had turned out to be true.

"I can understand that a stranger moving in, an outsider, is always viewed with suspicion," Ingeborg O. said. "I've been here a few years already, but people still avoid me a great deal. They call me German because Jöran Thomansson brought me here from Stettin, but I'm a barefoot Swedish-Finn like the rest of them here, for I'm originally from Betna," she explained. She emphasized her speech by gesturing with her hands, and her accent had a distinctive Swedish rhythm.

"Why were you in Stettin?" I asked. The city was known as a Prussian harbour through and through, though it had already belonged to Sweden for about twenty years, that is, ever since the end of the thirty-year war.

"My first husband was a soldier. He took me along and promised me that in Stettin we wouldn't want for anything," Ingeborg said.

"But it turned out to be the opposite?" I was curious.

"Yes, he had to go on war manoeuvres in Poland and he died there," Ingeborg answered. "I sat days and days with my newborn daughter at the city gates waiting for the lists of the dead. His name was on the third one."

Sitting at the gates carried a serious implication. On the witness stand Agnes Markusdotter had said in her statement that it was there, specifically, that Ingeborg O. had learned the skills of a soothsayer. She had confessed to Agnes that a strange woman had approached her and said she would learn her husband's fate by picking up a stone from under the last gate he had passed through. If nothing moved on the rock's surface, the man was dead, but supposing even an ant ran across it, that would mean the person she longed for was still alive. And when Ingeborg and the unknown woman had together turned a rock upside down, they had to agree they saw no life on its surface.

"Didn't it occur to you the strange woman could be Satan dressed and masked to appear as an ordinary married woman, and the turning of the stone together meant the sealing of a union?" I asked.

Ingeborg laughed. Her laughter carried both resonant and deeper tones, as if someone had dropped silver spoons on the dungeon floor.

"Oh no, she was a friendly person who felt sorry for me and the child. If only the Judge had been there and seen for himself, then ... ," she said, full of trust.

She had undergone such hardships that being locked in a prison couldn't throw her off her stride. And she had learned that as long as she had faith in herself, she would get through even the worst of times. No one needed to come and tell her that life was a battle; she if anyone knew that to be true.

"Then Jöran Thomansson came and rescued you?" I asked.

Not then, yet. Jöran Thomansson had actually only come when she already knew she'd get through, when the worst was behind her. But she had followed his suggestion since he had convinced her Åland was the most beautiful place in the kingdom of Sweden and the whole world, a place where no one lived in misery. Just like Stettin, according to the first husband! And again she was foolish enough to follow a man to his paradise.

I was interested in knowing how she had made her living after the death of her first husband. How had she supported herself and her child? It would be easy to arrive at a hasty conclusion about there being all too few choices available to a woman who was alone.

She wasn't insulted. She rested her elbows on the window sill, cheek in hand, and smiled.

"Jöran Thomansson wouldn't like it if I told anyone. He's ashamed of what I was doing," Ingeborg answered.

"I think in this situation I have to be honest," she continued sanctimoniously.

"I'm not a bit ashamed, but the island men are so old-fashioned," she continued.

Ingeborg had become a member of a troupe of clowns and jesters. They had staged street theatre and popular magic. First she had been the target for a man who shot flaming arrows at her; later on she had acted on stage.

"They staged foolish mimes that portrayed the Fall. The audience was crazy about them," Ingeborg said.

"Which part did you play?" I asked.

"Some of them would have wanted me to be Eve, because the woman playing Eve was fat and old and when she made her appearance on stage in a transparent, flesh-coloured costume, people whistled, they were so disappointed. But I thought it a poor role," she explained.

She almost laughed, remembering Adam stomping onto the stage that had been hurriedly set up on top of barrels. Adam's only garment was a belt made of hazel leaves, and a stray goat threatened to do away with his costume. At times the Devil had influenced their plays so that people had threatened to make them leave the city altogether. But she herself had also had fun as Hanswurst while the audiences had howled maliciously.

"Hanswurst?" I asked. Ingeborg was astonished that a

civilized person like me didn't know anything about Hanswurst.

"He is a jester, a pathetic idiot dressed in a colourful costume whose nose the other actors twist all through the play; it's a very important role. Hanswurst is a fool and it's he, particularly, who draws comments from the audiences," Ingeborg explained.

I thought the role sounded awful. I couldn't understand why she would be so anxious to play it. In doing so she knowingly humiliated herself in front of the audience, that's all. But apparently I had misunderstood the story, and this woman had the patience to set me right.

"The essence of it is in that the audience laughs at itself," she said.

"How so?" I asked.

"In the end, even the dumbest people realized that what was being mocked there was their own everyday stupidity. That is exactly what I showed them," she insisted.

"I can't believe country people to be that ingenious," I argued.

"I went to a lot of trouble to make them understand," Ingeborg answered. "I knew I had achieved my goal when suddenly everyone was silent. It was a magnificent moment."

Before long, the role had begun to bore her. "One gets tired of everything," she said, stressing the last word. "I decided then I'd have the people cry for the poor fool."

"Did they?" I asked.

She smiled. "In some way at least they were moved, but the troupe didn't like that, because the mime was only supposed to be amusing."

I was curious to know how she had made the fool into a tragic figure. She admitted it had been a true challenge. "I realized that the more heartbroken Hanswurst looked, the more people laughed. That's when I got the idea of having him smile bravely in the face of despair, and that really made an impression on the audience," she explained.

"Why do you suppose that happens?" I asked.

"People can't laugh at bravery! When a fool stops feeling sorry for himself, he evokes sympathy in others," Ingeborg said.

Appropriately, Jöran Thomansson had come into her life just when she had argued with the troupe whether mime should be allowed to make people cry or not. She hadn't wanted to go back to the initial interpretation, but the other actors couldn't accept the new. She could have solved the problem by taking on the part of the veil-clad Eve, or by being the target for the steady-handed flame-thrower again, but the dreams the sailor had put in her mind won out.

It didn't occur to her that the story could make her situation decisively worse. Being a good actress, she could be acting all the time!

The case was certainly not an easy one to explain, and I found the idea of having to make clear to her that I couldn't, under any pretext, free her right then, disagreeable. In addition to everything else, a suspicious looking scar was found on her buttock, which the Provost tended to believe had diabolic origins. Personally, I was prepared to minimize the scar's value as evidence, for I had just read Michael Freude's recently published work *Gewissens-Fragen von Processen wieder die Hexen* which pointed out it was possible for Satan to play games and lead people astray with those signs of his, but Kjellinus and the men doing jury duty still considered the sign important. It was, after all, precisely signs like that one which had previously determined the necessity of torture.

"We ought to obtain some kind of clear proof either for, or against; otherwise we're forced to depend on the Provost," I said apologetically to the prisoner. She looked at me perplexed.

"Doesn't the law say no one is to be tortured without reason?" she asked.

I was quiet for a moment, then I braved the answer. "We do have a reason. All the witnesses' statements and the sign on your body," I answered.

The dark pupils in her eyes grew larger; the reflection of my own small shape slowly melted into them. "But they aren't real reasons," she said, frustrated. "I haven't harmed anyone; I've only given comfort to others."

She couldn't understand. She couldn't fathom that a mortal being didn't just get a soothsayer's gift out of thin air. That the turning of stones and the searching for living things on their surfaces was no harmless trick. "How would I be tortured?" Ingeborg asked.

She had stood up. The calm and good-naturedness I had so admired in her were gone.

"Provost often gets what he's after by crushing the fingertips," I said, ill at ease.

She still thought I was playing a game with her. She believed it to be some sort of a tasteless joke that she had to rise above. She wanted to play that kind of role and I, for my part, wanted to believe her. The more time I spent with her, the more convinced I became she could never have sunk to such loathsome depths as the earlier witches I had sentenced. But by what means could I convince the jury and also Bryniel Kjellinus, whose opinions bore the authority of the Church and weighed a great deal.

Although the rules of jurisprudence had been removed from the Church's authority and given to secular judges, as witchcraft and lewdness had clearly been on the increase lately, it was emphasized from many quarters that since the crimes were aimed directly against God, there was a need for an expert to represent Him on earth. Also, since the punishments were meted out in accordance with God's, or Moses' laws, familiarity with the Church's view of the matter was particularly important. Legal experts had to agree, reluctantly, that crimes of witchcraft were out of the ordinary. Should there be any errors in the handling of them, God's severe and bloody punishment could result as His wrath descended upon the whole land and its people.

I couldn't think of letting Ingeborg O. go free simply because I had difficulty imagining her guilty. The doors of the prison wouldn't open for her just because I loathed the thought of her fingers, which had made such charming gestures, being torn to bloody lumps.

"I'll see what I can do on your behalf," I said when the guard came to let me out of the cell.

Ingeborg cast a strange look at me and I left quickly before she had time to say anything.

SEVENTEEN

Chapter Seventeen, *in which the Judge gets to know his prisoner in greater depth only to realize he doesn't know her at all.*

"THE FOOD IS NOTHING to brag about, but the view is grand!" she said when I visited the cell for the second time.

The scenery beautiful? She seemed in gay spirits and content as she said it. It wasn't sarcasm, then, but an allusion to the fact that nothing had happened to speed up her release. Would I ever learn to know her?

After I stepped inside she no longer looked out the window. It was as if she wanted to say, you are more fascinating. She wouldn't stay long in one place, at times she sat on my right, at times on my left. Sometimes she just stood in front of me and looked at me with attentiveness and curiosity while I was explaining her situation to her. It seemed as if my words were not as interesting as something in my appearance, perhaps in my demeanor.

I started to feel uncomfortable. Was she mocking me? Why did she flash that "well,-it-went-well" smile of hers when I had finished explaining her gloomy situation to her? And why did I make speeches like some kind of an idiot instead of interrogating her?

But no. She sympathized with me because of my burdensome task; she wanted to show her appreciation for my efforts in presenting matters that were unpleasant. It was ridiculous and unbelievable, but true, nevertheless.

"… So that all in all, sad to say, there's some rather weighty evidence against you." She was silent. I asked what she was thinking about.

"Once in Stettin I had an opportunity to eat river trout in fine company; a Russian gentleman wanted to treat the troupe. I won't ever forget how good it tasted." Ingeborg answered.

Was it a question of some kind of feeble-mindedness I hadn't come across before? Was she mocking me? Or was she really remembering a dinner of river trout?

"If you don't confess, you'll most likely be tortured," I said in a stern voice.

"Surely not?" she asked. A small wrinkle between the eyes showed that my words made her sad.

"Oh yes, and I'm not saying this for the first time."

My tone was openly admonishing. Was there any sense in her remembering long since chewed-up fish, and some Russian lecher, when right now the question was about life and death?

And, in the end, how did I know what she was alluding to with her story about the river trout? Had not the Russian aristocracy always known how to turn things to its advantage? The man would never have treated a whole group of people to an expensive dinner unless he was sure of being compensated for it. Was I so very wrong in believing that Ingeborg especially, the beautiful, talented jester of the troupe, had been Sir Russia's greedy target? And everybody knew actresses weren't unduly concerned about their virtue. All the while I had been feeling sorry for her so I ached inside, she had been remembering her tawdry love stories.

She spread her arms wide. "But I'm innocent."

Innocent or guilty, but practically dead. That is what I ought to have told her. Don't think about yourself, girl; here you won't get sympathizers by lifting your skirts; I ought to have said that to her.

Instead, I said, "I'm sure that's true, but the evidence speaks against you."

She sighed and looked at me in a conspiratorial way as if to say, we certainly are up against a knotty problem. She looked at my hands. At first I thought she was interested in Freude's book, which I was absent-mindedly fingering, but when I put it away, her eyes didn't follow the book, but my hands. What was it about them that caught her attention? They were not ugly, quite the contrary. I thought they were the best part of me. Not too small, not too large, the back of the hand thick, in part marked by dark hairs, fingers long and sturdy. Did she consider them expressive, perhaps reflective of intelligence? Ambrosia had said long ago that I had unusually beautiful hands, that I was going to do wonders with them. No one else had noticed them, though.

I swallowed. She also swallowed. What was happening?

"My predictions have never caused any harm to anyone," Ingeborg said, surprisingly matter-of-fact.

"That is not the question, but ..."

"What then?"

I shrugged. "Witchcraft is witchcraft," I answered.

She bent down very close to me. I felt her breathing. "Is it witchcraft if one wants to comfort a person who is suffering?" she asked with gentle patience.

I grabbed Freude's book as if it were a life-saving rope. She must have seen my hands shake. "*Wofern die Hexen und*

Zauberer keinen ausdrücklichen oder heimlichen Pact mit dem Teuffel gemach, und dem Teuffel sich mit Leib und Seel zu eigen gegeben noch mit unreinen Geist sodomitische Schand verübet ... ,"
I read, my face scarlet, not looking at her.

Ingeborg got up and walked from wall to wall in the cell. Six and a half steps and a turn. I stopped reading. Six and a half steps. No turn.

She stood with her back to me. Was she crying? It had taken this long for her to understand the mess she was in. Poor girl! Poor little girl! Oh no! She was a woman, not a girl. But how sorry I felt for her at this shattering moment. I dared look at her now, at her back. Unlike the usual straight posture of her shoulders, they were slightly bowed. The curve of her neck seemed all the more fascinating, her midriff wasn't exceptionally small, but attractive in an unassuming way, the behind was round as it should be, and the legs, yes, they were uncommonly long.... What a waste! I thought. And I grieved all the more for her sake.

Should I hand her a handkerchief? Did a woman of her class understand such a gesture? Before I had time to decide, Ingeborg turned around.

"I tried very hard to remember," she said, "I tried to remember how the purple-petalled flowers smelt, the ones that push through the soil early in spring. I tried to remember, but for some reason I can't recall it in my mind."

She didn't smile because the matter preoccupied her thoughts. She questioned me about the name of the plant, but I didn't want to say anything.

"When all this is over and I get home ... ," Ingeborg started, but when she saw the expression on my face, she corrected herself as if to appease me, "*If* I get home, the very first thing I'll do is to look for those flowers till I find them, gather my room full of them because they have such a nice smell," she said.

"I think you better forget the smell, because most likely you'll never smell it again in any case," I roughly retorted.

What was the matter with me? Where were my composure and my cunning now that I needed them more than ever before?

"I mean that you must confess, at least in part, to the accusations directed at you, demonstrate willingness to cooperate," I explained hurriedly in a soothing tone.

Obediently, she began from the beginning. What did I want to hear? She could talk about her childhood a whole week, if need be, but who could possibly be interested in that. When her mother died, her father was driven nearly crazy by his flock of screaming children. He had rocked the twin boys to sleep in the cradle with a riding whip. Granny had interfered but nearly got the whip herself when she wasn't able to make the children stay quiet. When the boys grew up a bit, her father had nothing against them, but he never really knew how to appreciate his daughters. Was it any wonder, then, that she was in such a hurry to get away from home?

One incident in particular stayed in her mind. She hoped I didn't think it involved witchcraft, though it was a strange happening. The master of the manor house had told them to carry away a pile of twigs from behind the house and burn them. When the twigs at the bottom of the pile were picked up, a nest of vipers scattered in all directions. There were about fifteen or twenty of them. One passed over her bare foot, but, as if by a miracle, she was spared. But the protection had come from Heaven and not from Hell, that I had to understand. Was that not reason enough for her never to be able to be in league with the Devil? When she already had a better bond ... but she had been horrified, real vipers and at least fifteen of them....

The story was told in a tone of easy chatter; reverence was far from it, though the words might have indicated reverence.

In the end, I couldn't be bothered to analyze what she said, for I believed her to be too clever to say anything that could be used against her.

I watched her and was no longer annoyed. She was a good story-teller, and she often looked at me searchingly as if making sure our thoughts were focussed on the same things. This order of things had a calming affect on me; she talked and I listened, just as one ought to do during an interrogation.

"... Once he took me along torch fishing, although usually only the boys were allowed ... I remember the beautiful, reddish flames above the dark water ... I thought they were mystical flares, souls of stillborn children that danced on their tiny toes on the water's membrane ... everyone laughed, even Father, although just to make sure, he smacked me on the ear because he wasn't sure whether I was being irreverent or not...."

I understood the father. What had made her spirit fly so even now? My presence?

The more I examined the case and thought about it, the more convinced I was of my mission. She was happy, almost exuberant in my company, and that was astonishing considering her situation and these circumstances under which we were meeting. But something about me filled her with faith and courage.

I began visiting her as often as possible. As might be expected, I didn't get anything out of her, nothing that might have supported the legal case one way or another. At times I was ready to agree she must be a witch. How else could she have taken such a lasting hold on me?

But whenever I saw her, evil thoughts fell away. She was an exceptional human being. That's all.

CHAPTER

EIGHTEEN

*Chapter Eighteen, in which the Judge drinks to excess, hears
bitter claims from his friend the Major's mouth and is
forced to concur with some delicate matters of fact.*

THAT NIGHT I DRANK too much. Major Berg — the Captain
had had a promotion — was visiting us and appeared to be
slightly astonished at my eagerness to have a fresh bottle
fetched again and again from the cellar. "Is everything all
right, dear brother?" he asked. I assured him there was nothing the matter with me.

The Major tapped on the piano lid and put his glass on it.
"Man is constantly learning something new," he said.

Such depth of thought, I said to myself.

"What have you learned today?" I asked.

"I've learned that a capriccio is not a cheese but a compo-
sition for a musical instrument."

I wondered whether he was serious, or whether my war-
minded friend was capable of taking an ironic look at himself.

"Is that so? How did you happen to pick up such a nugget?"

He said Parson Kjellinus had played the organ for him. The same organ I had arranged to be transported to the island.

"I had no idea you were such good friends," I said.

The Major thought it strange this was news to me. "Of course we are; we're really very good friends," he answered.

The Major told me the Parson had often praised the musical scores I had brought with me from Tartu and bemoaned the fact there weren't good enough singers on the island. There were droves of women, of course, but both he and the Parson agreed women's voices were not appropriate for singing in church.

"How sad that we don't have a decent enough school here where boys could learn to use their voices," he said.

"I, on the other hand, feel the Parson hasn't even given the matter a serious try," I commented with some malice.

"How so?" the Major asked.

I wanted to know if Kjellinus had mentioned that among the scores was also a manuscript for the Passion Play. The Major remembered they had talked about it, but it was of course clear that such an elaborate staging could never be realized in these backwoods.

"Passion means both passion and suffering," I said.

"I guess so; what of it?" the Major asked.

"Isn't it strange that both can be expressed by the same word?" I answered.

But one could tell by his distracted expression that to the Major the observation was neither strange nor interesting.

"Of course there are those for whom suffering, particularly the suffering of others, is their passion," I argued.

The Major looked at me for a long while. "Have you had too much to drink, brother?"

Elsa brought in the checkers. She glanced at me, annoyed. I was clearly breaking the rules according to which we were permitted to exchange only polite, vacuous comments. We were allowed to be bored — charmingly bored — but not to get agitated. To express risky, disturbing ideas was as improper as Elsa exposing the fact that under her dress, the shade of which was *bleu-mourant*, the steel-spined corset caused her merciless discomfort. Everyone knew the corset was there, but one had to pretend ignorance.

"If Kjellinus loved music as he claims, he would do all he could to stir the island's interest in a life of music," I said.

My stubbornness began to irritate the Major.

"What the hell do you have against the Parson?" he asked.

"But there's zeal enough for two when it comes to wrenching confessions from poor prisoners," I went on.

The Major reminded me there was a time when I had spoken highly of Bryniel Kjellinus as an interrogator. I had praised his reason and effectiveness. "Why the sarcasm now?"

Yes, why indeed? The Parson had fully mastered the doctrine of witchcraft; his focus on it was sharp and unrelenting, and now he had decided to bring Ingeborg O. before the court and would drive the death sentence through, no matter what I did. There was no doubt Kjellinus was mad in his persecution mania, but mad in such a way that he had lost all but his intelligence. There was no pity in him, no healthy questioning of his own opinions, no bursts of empathy, no ability to abort or give up.

"He is too cold a person to understand anything as beautiful as music," I insisted.

"The Parson? His knowledge in that area is very thorough," the Major answered.

"That might be, but how could a man like him understand

the tragedy of the Passion when he would have been ready to nail Christ to the cross himself if that could have been instrumental in furthering the birth of the Church," I said.

A heavy silence ensued. The Major raised a finger to his moustache which, in keeping with the current fashion, was a thin barely visible line above his upper lip. And Elsa, who had our youngest in her arms, a sturdy, healthy girl, looked at me with loathing as if I were the boatman of the island of lepers who now and then rowed in front of Kastelholm castle displaying his flags of warning and collecting the diseased. There was no doubt about it, none of those present would step into my boat!

"But you would have been the judge who did the sentencing!" the Major said.

I was stunned. Was the Major not a mere fool, walking around with a ridiculous big sword hanging from his belt and making women smile, who supposedly knew nothing about depression and suspicion? I had always thought there was something dog-like about him, something of the ignorant animal who happily entered wars, mated without much thought, and in the end, pierced by an enemy spear, died with a whimper of surprise. Making nasty comments didn't belong among the skills of such a creature.

"Are you claiming that as judge I don't pursue justice?" I asked. I didn't know if I was hurt or merely astonished the Major had so effortlessly found the path where I was most vulnerable.

"A queen comes to mind; I seem to remember she was the spouse of Philip the Second. She got furious about a valuable pair of stockings given to her in public as a gift," the Major said.

"What about it?" I asked.

"She flung the gift to the ground in anger and told the giver he was a colossal fool for not knowing that the Queen of Spain had no feet, or at the very least they were not to be mentioned!" the Major answered.

I poured the Major and myself another glassful. I didn't know what to say. Did Kjellinus gather evidence only to comply with my unspoken wishes? Were his deeds not, after all, inspired by his own stubborn dreams? If that was what the Major was implying, in that case I could make sure that the torture of Ingeborg O. would never commence.

I picked up a handkerchief from the floor, the one I assumed Elsa had dropped for the Major's benefit. It had powder stains on it and I realized it wasn't meant to be found; picking up this handkerchief and handing it back to its owner would have constituted a vulgar, tactless gesture.

Elsa's unaccountable tricks continued to teach me the nuances of the tiresome game women played with men at their expense. That's why women weren't interested in ordinary games. They found chess boring because in the world of emotions and desires one could make much more exciting moves. What did the red queen threatening the king mean when one could just as easily have a living man on his knees?

How could I know that Ingeborg hadn't played a game of conquest with me? I suppose the will to conquer a man is multiplied many times when one's own life is at stake.

But what had Ingeborg actually done? She hadn't flirted with me, nor spoken of inappropriate things. I had simply become fascinated with her, fascinated with a prisoner who was unlike any other. That's all. How could I burden her already bowed shoulders with the guilt I felt for my own restless thoughts? Had I not been bewildered by her naturalness and unusual vivacity, aspects of character I hadn't found in anyone else? Good God! I made judgements about Elsa who saved egg whites in order to make masks for herself, a woman who thought about her every word and deed, who thirsted endlessly for proof of her desirability. And I thought being familiar with such things made me capable of understanding a person like Ingeborg O.!

The more I drank, the more I longed for her, the prisoner. I decided I would go to her first thing the following morning. As a formality, I would organize an interrogation after which she could go where she belonged. To freedom. And afterwards, some day after an appropriate delay, we could approach each other under different circumstances.

I didn't want to assign a specific format to our meeting. There was desire, of course, but the rest, the more important part called for a context worthy of it. While I was sitting with Elsa and the Major with a glass of wine in my hand I declined to think what it might be.

NINTEEN

Chapter Nineteen, in which the Judge familiarizes himself with Ingeborg O.'s strange writings and makes an important decision.

𝓕EW KEEP THE PROMISES they make to themselves while drunk and I was no exception.

Ingeborg simply couldn't be set free, but with Dunte in mind, I prevented the instigation of torture. I visited her often, and to avoid suspicion, I gave Kjellinus permission to conduct close questioning, emphasizing there shouldn't be even a hint of coercion.

At the beginning of March, the Parson came to tell me he had made a thorough search in the cell in order to establish whether any diabolic tools could be found. None had, but instead he had with him some papers full of writing.

"I can't understand where she would get writing tools. The fact that she knows how to write is amazing in itself," Kjellinus said.

Frightened, I looked at the papers.

"I don't know; her father was a bailiff, perhaps he taught

her to write so that the girl would look after the bookkeeping for him," I answered. I knew that only a few years ago a young boy had been sentenced to death because he had surprised everyone by writing in Latin, a language he hadn't known before. Theologians agreed that occasionally the Devil liked to play games by bestowing the skill of writing on someone because he wanted his contracts with these poor fallen souls in writing.

Kjellinus laid the papers on the table in front of me. "You'll want to familiarize yourself with them in peace? You'll find me in the vestibule when you're ready to discuss them," he said.

I understood the decisive proof would be found in these papers. I poured myself a glass of wine before I found the courage to read them.

I'll copy the writings here, because I want you to understand why I did what I did. I've corrected the grammatical errors, which were plentiful, and the slang expressions, because repetition of such clumsiness is of no use to anybody.

February Anno 1668
I didn't dare ask the guard the date; he might have become suspicious. I know it's the end of the month, but finding out the exact date requires care and caution. It's important I note everything down so that later on I can prove to myself this hasn't just been a nightmare, but that I have been here in this ugly, cold, stinking cell in the flesh. I'm very unhappy, but also cautiously optimistic. Today I was given some gruel to eat; they call it soup. The bread is hard but passable. I miss my daughter Magdalena very much.

February Anno 1668
I shouldn't write every day because I might run out of paper if they delay letting me go. Today was a lucky day for me. I

was allowed to wash myself. The wooden tub was old and partly moss-covered, the bottom felt slimy, but after a bath I felt like a new person. Am I mistaken in believing that this happening means a glimmer of freedom?

February 25 Anno 1668
I managed to find out the date yesterday, but I forced myself to have a day in between when I didn't write. That was good, because much has happened today. I've been both promised freedom and threatened with torture. They can't be serious about both, but is it too reckless of me to believe in the former? I'm thinking of my daughter, Magdalena, but also someone else tortures my thoughts. I ponder what's at stake now.

February 27 Anno 1668
It was a restless night. I couldn't sleep because a peculiar unease bothered me. I haven't even worried about torture because the Other occupies my mind. We were given pea soup today, which wasn't very good. I ate it to the last spoonful, nevertheless, because I want to stay healthy. Otherwise I'm not hungry. I miss my daughter.

February 28 Anno 1668
A miracle happened. He has made it clear he'll rescue me from here. He doesn't want to see me die. It can't mean anything else but that I'm very important to Him. Am I becoming crazy, or has my hard luck truly taken a turn for the better?

March 1 Anno 1668
I can't think of anything but Him and my rescue. During the night I heard a woman's mad screams from the other side of my wall. I don't know what it means. Do they keep us here

till we lose our minds? Am I about to lose mine when I long for my Torturer so? I hope Magdalena, my daughter, doesn't worry about me too much.

March 4 Anno 1668
Why hasn't He visited me for four days? Have I disappointed him? What have I done or said that was wrong? Perhaps my looks are becoming repulsive since I can't tidy myself or change my clothing. I'm very unhappy. It's been raining outside for two days, and during the night there's an awful draft here. At moments like these I almost wish they'd do something decisive in my case, whatever it is, as long as this torture would be at an end.

March 5 Anno 1668
Perhaps I'm already confused about dates. I'm not sure. I was given a blanket today. In all friendliness the jailer hoped that I would soon get over my cold. I ate sprats. I remember how I loathed setting nets and hauling them in at this time of year because it's so cold out at sea. Now I'd be happy to do that from morning till night. I wonder if Jöran Thomansson takes Magdalena along in the boat? I hope he remembers to be careful.

March 6 Anno 1668
He came today. He appeared as if from nowhere. I turned my back and there he was. I was so glad tears came to my eyes. We talked a long time. I wanted to touch him, but did manage to restrain myself. Love triumphs even over the hardest luck. Now I know that is true.

March 7 Anno 1668
Today they talked again about torturing me unless I voluntarily admitted my wrongdoings. Just when I was in an optimistic

frame of mind and certain of my rescue. They gave me soup to eat that didn't taste like any food I could recognize. I was so upset by this uncertainty that after I had eaten, I threw up. The guard said I better wipe it up before I got into trouble. When I said I didn't have a rag, he told me to use my skirt or my hair. I can't understand why he's so nasty. I miss my poor Magdalena.

March 9 Anno 1668
Today they stripped me naked. A red-coated torturer examined me from head to toe. I was freezing and he stuck me in the back and buttocks with needles. It hurt terribly. I don't understand why He didn't prevent that from happening. Nothing can happen without His knowledge, that I believe. Have I been a disappointment after all? Or was this the last examination before I'm set free since during the interrogation nothing came up to warrant torture. I wished He had been present and seen how it hurt me. He could have also seen then that under these stinking rags I'm still quite a passable woman. My food today was oat gruel.

March 10 Anno 1668
I'm lonely. Very lonely. I long for my daughter Magdalena. If He doesn't help me, will God, then? After all this?

After I finished reading, I poured myself another glass of wine. Then yet another. The papers were spread before me on the table. I looked at them, at the unfamiliar handwriting which I couldn't call beautiful and I felt like laughing triumphantly. One couldn't be mistaken about the contents of the writing; she was in love with me. It was a miracle, against all the laws of reason, but it was as clear as day.

The sound of Kjellinus' steps carried in from the vestibule. That instant my mood sank. That beast had seen these pages, read the confessions written in Ingeborg's heart's blood. The thought was unbearable; it was infuriating. On top of everything else it couldn't be but fatal for Ingeborg and me. Good God, just when everything might begin, it all had to end.

I asked the Parson to come in. He was first-rate at pretending; you couldn't see a trace of glee on his face. He sat down on the Lübeck sofa and raised one ankle over the other knee.

"Disturbing proof, isn't it?" he said.

I looked at the papers as if I couldn't remember what they contained and didn't say anything. I had decided to deny everything; the only sensible thing to do in this situation.

"As far as I can see the fact that she admits having seen the Devil is a decisive proof; not only seen, but even dreamt about having intercourse with him," Kjellinus announced. I swallowed, surprised. He couldn't be serious, of course.

"Without a doubt, strange writings," I answered.

"Strange but, on the other hand, quite explicit. 'I long for my Torturer so!' I would consider that to be a full confession," he said.

I realized immediately that the Parson had already planned everything before reading the notes. Their discovery had truly been a lucky strike for him, a much better booty than any witch salve had ever been. With the help of these papers he could easily obtain permission to commence torture because it was clear if I now argued against it, I would be confirming my own guilt.

"You want her to be tortured right away?" I asked despairingly.

"Precisely! Who knows what might happen if we procrastinate. She believes the Devil is plotting to set her free, and it could even be true," Kjellinus answered. He told of a witch-court sitting on the mainland where a male witch had managed to escape on his way to the courthouse. The prisoner had simply evaporated from between his blankets, and Satan's only sign had been a loud, thunderous noise in the sky.

"This has been a tiring matter for us all, and therefore it's good that it'll be over and struck from the order of the day," the Pastor said.

I gathered the pages into a neat pile. "Perhaps there's reason for me to study these for a day or two, and then ..."

But Kjellinus didn't give in.

"We must strike while the iron is hot; the prisoner is now beside herself because these papers were found, and surely it would be easy to get her to talk. If we drag our feet, she might imagine the game isn't played out yet and be all the more stubborn in resisting us," he said.

We looked long and hard at each other. He must have known how I felt. There was nothing to indicate he felt sorry for me.

"All right," I said. "Call the Provost for tomorrow morning. I myself will be present."

He walked towards my desk, but before he had time to touch them, I put my hand on the papers. "We'll meet tomorrow," I said. He nodded and left.

CHAPTER

TWENTY

∽

*Chapter Twenty, in which the Judge carries through his
fantastic plan but harbours, nevertheless, a sense of despair.*

J CARRIED ON my drinking after Kjellinus had gone. I read
Ingeborg's touching scribbles over and over again. By the
time evening came, I knew what I had to do.

I went out to the dusk-filled courtyard where rain was
pelting down. I called for the field-hand. No one answered; I
went back indoors to get my warm cape and thrust yet another bottle under it. Close to the barn, I called for the field-
hand again, this time by name. The door to the servants'
common room opened, and a dark shape approached me
without haste.

"Harness the horses and get the buggy ready; I have to
go for a drive!" I ordered Torsten. He stood still, slightly
stooped, as he had been lately.

"Is it worth it? Isn't Sir Jurisdictional District Judge in
too poor a condition to go out into the dark night?" he
answered.

Had he been closer I would have slapped him. His words made me so angry I shook with rage.

"Who are you to advise me, you damned worm of a man? I wish you had enough wits to hang yourself, but first harness the horses for me," I yelled.

"Fine," he answered. He started to walk slowly towards the barn, as befits a beaten man.

"What is fine?" I asked after him. Torsten turned his head.

"I'll harness the horses then, since the master so wishes," he said.

When he had the job done and walked the horses hitched to the buggy close to the front steps, I asked if he wanted to come along. There could be wolves out there or something else unexpected, I thought. Just to be sure it might be good if there were two of us.

"Of course I'll go if Mr. Honourable Judge so desires," he answered.

"Go and get yourself a coat," I ordered.

He followed my order, directing his steps towards the servants' quarters. As I watched him go, it seemed as if he didn't drag his feet quite as detestably as he usually did.

On the way I offered Torsten a drink and he didn't say no. Torsten handled the horses and I sat next to him, whistling. Giving the horses commands, Torsten looked as alert as before, or else a couple of drinks had resulted in miracles.

"Do you know what? I think you're pretending something all the time," I said.

He didn't bother to answer.

"You like to play the role of a beaten man. I'm sure you find it very amusing," I remarked.

"I guess that's the way it is, if that's what the Judge thinks," he answered.

I wouldn't allow him to depress me. If he had decided to demean himself, what could I do about it? I had a big task ahead of me. Perhaps the biggest challenge of my life. Life had offered me a chance for heroism and may God spare me if I let the chance slip by. My task was mad, impossible in fact, but that's why it intrigued me all the more. *Amor vincit omnia!* An aristocratic woman had embroidered those words into a tapestry depicting the goddess of love standing astride a lion she had just conquered. Love triumphed over every obstacle.

"Where are we going?" the field-hand asked.

"To Kastelholm," I answered. "I have an extraordinarily important duty to take care of in Kastelholm," I said and felt very tempted to confide in him. "I'm not as miserable a man as you imagine," I assured him. He took a gulp from the bottle I offered him.

"No one calls a man who shares his liquor miserable," Torsten mumbled.

He smelled a little of sweat, but not enough to disturb me. I felt good having him along. It would have been dreary to travel alone in the rain and dark, and though he didn't talk much, his presence gave me courage.

Kastelholm loomed larger, more grey and desolate than I remembered it. Was I really intending to rob that silent giant of something? How would I manage that? It wouldn't voluntarily give up anything it had once swallowed.

"My purpose is to free a wretched human being kept there unjustly," I said to Torsten.

He brought the horses to a halt.

"Wouldn't it work better in daylight?" he asked.

"No, the situation is no longer under my control. There's a conspiracy against me here," I confided in him.

Torsten nodded and commanded the horses to go on again. "I understand," he answered.

I showed him a place beside a large tree where I wanted him to wait for me. It was so dark he was invisible no matter where he stood, but when I got back it would be easier to find him under the tree.

"Doesn't it look a bit odd, the Judge arriving at the castle without a buggy?" Torsten asked.

After a moment's pondering I admitted he was right. I couldn't sneak into the prison like a thief. I tried to remember why it had at first seemed necessary that I leave my transportation further away, but I couldn't find a sensible reason for it any longer.

"Good, we'll go to the courtyard together, then!" I said.

The jailer came to meet me with a coat flung over his shoulders. When he saw who I was, he was in a hurry to make sure he looked properly dressed.

"What on earth has happened?"

"I've received disturbing news that prisoner number sixty-five is planning to escape tonight," I said, stepping unsteadily down from the buggy. "I want to come and see that nothing unusual is going on," I said.

The jailer didn't know what to say. He had to notice I was drunk. He couldn't do anything, of course, but go ahead and show me the way.

"No one has told me anything about a conspiracy!" was his worried answer. I was too excited to think of any more excuses. We walked along the echoing corridors without exchanging a word, the guards fingering their key-rings when the jailer pointed at locked doors.

Clatter of boots, great emotion. Anxiety and triumphant longing, while the glow of drunkenness lit the dark stone walls.

Those were probably the last impressions left to me from that journey that I could be sure of. I can't remember how I explained to the jailer my wanting to check on things myself, and alone to boot. It was painfully clear I couldn't manage to sound very convincing.

I've been probing my memory, enticing it with good and bad, but it's willing to release only a few poor and confusing glimpses. Perhaps one ought to be thankful; I can imagine myself having been a hero; I can come up with honourable offers and tender meetings; I can see the prisoner coming into my arms, out of her mind with a sense of relief and longing. I can feel her against my chest, my stomach, my heart, my limbs, my groin; I can believe us having lost our self-control; me experiencing the skirt sliding up the leg; I can hear her breath being held back, yet filling the whole dungeon; I can imagine hearing the crazy whisperings of a woman in love; becoming bewildered about my own toughness and her gentleness; being surprised about my self-control in realizing — in the final moment — that a prison cell could never be the proper place for us; softened, making myself and her promise to guard this passion for a while yet.

But what am I doing? I insist on providing myself with the role of a fool. What possible evidence is there to support such a stand?

I remember hanging the lantern from a bracket on the wall, and the creature who brushed off bedding-hay from her clothing. It had to be Ingeborg. I had woken her up then! Of course I had, since the cell was as black as night when I arrived. She was frightened, very frightened. It's possible she may even have screamed in fright. Why shouldn't she? The poor girl must have thought she was being taken out now — in the middle of the night — to be tortured. Was I man enough to calm her down, to indicate by a few tender sentences that she was completely safe? Although I don't remember exactly, it is possible I stuttered and mumbled the words in an incoherent stream which frightened her all the more....

A pail toppled over. That much is true, because I remember swearing when the water splashed onto the stone floor. The pail got overturned when I stumbled over it, but I myself didn't fall. Of that much I'm certain. Why can't I forget about the pail and remember her words and gestures instead, remember something else besides the frightened looks and retreating steps caused by the initial fright.

We talked about her diary. At least I talked about it. She was strangely silent. Did she still believe this was an interrogation? That I had come to humiliate her because of those honest lines. "Did he show them to the Judge?" Emphasis on the last word. That kind of a sentence comes back to haunt my mind, and her voice, which was full of anxiety and horror. As if I should have been the very last person on earth allowed to see them. Or that she thought it cruel that the Parson had passed the diary on and not dealt with it in confidence. Why does it bother me? A person in love fears nothing more than making a fool of herself in the eyes of her beloved; what is more paradoxical and true than that?

I can remember the wall against which she had withdrawn when I touched her. I remember the dry lips, the moist mouth and the hair that fell from a wool head-covering and tickled my face. But why don't I remember her arms around me? Why don't I remember my hardness and her welcoming softness?

I must have offered her a plan for escape.

But what did she say? What did I say? Surely we couldn't have been arguing? Not so soon and not under those circumstances? Something had made me think. When Kjellinus arrived with the jailer, I was sitting in a corner, Ingeborg on the other side of the cell, but that wasn't because either of us was upset. Perhaps we had heard the steps and decided to salvage what we could of the situation so as to avoid suspicion.

The Parson was very polite. "I heard you were here

conducting an interrogation. Have you found out anything?" Or something like that. Restrained and unaffected phrases to a man who sat drunk and speechless in the cell of a dangerous prisoner at an insanely late hour.

Later on, not the next morning, but about a month later, I asked Torsten if I had said anything about what happened in the prison. He maintained I had uttered only one sentence. The rest of the way I had slept with my head against his shoulder.

"That woman is a bitch!" I had said to Torsten.

"And what did you say to that?" I had wanted to know.

"Aren't they all!" he had answered.

When I woke up late the next morning, I was very sick. In the afternoon Parson Kjellinus sent word they had obtained a satisfactory, albeit not a complete confession from Ingeborg.

TWENTY-ONE

ᗡ

*Chapter Twenty-One, in which the Judge becomes ill
and ponders the essence of suffering.*

A PECULIAR ILLNESS made me weak for several weeks. I
didn't have a cold, but I ran a temperature which got higher
every time I tried to look after my duties. Parson Kjellinus
thought it obvious the witch had practised *magiam divinatoriam* on me that crazy night when I, with no precautions, had
tried to expose the Devil's plans. Despite that, I forbade any
further torturing of Ingeborg since, according to the jailer,
her hands had become inflamed and she was in bed with a
high fever.

At home Elsa fussed over me the same way she fussed
over the children when they were sick. She brought cold,
then hot towels, made me drink juices and breathe healing
steam. She had a woman come and cup blood twice a week,
and she sat by me during the process, stroking my free hand.
Last thing at night she came in to see that all was well. "Dear
man!" she said while fluffing up my pillows. "Dear Elsa, my

darling," I answered.

I began to cling to her in a desperate, sexless frenzy. It calmed and comforted me that she was so ordinary, safe, and motherly. Had I, long ago, called her a coquette and a hypocrite? She who in her caring was the truest of women! There was no doubt that she alone saved me from impending disaster, and that she did it with the power she derived from her usual, everyday behaviour.

For instance, the more tasteless her clothes and the less they flattered her, the more I liked them and the more she was able to comfort me. Broadcloth, wool or linen brushing against my hand in passing spoke the language of forgiveness.

There was nothing surprising about Elsa's care. I was the breadwinner and if anything happened to me, that would have meant a miserable fate for Elsa and the children. Her inheritance from her father was no more substantial than my financial resources, and she, as the mother of six children, could hardly hope for remarriage. But I couldn't believe, just the same, that her tenderness was mere manipulation.

I was her husband. That meant I belonged to her, and Elsa had a strong need to nurse, care, watch over, nurture, improve and love all her property; when I was in a helpless situation I was, for the first time in a long while, clearly dependent on her just as the children were. That is why she felt this tenderness for me.

Elsa didn't like the fact that Bryniel Kjellinus kept bothering me with matters of work since the visits obviously tired me. "Dear man, is it worth your while? ..." she would ask, worried, at the same time helping me put on my dressing-gown.

The Parson never used the chair Elsa pointedly had someone fetch and position at the foot of the bed.

"I would think that in this case the death sentence can be pronounced without actual proof of her union with Satan, for hasn't she, in any case, led people astray and employed secret skills? But the problem is how to get the jurors to agree to the severity of the punishment," he once complained.

"Don't they believe her to be a witch?" I asked.

The Parson shrugged. "They do believe it, but referring to the *Carolina Constitutio Criminalis*, they remind us a person practising magic need not be punished by death unless she has caused some damage," he said.

I couldn't agree to have my sickness used as proof. The Parson did admit the matter was a sensitive one for him as well since, after all, I was the judge in charge of the case.

"What if we found support in books for the fact that soothsaying, with the aid of scissors and a needle, is *crimen exceptum* and not possible without the Devil's help?" he asked.

I said I couldn't remember reading anything specifically about scissors and a needle, but he wasn't convinced, and he thought that perhaps we might together familiarize ourselves with works that were central to the case.

A clear reference was found in Andreas Kesler's *Protevangelium, scholasticè & theologicè explicatum*. On pages 360-361, figures, letters and such were said to have magical powers which, without a doubt, emanated from the Devil. And Arnold Mengering in his work drew the natural peripheries of magic so plainly in *Erothema Catechtetich* that Ingeborg's tricks could no longer be considered harmless.

The Parson left satisfied; I became all the more ill.

"Why doesn't he take care of the matter by himself? Rather stupid, not able to read books without you," Elsa said, collecting the books strewn all over the bed.

It happened exactly as Kjellinus had foreseen. The jury was against the death sentence. The Parson had, nevertheless, decided to get what he wanted, and in the end the sentence was beheading and burning. While submitting the decision to

Turku's Court of Appeals, I made a separate reference, nevertheless, to the opinion of the jury and Dunte's opinion which opposed the death penalty. Would it be possible that the jury's and Dunte's views would be enough to overturn the sentence I had given?

I didn't look at Ingeborg as I pronounced the sentence. I felt sick, my heartbeat was accelerated, I had mild breathing difficulties. When I got home Elsa was horrified at my condition and I confessed to being in a miserable state, but not ill enough to go back to bed. Elsa's face showed signs of disappointment.

"Are you sure then," she asked "that the illness won't come back all the worse because of it?"

"No, I don't believe so," I answered.

Instead, I spent sleepless nights blaming myself for cruelty and weakness, but I took comfort in that the Court of Appeals would surely adjust the sentence to a more charitable one for the accused. I didn't know whether Ingeborg deserved mercy, I didn't know whether she was a witch or not, but I didn't want her to die.

I waited. If I think of my life as a musical score, as I often do, then the sign of execution for that period would be *grave molto grave*. Days and nights passed in slow and heavy procession; sometimes it seemed as if they didn't pass at all. Time, which I had long ago pronounced dangerous because it carried me too fast towards the grave, had now turned to stone.

Once, before trying to fall asleep, I remembered a German naval doctor in Tartu who showed me a passionflower under glass. The doctor told me he had examined many such climbing plants and noticed two logical phenomena in their growth patterns, triplicity and quintuplicity. The doctor said in the souls of some plants there were shapes seeking harmony. In the passionflower there were "thirds" and "fifths" which created, as in music, their shape in intervals.

People thought the doctor was crazy, but he knew all the plants that had healing properties, and he played the flute like an angel.

I didn't think it extraordinary that the doctor drew a parallel between harmony and suffering. After all, the beauty of a Passion Play was in that it told a tragedy in a way people found moving. The Jesuit missionaries who had found the first passionflower gave it its name for metaphoric reasons. They linked the plant with the history of Christ's suffering; the lobate leaves were the torturers' hands, the tendrils were the rope, the corolla the crown of thorns, the five petals the wounds, the small thorns the three nails used in nailing Christ to the cross.

Thinking about it, I realized that suffering is actually beauty of a kind. At least that is what people used to believe. If a human being had to suffer a great deal, her life hadn't been for naught. The more evident the pain, the more it brought emotional gain to those who witnessed it.

When Ingeborg O. anointed herself with her menstrual blood as an expression of her despair, it was an unpleasant sight, and yet it disturbed me. Her deed, despite its loathsomeness, had dignity because it was born of great suffering. Deep inside, all of us who saw her had to respect her because she suffered on behalf of all the ordinary, anxious, cowardly and timid people. We had been taught there was a set amount of suffering in the world and some people had to bear more of it so that human existence could be justified by its contrasts.

For that reason it wasn't important whether Ingeborg was a witch or not. For that reason there was no sense in my staying awake night after night.

It was true that what befell the rest of us was an easier life, but inseparably there also was always the sense of guilt and gloom of the ones lucky enough to be spared suffering without any effort on their part. Our only chance to experience the strength that suffering illumined, the strength that freed us from our worm-like existence, was to search for it in the arts, where it appeared in a refined and enjoyable form. Someone like me was the perpetual listener and watcher, never the focus of others' watching and listening. Deep inside I had difficulties accepting this because everyone wants to have an effect on things, to touch others and leave a lasting impression. But naturally I wasn't willing to pay the price. No one, with the exception of Christ, voluntarily paid the price, but the fate of some of us was to be born passionflowers.

That's what I thought at night when I lay awake pondering my role in Ingeborg's fate.

After a time the Court of Appeals confirmed the death sentence.

TWENTY-TWO

ℭ

Chapter Twenty-Two, in which the Judge ponders the devilish alchemy of falling in love and suffers a peculiar attack.

*T*WO YEARS. For two whole years nothing happened, and I began to believe it was all over. Without wanting it, the two years belonged to Ingeborg.

She robbed me of my interest in reading. Life didn't meet the expectations found in books. Still I tried to read more than ever; I ordered the latest publications, made a shopping trip to Sweden, borrowed books from the libraries of friends. But however the task began, sooner or later I ran into her. She stood like Hanswurst, jesting and mocking at carefully thought-out theories. I began to doubt that the morality of life had anything in common with the morality of men who sat in monasteries or in philosophers' chambers and let the quill fly.

The changing scene outside my library window always had her in it. When I watched the leaves fall from the oak trees, it no longer surprised me that they floated down, but that they had one day climbed up the tree. They had done it in secret; I couldn't testify to their long and arduous trip up to branches that stretched their limbs high above. Only to fall down? To experience a few moments' relief in the biting autumn air, after which the only thing left for them was to become earth. Why was it so easy for them when a human being, when Ingeborg, resisted the termination of her existence by crying out and writhing, gulping air to the very end?

On an August night when the wind spread the smell of a bitch in heat over the island, impassioned by the sea and the ripening wheat, and when no one had wits enough to sound an alarm because of the expression gleaming in every man's eye, I took myself a mistress.

Her name, like the name of my oldest daughter, was Ilia, and I ended up with her because of all the women within reach, she reminded me the least of Ingeborg. By my estimation, she was pretty and stupid. Later on I realized I had been wrong on both counts; with time Ilia turned out to be both ugly and smart. But even with my eyes closed I couldn't forget the fact I took her in order to cheat on Ingeborg, to silence her.

My relationship with Ilia, a servant girl, was cynical and uncomplicated. No child-minded emotionality ever interfered with our down-to-earth lovemaking. When she spread her legs for me with polite nonchalance, I was deeply ashamed about the naive foolishness into which I had sunk in imagining I was in love with Ingeborg. Ilia taught me that a woman is to be taken without speeches, without feelings, and without wrapping passions in ridiculous lies. She wasn't worried about getting pregnant, and neither did she. She didn't expect to be kissed when I left her, but she didn't mind small gifts now and then.

My own fall from grace didn't make the task of pronouncing judgements on whore-mongers any more difficult than before. I had my law books, I looked up the appropriate sections in them and pronounced a sentence befitting the crime. Nothing had changed but me. The thought of metamorphosis hiding in a judge's robes had at long last become clear to me; the judge represented the spirit of justice at the Assizes, not his own persona. I had said that many times, but now I understood what it meant. I couldn't let an adulterer escape punishment because I myself was one of the offenders, any more than a priest could refuse to hear a confession based on the fact that he also had sinned. In his cassock a priest was God's tool, and I was the tool of justice; a human being couldn't be guilty of a greater hubris than to imagine he could ever, as an individual, reach the level of actual metaphysical metamorphosis.

I ended the relationship because it hadn't freed me from Ingeborg; rather, in some insidious way it attached me to her even more strongly. That is when Ilia got worried about her place in Heaven for the first time, and fell into a mood that came close to being hysteria.

"I have to see the Pastor and confess my sins, otherwise I'll have no peace," she moaned. She knelt down as if she were praying, my semen running down her legs, and she grieved aloud about the damage done to her soul.

I looked at her with dread.

"If I bring twenty thalers, will that give you peace?" I asked.

Ilia got up, wiped herself with the skirt hung over the edge of the bed and dried her eyes.

"Really and truly?"

When I brought her the money the following evening, she undressed herself as usual and lay down.

"No, I can no longer afford to increase the burden of your sins," I announced and left her looking surprised.

I can't lie that I didn't feel a stab of conscience; I had,

after all, almost half a century's attachment to the Lutheran spirit; trials and acts of self-conquest and their collapse couldn't happen without pain. But I surmised dimly that at an older age and closer to death I would be given an opportunity for more proper and serious regretting.

But Ingeborg! She had set a trap for me, one from which there was no escape. For the two years during which I didn't have to handle a single witch case I spun in the hole she had dug for me, tearing at the edges, making them all the more bare the more I tried to climb to freedom.

With time insignificant matters became more important than great shocks. I no longer felt anxiety when I remembered her hanging from the noose like a fractious child — "I don't want, I don't, no, you mustn't" — but rather when I tried to remember word for word something she had said in passing. I was certain the truth about her and myself could be found in her words, the truth I couldn't find alone. But as I probed my mind, I could catch only the trivialities I myself had let drop; I couldn't recall her words with any clarity. Perhaps it was too wearying in the end to satisfy myself with the non-existent findings, so I made one up.

"You can teach pity even to a beast, but not to someone tortured without reason," she said. And she smiled just enough for me to see her strong, even teeth. "So you didn't at least out of pity ... ?" I asked. "Oh no!" she answered. "No, no, a torturer isn't pitied, that much is certain!" she stated. "Well, out of hate, then? Or in order to use me to your advantage?" I suggested. Her hand, made into a fist, opened and motioned in a gesture of helplessness. "When there's this little time, one doesn't use it frivolously," she said sadly. "But how can one fall in love, generally speaking, when one knows it's all coming to an end?" I went on. She came closer to me. "The more precious the gift, the more beautiful the burden," she answered.

Of course no such conversation ever took place. But it could have, if thoughts had been words. Thinking about these conversations was ridiculous, it was sentimental and foolish, but I couldn't put a stop to it all the same.

Why did it matter so that Ingeborg, the woman to whom I had handed the death sentence, was fond of me, had fallen in love with me? And if it was so momentous, why hadn't I simply walked into her cell before the beheading and asked her about it? Was it because I was ashamed, or because I was afraid of the answer I would get?

Even Elsa was no help. When I was thoroughly fed up with having my hand as my wife, I'd go to her. But the night together would shrink into a couple of groans and moments of detestable stupidity, and I would sneak back to my own room with a sour taste in my mouth.

A night came when I couldn't even manage that. I stood at her door, watched her, my wife whose nightgown fell seductively from her shoulders. Under the lace I could see even lighter skin, soft as foam, flesh humbled by waiting. She crossed her legs, the sign of self-preservation and moral indignation, but took care that between her legs there remained visible a tempting portal.

"Don't even try to touch me," she said.

I was horrified. Is this what we had come to, the finest girl in our society and me? ("Listen friend, what's the name of that beauty, the one with big, innocent eyes?") Is this what had happened to us although together we had sworn the vows that promised to gild our whole life? The wedding night was far from a rape, and later on when she no longer felt any pain, the ritual had — at its most ardent — bordered on the beautiful. I remember a night when I had fallen asleep with my hand on her breast and she hadn't taken it away even after she saw I was asleep. How had we come to where we were now?

In my thoughts I went to her, pulled the nightgown down to cover her feet and stroked her hair. In reality, I withdrew towards the door and mumbled something as an explanation. Had I behaved according to my thoughts, she would have struck me out of a sense of humiliation and disappointment, I was certain of it.

"Please forgive me," I said.

"What?" she asked. She masked her upset; I turned away before understanding gave way to naked rage. I heard her call something after me. Only at my door did I understand what she had said.

"I never wanted you in the first place!" she said.

I opened the door into a night where crickets set the beat.

"I know," I answered.

I didn't have shoes on; I'd been in the process of undressing when the thought of Elsa came to my mind. I hadn't changed into a nightshirt because I had noticed how my wearing it irritated Elsa. If I had to gone to her, it would have been better to penetrate her chamber like a thieving Cossack who lowered his pants only as much as insolent copulation demands.

For the first time in forty years I felt bare ground under my naked feet, the night-damp grass and the rough sand. I took a few running steps; it felt incredibly good. The ground was one vast shadow; my feet didn't know what they trampled. But the running wasn't groping for the way, it swallowed a sliver of road that grass had overgrown, low shoots of hazel bushes, carefully marked edges of wheat fields. I felt I was running on abandoned land; people had deserted everything for a whole night and escaped somewhere. And we abandoned ones took measure of each other. In the scent of a dense dusk.

I was crying all the while, of course. That's something you clearly guessed, correct? When a man runs barefoot over hills and dales for the first time in forty years without giving a thought to getting thorns in his feet it must be because he is crying. I didn't see the barely visible white birch trunks, the sight of which had filled me with enjoyment when I was younger, didn't see the stardust, nor hear the peaceful droning of the sea further on, but I cried for all the times I had not expressed my anxiety, my distress, my despair, my fear, my misery, my pity, my fear of death, my hatred, my pettiness.

Yes, I cried. So what? Forty years or more is a long time to show a stiff upper lip and keep inside something that preys upon you in a world where windows could open at night, but never during the day.

At some point I had to stop. In the end it was ridiculous to run up and down the hills in the middle of the night. When the body started to tire, intelligence began to mock. I was pitiful; what possible use did I think this kind of an attack had?

I sat on the edge of a ditch and felt something slimy under my hand. A fragile scent, familiar and comforting, spread from a crushed plant. It came from somewhere far in the past, from the time when one didn't yet look into the past but gathered experiences like a bee gathers nectar. How far back would one have to go for the shadows not to be visible? "Why don't you have a husband like everyone else, Ambrosia?" And the answer from a cloud of smiles: "A maid knows what to do when no one marries her, she manages without!" "I'll grow up to be your man, Ambrosia!" The brush of a cheek and kisses. "So you will; it certainly pays to wait!"

No, the memories couldn't keep one warm indefinitely. The world hadn't gotten uglier since those days, only I had let a crippled, loathsome creature in for a visit and it had decided to stay. It had no name. And even if it had, it wouldn't come forward when called, but hid waiting for the worst possible moment to emerge. I was the one who had let it in, and I was also the one who had to drive it out if I wanted to be free. But how did one get hold of it? It was like an old dog; when provoked, it bit through the flesh all the way to the bone.

"No fear of God, only the fear of death," Ingeborg had once said. Now I felt there wasn't even the fear of death, only the fear of one's own inner world. If I prayed at all any longer, the prayer went like this: Don't make me be alone with it!

But enough about that! It was night, a blue mist floated above the fields. Why wouldn't I let that be enough for me. Only a crazy man searched for ugly sights when there were others. The night and the mist, the scent of love and grain. Had I become a farmer, I wouldn't have sat there grieving. I would have had two clear thoughts: plough and sow, in the ground and in the womb, bread and children! But a judge, he cuts down what others have sown, he cuts away damaged branches, he takes chaff instead of grain, he ploughs death where others plough life. That's why there was no sense in expecting much even of love, not the right ploughing or sowing, for where would the justification for it be?

Unless there existed a woman who would give me back the man in me. The kind of woman who had power. Flesh from my flesh, bone from my bone. Yearning only for me, because I alone could fill her arms. I must not believe the woman who had died was the only one. That was too inconsolable.

Why did it all depend on so little? The line of a nose, a way of answering questions, a random sentence, and the matter was won or lost for all time. What devilish and finely tuned alchemy hid behind loving?

I tried to feel for the plant that gave off the pleasant smell in the dark, but I merely managed to gather a handful of hay. When love puts in an appearance, one doesn't know enough to take hold of it because it seems too good to be true, I thought. When one had become used to burying expectations in work and principles, one was reluctant to give them up.

I stood up. There was a slight wind from the sea and the bottom of my feet were sore. There's not much left of life, I admitted, returning humbly through the gate to the yard. If only one could say one had loved someone, that might work as a defence.

I decided if Elsa was waiting for me, even if only to tell me off and start a quarrel, I would take her seriously and try to like her the way she deserved to be liked. She was an exceptional mother, had good social skills and much more; why wouldn't I be able to feel genuine fondness for her? And if my sudden leaving had made her so worried that she had come all the way outdoors, I'd truly try....

Elsa was not out in the yard. When I peeked through the door into her room, I saw her sleeping soundly with the cover tucked under her cheek. I went into my own room and lay down without taking off my clothes. Just before falling asleep I thought I heard crying from the other side of the wall. Perhaps she had been waiting, after all; perhaps she would have considered softening only if I humbled myself and went to her. But when I thought of all the pretending with which she would, in any case, start it all, I no longer cared how things stood.

At dawn it began to rain. The rain continued without pause for three weeks. In August the drops turned into ice pellets. Hail brought frost with it. Nearly all the harvest was lost. That winter a large number of people died of hunger.

CHAPTER

TWENTY-THREE

⌒

*Chapter Twenty-Three, in which the Judge sentences a
church thief and must worry about Torsten, his field-hand.*

CATS AND DOGS disappeared from houses. Some claimed the
hungry dug carcasses up from the frozen ground and ate
them unthawed. The luckier ones made ersatz bread out of
tree bark, linen seeds, roots, and acorns. People died along
the roadsides. When a body lost its limbs at night, people
feared there were not only wild animals around, but also beggars. The most desperate ones crossed the ice hauling a row-
boat as a makeshift sled and went to sell their children as servants to people in Stockholm. They thought the King was
giving city people wheat. The few who reached the city saw
the capital's streets full of beggars and the dying. In the
spring the fishermen got pitiful hauls in their nets. Burial
bells rang late into the summer.

During the winter Assizes a sixteen year old boy who had
stolen communion bread from a church was brought before
me. Since he had no prior record, he would have gotten off

with only a fine or some time in a work camp. This was in accordance with light sentencing, the right given to the lower courts some time ago, but the rule couldn't be applied to anyone caught stealing from a church.

"What happened to him?" my field-hand Torsten asked on our way home. He had livened up a great deal during these two years. I could say he had gained self-confidence from the humiliation I had experienced; after the trip to Kastelholm, his posture didn't any longer so much reflect the fate of the down-trodden.

"The boy? I was forced to give him the death sentence," I answered.

"Why?" the field-hand asked.

"In accordance with the order of punishments decreed by Queen Kristina," I said. Torsten shook his head.

"I don't understand how a ruler can demand the death sentence when people are not even given enough food to keep them from stealing to stay alive," he said.

His neck was red and he didn't look at me.

"You're a revolutionary!" I announced, surprised.

"No, I'm not," Torsten argued. "If I were a revolutionary, I wouldn't sit here driving the merciful Judge to those sittings that for some reason are called dispensations of justice," he answered.

"Why do you insist on becoming bitter because of a thief you don't even know?" I asked, without getting upset. Torsten's peculiarity had earned him the special privilege of provoking me. I don't know if there existed even a single line that he couldn't overstep with impunity.

"There are too many people dying already; I don't understand the sense of killing those who have miraculously managed to stay alive," he said.

I wrapped the fur coat tighter around me; it was getting bitingly cold.

"You don't understand? If wrong-doers weren't punished, we'd soon have complete chaos here. Thieves would enter every house, even ours. That's where your charity would end, if your own plate was empty," I explained.

We had been lucky. There were enough cows to be slaughtered and enough wheat left over from the previous year in the storage bin.

I had felt sorry for the boy. A mere skinny, frightened kid who probably had done what he did because others had egged him on. But he was caught in the act of gulping down — disappointed — those dry wafers that tasted like paper. As if that wasn't enough, he had stuffed altar candles inside his shirt. The crime was one of the most brazen of its kind.

"That's not true," Torsten said. "If I wanted to give my portion of food to someone who was hungrier, that would cause a great uproar right away. After all, we're supposed to lie to everybody that in Judge's house there's hunger and misery so that beggars won't endlessly bother us," he remarked.

"If you think that's such a hardship, you can always leave your food uneaten," I jeered.

"But not give it to the needy?" the field-hand asked.

"What help would that be? One person doing that for a short while?" I said. "Is that how you'd clear your conscience?"

Soberly he kept his tongue in check. Who knows what twisted thoughts moved in his head at that moment? That his conscience was cleaner than mine? I who guarded full flour-sacks at the same time I was sentencing to death those for whom there hadn't been enough of anything to give? That I pitied people less than the horses in animal shelters barely able to stand, ones I couldn't make myself order to be destroyed?

My field-hand was welcome to harbour those views, although he ought to see that I had tried to help the hungry until finally their never-ending flow became intolerable. When, on two occasions, bodies were found on the front steps after a flock of beggars had departed, Elsa lost her nerve altogether. "What if the children become infected with something deadly?" she asked, crying, and suggested we pay the Church to hand out food to the needy on our behalf. I considered that sensible, and that's what we had been doing.

"The clergy are telling churchgoers that this punishment is sent to try us because of witchcraft. Soon the Judge will have to exercise sentencing again," Torsten said.

I didn't bother to answer him. I was afraid he was right; the nightmare couldn't go on without a scapegoat. And not all the wives Karin P. had named had been thoroughly examined yet. People's despair had grown so great they had to find a target for its release. I knew that a witch couldn't be behind all this; the hard times were testing the whole dominion, after all, but in times like these the weaker took comfort in the Devil's temptations to stay alive.

"Don't you ever find anything good to say about anything?" I asked the field-hand who was driving the horses onto an echoing bridge deck.

"I've been freezing half a day waiting for you, Sir. In that situation miserable thoughts come easily to mind," Torsten answered.

"Why didn't you come into the courthouse? It was warm in there," I said. He laughed a nasty laugh.

"I wasn't *that* cold!"

There was no question about it. I was the special target of his hatred. Just as before. I, who treated him kindly. I, who allowed him liberties no other master would have given him. And he accepted my magnanimity, callously used it for his own benefit, but didn't bother to disguise the fact that he despised me. With what right? And who did he think he was?

"Do you imagine yourself a better person than others just because you're the only one who goes on squeaking like an old hinge?" I asked.

He shrugged his snow-covered shoulders and didn't say anything.

"You can't do anything else but fan gloom, that's all you're capable of," I provoked him.

"I am capable of other things too," Torsten answered.

"Absolutely; you know how to shovel and haul manure, but that's one and the same thing isn't it?" I said mockingly. He didn't try to argue my point and we said nothing more to each other during the ride home.

Next day I heard Torsten hadn't touched his portion of food. Nor did he eat the following morning or evening. Even on the third day the plate remained untouched.

I found him in the cow barn.

"I've had just about enough of your schemes," I said to him. He stopped what he was doing and stood, hands on the backs of the horses standing on each side of him.

"What schemes?" he asked.

"In this house we don't tolerate whims! If you don't agree to eat your food, I'll see to it that you're force-fed," I told him.

The horses laid their ears back because of the sharp tone of my voice. The field-hand patted their backs to calm them.

"I don't believe the food would stay inside me, because I'm not hungry," Torsten said.

"Why aren't you hungry, if I may ask?" I spoke in a sharp tone. He kicked the hay at his feet.

"I just am not," he answered.

I became suspicious. What if he ate in secret? Wouldn't it be just like Torsten to smuggle food to a hiding place and then play the role of a martyr at the dinner table? I scrutinized him closely; he didn't look a bit skinnier than before.

But no. It really wasn't like him; if he had a role in that kind of farce, he played it as thoroughly as possible. He would never be able to bear the shame of being caught pilfering food, stealing my food.

"I'll let them beat you as long as it takes for you to learn to eat again," I said. Torsten shook his head.

"That would be a crime. There's no article that says a field-hand has to eat his master's food," he answered.

"If you don't eat, you'll commit suicide. That is a crime!" I argued, undefeated.

"Go ahead and sentence me after I've killed myself!" the field-hand answered and began to brush the horses with calm strokes. The horses were skinny but amazingly placid. Like the field-hand. I couldn't think of anything to say so I left him.

He didn't touch his food the next day either. Not in the morning, nor the evening. Elsa was amazed. "Is he crazy? In these times, when others would be deliriously happy if they could take his place at the table?" Elsa asked. The servants didn't talk about anyone but him. I heard he had stumbled in the morning on his way to do his chores. They all were certain it was because he was weak.

"It's very slippery out there," I reminded them.

"He's never stumbled before," the kitchen maid said.

"Except when drunk," I said cynically.

"Why don't you force him to eat?" Elsa asked. "We can't afford to lose a good field-hand."

"A witch has put a spell on him," my daughter Ilia thought.

"And he eats only invisible Devil food," Märta enthused.

After I got up from the dinner table that evening I asked that the field-hand be brought to me. The children, who had started to play a game of marbles, stopped their game to come and see what strange things would be found out about the field-hand.

"This is not a matter for children," I told them.

"Do they take him to prison?" Märta asked.

"No," I answered sharply.

"But he'll have to go to court for sure," Ilia argued knowingly.

"You dummies, how could a man be a witch!" Hans said, and laughed at the children's childishness.

I took my lantern and went to the cellar. Nowadays I didn't send for a servant when I wanted something to drink. I no longer hit my head on the low vaults the way I used to in the beginning. Broken bricks took on odd shapes in the light of the lantern; there were cobwebs behind the bottles. I would run out of stock before summer.

The field-hand was waiting in my den when I returned with a bottle in each hand. I took my time calmly pulling out the cork and pouring a glass half full. I sat down but left him standing.

"Why?" I asked as calmly as I could. "Why do you insist on shaming me?"

Torsten shook his head.

"Do you want a drink?" I suggested. He stood still.

"No, I don't," he answered.

"What do you want?" I asked and tried to restrain the revolt brewing inside me.

"Hans Kristiansson had a dog, did the Judge hear about that?" he asked.

"No; I'm not interested in other people's dogs," I answered.

"He didn't feed it, but couldn't make himself eat it, either. Hans kept it on a chain because he didn't want anyone else to kill it either, and it barked like crazy day and night," Torsten said.

"Hans should have killed it," I said.

"In the end Hans Kristiansson went right off his head listening to the never-ending barking, and he began to kick the dog to death, but it jumped at his throat and killed him instead. But it didn't eat him. The dog lay down beside him until it died of hunger," Torsten said.

I emptied my glass.

"I haven't kept you hungry."

"True, but while I waited in front of the courthouse, I saw a woman carrying a dead child in her arms," Torsten said.

"It's not my fault the frost destroyed the harvest," I said.

He smiled for no apparent reason and said, "I'm just fed up with everything; I don't feel like eating."

I was about to lose my temper, but he was standing too far away for me to slap him. He was too strong and sturdy for me to attack him. What right did he have to argue it was more honourable to die hungry these days than to stay alive. Honour was the privilege of my class, not his.

"You're joking!" I insisted. "In the end you'll cave in and start eating."

I ought to have taught him humility as the Major had advised me. Why hadn't I gotten rid of him ages ago, given him to the recruiters, why hadn't I sent him to war? I had sympathized with him for no reason and now he did this to me.

He was a heretic. He indicated by his behaviour that the world God had made didn't satisfy him, that it wasn't good enough for him. He had the nerve to say it was wanting, miserable and rotten. And in his eyes, I of all God's creatures was the biggest failure. What else could he be but a complete heretic?

"Dogs don't end up in Hell, but you will," I said and poured myself more wine.

He rubbed his eyes with his large hand, out of fatigue, not because he was moved, and said, "I suppose so!"

"Doesn't it bother you?" I asked.

He rubbed his whole face as if making sure it was of one and the same flesh. "I haven't given it much thought."

I couldn't stand looking at him any longer. "Get out!" I ordered. "Go and do whatever you want, but make sure you're nowhere I can see you!" I shouted after him.

When I went to the cellar again that night I hit my head on a low vault beam and dropped the lantern. The light went out and as I groped my way out in the dark I heard mice or rats making their horrible cheeping noises. The night was very cold and for a long time after I got indoors I had to massage my hands before I could feel them touching anything. The bed rolled around before my eyes when I dropped down on it. I fell asleep right away, but I woke up in the small hours of the dawn with a bad taste in my mouth and stayed awake until morning.

Before I began my work, I inspected the grain storage and gave an order to slaughter one more pig. The situation looked bright enough so that I also ordered the feeding of beggars to resume.

"Only a few bowls twice a week," I comforted Elsa.

"What about the diseases they bring with them?" Elsa asked.

"The food is to be handed out at the back of the barn; they're not to be allowed closer," I answered. To my amazement she didn't say anything more against it.

In the evening I was told the field-hand had eaten a little of the soup. When I saw him in the yard, I couldn't keep from mocking him.

"Didn't I say you weren't man enough for it?" I said. The cold wind blew his lambskin vest open and his ears were red from the biting wind.

"That's the way it is; I got hungry and I ate," he answered.

We smiled. I can't remember when last we had smiled at the same time. Then his triumph became unbearable. I stepped closer and slapped him with all my strength on the cheek.

"You make sure it doesn't happen again!" I shouted.

He nodded, but didn't bend his head nor raise a hand to his cheek.

TWENTY-FOUR

*Chapter Twenty-Four, in which the Judge will have
the nasty Greta M. to interrogate and will hear
worrisome stories about close friends.*

GRETA M. was a parson's daughter, but a devil of a woman. She was nearly sixty, nasty and unscrupulous. Her nastiness bothered people particularly because she had a sharp mind and tongue.

A devious nature wasn't enough to make a witch of anybody, but many witnesses knew that the ills Greta wished upon others also materialized. Greta always cursed others when things didn't go the way she wanted. No wonder Major Berg feared his wife's sickness was Greta's fault because she had, in a moment of hatred, foretold it would happen.

After a two year respite I was almost anxious to take on a new case. Greta M. was one of the women Karin P. had named as witches, but this second denouncement by Major Berg was a surprise. Was I expecting to shed light on Ingeborg's case with the help of this recent indictment, was that the reason for my interest? When one had been forced to fence with a ghost for two years, it felt good to have a real opponent. The fact that the case had become known all the way to Sweden and Germany didn't matter. I often left my colleagues' half-read letters of praise in the recesses of my desk where they remained and turned yellow without my taking the trouble of even mentioning them to anybody.

"I only asked God to punish Major Berg for his evil deeds," Greta said. She gave me and the jurors sanctimonious glances. Major turned red with anger, or was it fear?

"Why did you ask for misfortunes only from God?" I asked.

Greta got angry.

"God will also punish the Judge for asking those kinds of questions."

The Major demanded the words of the accused be remembered, because should suspicious misfortune befall him or his house, he would consider Greta to be the cause of it. As for me, I asked the jurors to be witnesses and at the same time noted down that I had been threatened. The accused wore a mocking smile.

The matters that had seemed suspicious to the Major were examined again. During the Major's long stay in Spain, his wife, who had remained in Stockholm, had become seriously ill. That didn't surprise me; Kristina had always been sickly and when one considered the fact that the Major's long foreign trip had had an unhealthy effect not only on his wife but on my wife as well, it was a painful matter to bring up in court.

There were many statements against the accused. The stories about life in Greta's childhood home caused the greatest astonishment. Her father, Martin Buscherus, Lemland's parson, who had passed away, appeared to have favoured the most peculiar hobbies and modes of social life at the parsonage.

It was even necessary to have the jurors examine whether the way Greta's mother, the mistress of the parsonage, entertained guests could be seen as extraordinary hospitality or outright whoring. When two of the jurors tended to support the latter, Sir Martin had wished them to go straight to Hell, and it so happened that soon after the sitting, the two men had drowned.

"Mother got a bad reputation because she couldn't stand sitting in corners looking like she had swallowed poison, the way the other wives of the clergy did," Greta said.

"She chose depravity instead?" I asked.

"Father didn't complain about her behaviour; doesn't that say something?" Greta answered.

The jurors shook their heads; they didn't want to speak ill of the dead, but rumour had it that liquor fumes had clouded the dead parson's judgement in a number of ways.

"Greta drank as much as the rest of the family, although her brothers were more wanton!" one juror stated.

"Her brother Måns was in the habit of bragging that his father had given him a book with which he could do as much good or harm as he wished," he added.

"Not one of you understands a joke," Greta answered.

"If Måns knew a field-hand was after a pretty servant girl, he used the book to get the girl for himself," the juror said.

"Women just liked him, nothing could change that," Greta said.

The Police Chief, Per Andersson, stated that when Greta was very happy she had a habit of saying, "Even if I were in Hell right now, I'd still brag about how much fun I'm having." Her dead brothers Daniel, Måns and Nils had used the same expression.

"Don't forget Isak!" Greta said.

"Why did you swear like that?" I asked.

"It was a cliché, not swearing. I don't suppose the Judge

has ever enjoyed himself thoroughly, or had real fun, if he has to ask that," Greta answered.

Later on, Greta told me she very much missed her years as a girl at the parsonage, and her four brothers who had been the only people in the world with whom she could play jokes and have fun.

"Isn't anything else fun except lewdness?" I asked.

She gave me a long look filled with an old woman's condescension. "That's precisely the question all the time. You can find only ugly names for what you don't understand and what is not within your reach."

"What is it then?" I wanted to know.

"Not everything can be explained," she answered.

"Your brothers had bad reputations," I said.

"We, the whole family, always have had, but that hasn't made us bad," Greta answered.

She had cut her hair short, because she couldn't stand the thought of the hangman's helper doing it. With her large ears she looked like a little boy who had an old person's spotted and wrinkled skin. She was angry that she hadn't been allowed to keep her jewelry; she was especially sad about her earrings. "Then everybody would have stared at them and not my protruding ears," Greta said. Here again was something I would never learn to understand, the vanity of an old woman in a situation where one would have thought her to have worse things to mourn. "After all, it's my funeral, is it not?" Greta insisted. "A person should have the right to decide how to look at her own funeral," she maintained.

"Not in this case," I answered.

"Well, I suppose it's asking too much that Nils would be picking jewelry from my severed head," Greta said. She began to laugh nervously.

Her fate was determined by the fact that all too often she had wished her fellow human beings ill.

"Misfortunes happen to people, what can I do about it? What possible joy do you think I got from the fact that Justine's newborn baby died?" she shouted.

"She insists you cursed misfortune upon her," I answered.

"She is crazed and stupid," Greta said.

Greta M.'s attitude made it impossible for her to win the case. At times it seemed as if she didn't care very much either way. However, her original decision to escape to Sweden after she heard the Major had returned to the island was an indication of something else.

"I knew he would take out an indictment against me," Greta said.

"How could you know that beforehand?" I asked.

"A son of a bitch of a man like that always does the worst thing possible," Greta answered.

"That kind of language isn't appropriate here," I said.

"You're the same yourself," she said.

Greta simply would not bow to anybody. Her husband stated she'd said the night before the Assizes that this thing would cost her her life, but Devil take it if others wouldn't follow her. "Why would you be sentenced to death if you haven't done anything wrong?" her husband had asked, but Greta hadn't replied to the question, she had just started to get ready to leave.

"After all, I'm neither blind nor deaf. Have any of the women you have decided to get rid of for disturbing your peace gone free?" she asked. She was in the same cell Anna B. had occupied in her time, and the strange notations Anna had made still covered the walls.

"We can't let witches live," I answered.

She laughed; she had many teeth left, but they were dark and split like old sauna rocks. "Shall I tell you what witchcraft is?" Greta asked. "You think up laws and sins in order to protect yourselves, but you realize they also protect others against you. That's why you had to think up witchcraft as an excuse to kill people who cannot be judged according to ordinary laws," she said.

"The Law does know what witchcraft is," I argued.

"But it doesn't mean anything; every judge can give his own interpretation any way he wants," Greta answered. "But be careful. There will be a day when that too will turn against you," she added as a threat.

Greta raised her feet onto the sleeping boards made especially for her because she was so frail. While sleeping on the floor, her joints had deteriorated to such a degree she couldn't get up on her own.

"That is paranoia! Why would I, or anyone else, want to get rid of you for any reason other than that you are spreading heresies on the island?" I said, astonished.

"You can't stand those who see right through you like I do," Greta answered. One blue-veined hand rubbed her aching knees, the other pointed at me. "You have to silence all those who are able to tell what useless creatures you are."

It annoyed me that she was in such poor health we didn't dare torture her. She had a habit of daring us, "You don't use torture because I would let too many unpleasant truths come out."

"Such as?" I asked.

I couldn't understand her hints, and I ended up presuming her to be bitter about the fact that she had to change her comfortable days as a parson's daughter to being a sexton's wife, and later on move into even worse circumstances as her husband was fired from his position because of drinking.

There had been questions about a ring belonging to the Major's wife and the quarrel about it had, in its time, reached all the way to the Assizes. There were rumours that Greta had offered to sell Olof Beckius, the parson at Jomala, the same kind of ring Kristina Berg had lost at a wedding in

Norby. Furthermore, they found out that Beckius' son had sold the ring in Turku. The Major believed the chain of events to be proof of Greta having stolen the ring, but the matter had remained unresolved.

"Isn't it clear? When they can't make a thief of me, the only thing left is magic," Greta said.

"Neither do I believe that you found the ring, because you didn't return it," I answered. I could imagine anything at all about that woman. She was as loathsome as I had hoped every person sentenced to death would be.

"I didn't find it," she admitted. "The Major's wife gave it to me."

"That can't be true," I argued.

Greta deliberately misunderstood my words. "No, that's right; in those years she was still the wife of a captain."

Greta told me an unbelievable story about the fate of the ring. Although I realized she invented it out of bitterness and nastiness, it always bothered me when I had anything to do with the Major and his wife. In Kristina's nervous laughter now rang the harshness of guilty feelings, and her habit of putting her hand under my arm nowadays began to feel like an unpleasant and intrusive gesture.

According to Greta, Kristina Berg had given her the ring at a wedding in Norby where she then claimed the ring had been lost. In the summer night Greta had run into a couple who had fled the noisy festivities to a field behind the parsonage. Greta said she wasn't in any way spying on them. The couple was well hidden in the shadow of a large oak tree, and she hadn't noticed them until she was right beside them. When Greta, surprised and unwilling, had to witness what in itself could be seen as perfectly natural goings-on happening against a tree trunk, there being no doubt about the nature of the goings-on, she had turned to leave. That is when the man had called after her and given her the ring, asking her not to tell anyone what she had seen. She had recognized the man to be Parson Beckius' son, and the woman to be Kristina, Mrs. Berg.

"That's where they made a mistake!" Greta said. "My eyesight is too weak to have recognized them in the dusk; besides, I don't recognize every naked man on this island anyway," she explained.

I was silent; I didn't know what to believe.

"What irked me was the fact that they had so little faith in a person they had to start bribing me right away," Greta said.

"Like a servant girl!" I said mockingly.

"Like a servant girl," she said and shook her head.

"Why did you sell the ring to Beckius then?" I asked. There was no sense in that, it wasn't logical, but I had forgotten that life and an angry woman were rarely logical.

"Out of spite! I've always loathed that idiot, and I wanted him to humble himself before me! I told Beckius where I'd gotten the ring and asked if he had any use for it, or would he return it to the Captain," Greta explained.

"And so the Parson bought it to rescue his son?" I asked.

"Bought it and then made his son sell it in Turku so he would get his money back, but greed turned out to be its own punishment," Greta added.

"Why didn't you tell that in court?" I asked. She loved blackening people's reputations; how come she had let such a juicy opportunity go by without taking advantage of it?

"For two reasons," Greta answered. "I felt sorry for Kristina Berg; I thought she might truly love the boy and when he drowned, that was punishment enough."

"What was the other reason?" I asked ironically, because the first didn't convince me.

"I was afraid of the Captain; I didn't know what he'd do when he found out about it and began to hate me, the cause of his shame," Greta reasoned.

"Now you'll die in any case!" I said.

"If I had destroyed the Major's family, he wouldn't have let it go unpunished. That's why I'll be silent," Greta said.

I didn't write Greta's confession into the records. I said to myself that those were the mumblings of an old, loud-mouthed woman. I had known the Major and his wife for years; our meetings had always been spent conversing in the same relaxed manner characterized by the tact and self-satisfaction of four well-bred adults.

I did get secret satisfaction from the thought that Greta's story was the truth, but the regular meetings of the four of us had become my shield which would never be pierced by a small arrow aimed at any weak point of our group.

I said to Greta I didn't believe her. She said she had known right from the beginning that would be my answer. And she smiled triumphantly as she was left to wait for her death among the lice and rats, while I went home.

CHAPTER

TWENTY-FIVE

*Chapter Twenty-Five, in which the Judge hears more
ugly allegations from Greta M. and therefore has
to ponder the essence of justice.*

"*O*UR FAMILY HASN'T been tolerated because we've been
openly what we are, what a human being is, while others have
lived that way secretly and only in their thoughts," Greta said
to me a couple of days before her death. "My father would
never have agreed to take part in these kinds of goings-on
where innocent people are being murdered, and yet they
called him a worthless man," she said and began, as was her
habit, to slander Bryniel Kjellinus who, according to her
opinion, was the personification of all that is abhorrent.

The Parson had once again offered to conduct interrogations and I had let him since I couldn't find a proper reason
for denying it. I would have had to include the Parson as the
representative of the Church's authority in any case, and it
was expedient to give him the role of an interrogator because
he knew the doctrine and lived in Sund.

"Mr. Bryniel presents himself as virtuous a human being as a church choirboy, but I know that he is a worse sinner than the Devil himself," Greta said. I didn't like the Parson, but decency demanded I interrupt the prisoner's way of talking about her interrogators.

"If you don't learn to control your tongue, I'll have you burned alive," I said.

"That you won't do because it's against the law. See, you have no experience at making threats. The Parson makes the prisoners bow to his will because he also carries out his threats," Greta answered.

I wanted to know what she meant, but she changed the subject. A little later she upset me by claiming — in the midst of talking about something else — that Kjellinus tortured prisoners.

"How do you think the Devil's sign appeared on your witches unless someone put it on them while they were in prison?" Greta asked.

"The Devil is apt to leave his sign or remove it at any time to confuse people," I said citing Carpzow.

"Sure enough, but the devil's name is Kjellinus, and he has burnt those marks on their flesh," she said.

That had to be a lie! How could Greta have known what had happened in the prison?

"I have my sources," she answered.

Her secrecy was an indication that she talked nonsense, but the matter bothered me.

"Why wouldn't the women have told me that?" I asked.

"But you were on the same side as the Parson, isn't that so?" Greta said. "Besides, Kjellinus knew enough to close their mouths by threatening to treat their loved ones the same way," she added.

"That can't be possible," I said, rejecting even the thought of it.

"How could the poor women know that?" Greta asked.

It couldn't and mustn't be true. Torture always had to happen in the presence of witnesses; secrecy and threats were not part of the essence of justice. But of course Greta was lying because she was bitter; I had to keep that in mind at all times. And yet! Every case had depended on us finding the Devil's sign; torture couldn't begin until a sign that was dead to the touch was found.

"You can't feel the burnt area once the initial pain is gone," Greta said.

"Not all marks appeared in prison for the first time; I saw some of them during the very first inspection," I said triumphantly.

Greta asked me to help her up, and I reluctantly obeyed. She took hold of me with her bony hands and turned me around so I was standing with my back to her. The old woman was too fragile and in too poor health to be dangerous, but still I was alarmed when she pushed my cape aside and pressed her fingers with surprising strength between my shoulder-blades.

"How many fingers?" she asked.

I tore myself loose. "One, of course. One!" I answered.

Greta shook her head. "No, two," she said.

It was true. In the evening I played the same game with my children. When you pressed someone's back with two fingers that were spread apart, the person usually felt only one. The prisoners were tested with a two-pronged fork: if they felt the prick of only one, the case was considered unequivocally solid. And most of the Devil's marks usually appeared on the back! How was it possible that not even the Provost knew the misinformation the human back could furnish?

I tried to calm myself with the thought that learning about this wasn't the whole explanation. Other tests had also been done, had been certain, although I couldn't — at this very moment — recall the details. I had often intentionally turned to look elsewhere because the sticking of spikes into human skin was to me an unpleasant sight. One thing was certain: Greta didn't say those things to save her own skin. There were so many instances of proof about her sorcery, and the ways she had been the cause of misfortune through magic, that she would be given the death sentence even without any additional confessions torture might bring about. She herself would not be granted mercy, however truthful her evidence might turn out to be.

If her claims against the Parson were true, what ought one then think about her statements concerning Kristina Berg? If the Major's wife who, in spite of her boredom, was the very image of Lutheran decency, if *she* would let the handsome sons of parsons make love to her in the most outrageous way, who was left to live by the values we were supposedly protecting?

I had to confess my own helplessness, but God knew I had tried, and in fact managed, to stay blameless for almost fifty years. Father had taught me to believe in an idealistic life and in conquering oneself for the sake of virtuous and eternal goals. It was precisely because of such tenets that my life had had its most important substance. Even after I myself had fallen, I had considered the shattered principles to be correct and valuable ones. That is why I was able to sentence whore-mongers and adulterers to death with a good conscience, I mean, if the seriousness of the case so dictated.

What if things were the way Greta had described them, that only those who had no opportunity to succumb to temptation remained without blemish? According to Luther, the human being is by nature rotten, but what sense was there in a faith that didn't make people any better than heretics and pagans? On the other hand, if even God is certain of our irremediable weakness, then why did He give us laws that cannot be followed and according to which some of us must sentence others to death?

Or did God demand that? That is what the theologians claim, and even I had found in the Bible the avowal "thou shalt surely die" which, to be sure, was contradicted in the same text. I didn't read the Bible much because — I'm ashamed to confess this even to myself — its lack of logic irritated me.

Some time before Greta M.'s case, I had sentenced a woman to die because she had broken the fourth commandment and hit her father. The jury didn't want to agree with my decision and expressed their opposition by saying that at some point everyone gets frustrated with older people when they're in the way. To my astonishment the Court of Appeals agreed, and the sentence was reduced. That suggested that not all commandments were any longer of equal importance; how else could one interpret the undermining of a case which clearly matched the description in law.

And if law could be changed based on the fact that all of us at some point or another mistreat our aged parents simply because they're underfoot, then how soon would the fact that we all at one time or another sleep around become reason enough to set aside adultery? And if laws would become utterly corrupted and devoid of meaning, what kind of a world would result: a violent, barbaric, chaotic hell.

No! I couldn't have drifted into an easier and more accommodating option simply because that seemed to be the spirit of the times. Carrying out justice also constituted violence, but that was using it to force people to be good and therefore such violence had its justification. I couldn't, after all, leave my children a world in which nothing was as I had described it to them.

Now you ask why I didn't look further into Greta's claims. And you answer that I couldn't stand the thought I might have sentenced innocent women to death. You believe the cases were not examined because I would have had to confess my mistakes. You suggest it's so very easy to find comfort in general philosophical arguments and ideologies when one needs to clothe one's naked fear and self-esteem.

But in the end, do not ideologies exist for precisely that reason, the glorification of selfish needs?

When a person lives a full life, he seldom makes up metaphysical theories, or if he does, they are like the thesis of euphoric madness, closer to art than science. But the thought of needless victims didn't frighten me because of their tragedy, or because of fear of damage to my reputation.

If the women were not witches, knowing that would only have meant the confession of one mistake in a long chain of mistakes. And somewhere in that chain there was a link which a sentimental person would call love. Had I supposedly squeezed it out of existence for no reason?

CHAPTER

TWENTY-SIX

*Chapter Twenty-Six, in which a witch is beheaded and
everyone waits for the miracle she had promised to happen.
In this chapter the Judge also hears strange suggestions
from his own wife's mouth and decides this time to act.*

GRETA M. took care that her beheading would be as big a
festival for the folk as possible. Towards the end of her
imprisonment she told the prison superintendent that a miracle was going to happen after her death. Erik Eriksson said
he understood Major Berg's house would burn the way
Greta's house would when it was used as her funeral pyre.

The Major and the Parson considered the threat worrisome enough to arrange an extra session of interrogation
because of it, an interrogation at which I too had to be present. The extra session didn't help matters much. Greta
spoke in twists and turns, admitted mentioning a miracle but
denied it a moment later. She referred to a sign which would
appear in conjunction with the communion, a sign that
would be a proof of her innocence, but just as the Major

began to look relieved, she referred to some serious misfortune still to come.

The Major lost his night's sleep and suggested to me that Greta's house not be used as the pyre after all. Perhaps that might calm those involved. So we agreed the Major would procure the necessary wood from his own tenants. Greta was noticeably more amicable because of this consideration; she even apologized to the Major and his wife for frightening them with her threats.

I heard rumours that the islanders were making bets who would be the target of the promised punishment. Would it be the Major who had informed against Greta and been her persecutor for so long? Or was it I, the judge, who in using my power had sealed her fate, the cutting of her throat? Or was it Parson Kjellinus, who wouldn't give her the last communion because she refused to confess she had made a pact with the Devil?

Kjellinus' decision — he said it was the joint decision of the island's clergy — bothered me. It proved to me how important he considered the fact that he could put down on paper the last-minute, complete breakdown of the will of the accused, including a full confession. He hadn't had a confession from Ingeborg, and for the second time he was in danger of not succeeding. But if the Parson believed so strongly that Greta had been in league with the Devil, then why didn't he fear her threats in the least? There was something so suspiciously contradictory in all this that it wouldn't let me rest.

Things turned out as I had thought. Greta went to her death without the last communion, and Bryniel Kjellinus' role was to be the master of ceremonies without a programme, in the midst of a carnival atmosphere. Wandering salesmen had taken a lead from prior beheadings and set up their booths around the pyre without permission. They had a record number of buyers since in the December cold many onlookers wanted to warm themselves with a freshly baked bun, a fatty sausage, or a hot herbal drink from which rose the tempting aroma of liquor.

I think the Parson was furious about Greta's stubbornness, but he didn't show it openly. Major Berg, on the other hand, was so obviously nervous that onlookers were at times more interested in him than in the victim. I too thought the Major's behaviour strange, considering that on the battlefield he had to face death eye to eye. Despite his shortcomings, I had always thought him to be a brave man.

When a couple of weeks had gone by after the beheading and nothing unusual had happened, the Major dared to joke about the case. But I noticed that in Kristina's presence Greta's case was never mentioned.

Nevertheless, in a moment of devilishness I once introduced the dead witch woman into conversation while Kristina was playing the clavichord a few steps away. The Major answered me with a stiff, restrained response, and Kristina started to make awkward mistakes in a simple piece of music. After that I didn't bring the matter up any more.

What astonished me even more those days was what Greta had revealed about a certain other woman. The case was fully in line with the witch doctrine; the accusations were as serious as any levelled against anyone among those sentenced earlier, and we even had the necessary number of witnesses. To my great amazement, however, I found myself working on the case alone. Bryniel Kjellinus wasn't the least bit interested in this witch; to him the case smacked of revenge because Greta had thought the woman was persecuting her. When I suggested the Parson should at least get involved enough to express an opinion upon examination of the case, he reluctantly agreed but, blaming the pressure of church matters, he forgot the whole thing.

Kjellinus wasn't interested! How did this case differ from

the previous ones? In no way except for the fact this was not one of the women Karin P. had singled out. But why should that have been particularly significant? Had the Parson simply had enough; had his Christian thirst for the blood of heretics been satisfied, or had the incomplete confessions backfired in such a traumatic way he didn't want to expose his authority to any more of them?

My principal interrogator's lack of interest made me a distracted and generous judge. After I had questioned her, I let the old woman go free without a judgement of any kind. The poor woman hardly believed her luck; she had prepared herself for the same fate her informant had received, and for weeks afterwards I had to send back various tokens of gratitude, from wheat cakes to legs of lamb. I didn't want to be suspected of accepting bribes.

"Sometimes I feel as if, unbeknown to me, Bryniel Kjellinus is playing some sort of chess game with live pieces," I said to the Major when we were at his house one evening.

"Surely not? Why do you think that?" the Major asked.

"Not all the pieces I offer him are good enough for him, and in the game that generally means they're no threat to the king. But what that indicates in real life, I have no idea," I answered.

"What damned pieces?" he asked, so innocently frustrated, though I had thought all along he knew what I was talking about.

"Or perhaps the game is already over and I just haven't realized it yet," I said.

At home Elsa told me I drank too much nowadays. I said that was because with a sober head I couldn't stand the people around me. Particularly the Major and his wife. Elsa said she was ashamed of me.

"Bryniel Kjellinus is not concerned with the woman I'm accusing and that bothers me."

"Perhaps that's because he's interested in young boys," Elsa said.

"What in the world ... ," I asked.

"That's what is being said!" she answered. I looked at her amazed, and she began to smile because she had managed to shock me. "That's what they're whispering!" Elsa said.

"Young boys visit the Parson so often it can't always be a question of some church matter," Elsa said. She told me some mother had asked her son what he was doing at the parsonage, and the boy had just blushed. That's why every caring mother told her son not to have anything to do with the Parson.

"That's a shocking accusation! If it's true, then ... ," I said, not knowing what the consequences would be. He'd have to leave his position? An indictment based on whoring? Was this my opportunity to get rid of Kjellinus?

"What if it's just slander?" I asked.

"It could be," Elsa answered.

I had no proof, not even a possibility of getting any, but the news drove me wild.

Besides, it immediately offered an explanation. Being inclined to love boys made his cruelty towards the poor women explainable, the passionate lack of forgiveness and the single-mindedness with which he persecuted them.

I spent a happy night dwelling on Bryniel Kjellinus' loathsomeness and worthlessness. Had not Greta M. also hinted in that direction; why hadn't I asked her more directly what she meant? One might have guessed that Kjellinus was not a man of ordinary vices; when he embarked on soiling his ministerial robe, he did it in the most despicable way possible. What a joy and relief for me!

If the Parson was so hardened and two-faced, it might not be impossible that he had deliberately arranged a trap for me that night I imagined myself rescuing Ingeborg. I'm sure

Ingeborg had known or at least guessed what was at stake at the time. That would be the reason why she had behaved so coldly, had humiliated me in order to save me from a much worse fate.

Before I had time to do anything concrete to clear the matter, Bryniel Kjellinus came to see me.

"There is one woman who hasn't been examined," the Parson said, and added, "I think this is a clear case of witchcraft."

*H*E IS TIRESOME, this judge of mine.

All the oddities and explanations he offers me now appear simply unpalatable.

— Let's make this clear once and for all, I want to get to the end of this matter as soon as possible. No more hocus-pocus tales, agreed?

I open the window to call to my youngest that he must wear a cap. Even if the sun is shining. The boy waves the plastic duck he had lost last autumn and laughs. One hand is made into a fist; I saw him pick up flies in front of the workshop, but he doesn't show them because he knows I would tell him to throw them away and go and wash his hands. Poor flies, groggy after the winter like me.

— I merely want to explain why I let Ingeborg O. die.

— As revenge. The one and only time I dared give in to my feelings, and she humiliated me! It's hard to endure being laughed at right in one's face. That is how I saw the situation, and so I stopped visiting her.

The Judge's place is no longer here. I want to clean him out of the house along with all the other useless trash that has accumulated during the winter.

He doesn't realize he is superfluous; he's stubborn.

— Do you maintain that you yourself have never wanted to destroy a person who has made a mockery of your love? You think, of course, that from wanting to actually acting on it is a long journey, because you haven't had an opportunity to use revenge without having to pay for it. But I did, and I used that opportunity.

A couple of weeks like this one and the window of my

study will be covered in greenery. Summer is coming. I can seal this room; it will cease to exist. I'm starting to live again. Without the Judge and the other ghosts. But there has to be a little feeling left for him still; he has, after all, led me by the hand through a winter that seemed interminable.

— Death is ... one cannot talk about it as one talks about shaking someone by the hair, or giving someone a proper beating. "She mocked me, I punished her by killing her."... One cannot talk like that.

— I didn't kill her, but I lacked the strength to save her, to fight for her life. There's a difference.

Exhilarating spring air flowed in through the open window. I took deep breaths, three, four times. Secretly I wished the Judge would no longer exist when I turned to face my room again. But he is waiting for me. Painfully patient.

— I'm honest. I understand this shocks you because you are the child of your own time. Your world is so civilized even the worst egoist knows enough to mask his disappointment and pretend it to be sadness over the misfortunes of fellow humans ... or something else like that.

The dog barks a warning: the boy is hanging onto the gate, looking longingly at the road he is not allowed to go on.

— There is also love of another kind, the kind that is born of something other than mere selfishness. I felt I had to say that though, actually, it had nothing to do with this whole thing.

— Of course there is, when we talk about childhood and the time of innocence. Before long, however, a person corrupts himself so that he is no longer capable of having pure feelings.

— You did have your children, after all; you could have had great comfort ...

— You don't know what it is to have to wallow in feelings which have become ridiculous. You don't really even try.

What else have I tried here if not that? The whole winter! But no, even now he isn't satisfied. I simply have no more strength; at some point I've lost my red threads. They are the kind that shine in the dark but can't be seen in sunlight.

— The world is full of people like me even if they pretend to be something else. And just wait, when they have a chance to show ... ! he gloats.

Why don't I kill him? Why not indeed? Liquidate him in some believable way; he stumbles, drunk, hits his head, freezes to death, is given the wrong medicine.

No, now I know! I'll have him kill himself. He commits suicide because he can't endure the evil he is guilty of. There! I have an effective ending, he compensates for his cruelty, appeases the enraged gods of justice with his self-sacrifice.

And then I can enjoy the spring and real life.

— The woman you admired died aided by you, you don't love your wife, your closest colleague is a monster, your ridiculous field-hand is morally superior to you. If I were you, I'd draw some conclusions from these things.

— What then? The Judge wants to know.

— That life is impossible. Why wouldn't you hang yourself, or throw yourself off a high cliff? That's it! Let him come up with one good reason if he can. I won't pity him, that much is certain.

The Judge looks at me for a long while and this time right through me.

— Because that is a coward's solution. And because it isn't true.

He looks at me and smiles. One would think the sun might melt him, disintegrate him, but no, there he stands and looks at me. "Because it isn't true!" he says. He teaches me; a murderer teaches me morality.

— This is an outrageous story. I don't like it.

— Neither do I, but it happens to be my life's story.

— You could have changed it while you were alive. Supposedly you had a chance to choose between good and evil like everyone else?

I want to go out with my children, play with the dog, turn up soil, plant rows and rows of carrots. I want to do good and joyful things, not dwell on injustice and brutality.

— Perhaps I had unusually bad luck? the Judge says.

— Perhaps the women you sentenced to death had unusually bad luck!

— They too. That's true.

TWENTY-SEVEN

ᏣᎦ

*Chapter Twenty-Seven, in which the Judge interrogates a new
prisoner, Margreta H., who is taken away from her baby and
brought to Kastelholm. Strange thoughts come to the Judge's mind.*

*M*ARGRETA H. was torn from her baby of only a few weeks
and taken prisoner to be held for trial. I let it happen because
I believed that at long last and with the help of this case, I'd
be able to get a grip on Bryniel Kjellinus. Why was the
Parson so anxious to accuse Margreta when the previous suspect hadn't interested him in the least?

Meeting Margreta upset me. She was quiet and humble,
didn't cast one accusing or rebellious look at us, but when she
was being undressed so we could search for a *stigma diabolicum*, her inflamed breasts, full of milk, judged us. This is
cruel, I thought, this mustn't continue. And when I saw how
extremely painful it was for her to have strange men see her
naked, I was ashamed of us, the interrogators. I was especially
ashamed when I understood how she vainly tried to cover up
the fact that her body longed for her child.

They found a suspicious mark on her back, and when the Provost stuck a needle into it without her knowing, she didn't seem to feel any pain. Permission for torture was therefore granted, but I didn't want to proceed. I reminded them, by referring to Delrion, Köning, Waldschmidt and Freude, that the Devil could at times confuse those investigating these things by inserting and removing his signs at will. Bryniel Kjellinus announced he favoured torture.

"It is in the best interest of everyone involved that this matter be brought to a speedy conclusion," he said.

Margreta was one of the women Karin P. had informed on and, in addition, her reputation was further blackened by a peculiar illness that bothered her especially on Church holidays. Her neighbour and the Parson could attest to the fact she was rarely seen in church during major religious holidays.

"Yes, I have been sick," Margreta testified. She stubbornly clung to her claim, but when her husband was brought in to be questioned and saw the thumbscrews, he immediately broke down.

"Margreta didn't dare leave the children home alone. She wasn't sick," the man admitted.

When I told the prisoner her husband had admitted many suspicious things in fear of torture, she began to cry.

"Am I going to be burned now?" she asked. "The way the others were?"

I didn't say anything. The situation — as far as I was concerned — had taken a troublesome turn. I had opposed torture in the hope that the case would come to nothing. How could I have guessed her husband would break down at the mere sight of the thumbscrews, which wouldn't have been used on him in any case since he was only a witness, not the one accused of any wrongdoings.

"Your husband asked me tell you the children are fine." She stopped crying. "The youngest one takes pap from a pig's bladder, and a neighbour comes in and breastfeeds him too," I said.

"He does take pap?" she asked. I saw she wished I would leave so she could give vent to her feelings of relief and fear. Now she didn't know what to do with her hands. "Does he really take food?"

"That's what your husband said," I answered.

"Did Lars say I'm a witch?" she asked.

"No, but he confessed you had uttered magic words and pretended to be sick on holidays," I answered. Had I wanted to be cruel, I could have said that seeing the instruments of torture, her Lars had been ready to sell her to death just to save himself from pain.

"Are you then?" I asked.

"What?"

"Are you a witch?" I asked.

"No, I'm not," she answered.

I looked at her eyes, red from crying. The sun came in through the bars and spotted her skin and my hands with warm squares. She had a mole on the back of her hand, in almost exactly the same place I did.

"Perhaps witches don't even exist?" I asked.

She thought I was joking. Of course, what else could it have been but a joke, I wondered myself, disturbed by the fact such a sentence had fallen from my mouth.

"Of course they exist," Margreta said. Scared and convinced of it.

"Yes, otherwise there wouldn't be any sense in anything," I answered.

"Are you disappointed in your husband?" I asked.

"I don't know, I suppose not," Margreta said. Behind her head, the Gulf was visible with little dots moving about, fishermen and children throwing flat rocks.

"Not at all?" I asked.

"You ought not to have threatened him that way," Margreta said.

Anger went through me like an unexpected gust of wind. Could a woman love a man who was so cowardly? How was it possible that some people could do anything they liked, behave in however condemnable a way, and still they were loved and defended to any lengths. But others, however good and just they tried to be, were beyond the reach of such emotions.

I realized it was useless of me to pity this woman, deliver ridiculous messages about pig-bladders and other unpleasantness when her only worry seemed to be that her husband shouldn't be badly treated. And who says her body cried for the baby; perhaps she longed more for that good-for-nothing husband who was all too ready to sacrifice his own wife.

"Are you not worried your children will be left in the care of such a weak-willed man?" I asked.

"He takes good care of them," Margreta answered. One could clearly hear uncertainty in her voice.

"Since he betrayed you once, he can betray the children also," I reminded her. The jailer's wife was in a hurry, you could hear familiar steps behind the door; Margreta's attention shifted.

"We'll probably get food," she said.

But I wasn't going to give in.

"He'll betray the children too," I reminded her stubbornly. Margreta shook her head.

"No, surely not," she answered.

"Why did you marry a man like that?" I asked. In my mind I wondered what was the matter with me, why did I behave in this idiotic fashion. Now you could see in Margreta's red-rimmed eyes the agitation of someone who's under attack. With agonizing concentration she pretended to be listening to sounds from the corridor.

"I'm sure they're bringing in the food now," she said.

"Weren't you able to get anyone else?" I asked.

Right then I saw for the first time a flash of pride in her.

"Lars was so handsome, the most handsome man on the whole island," Margreta said.

That's where it ran its course, then, the pursuit of wisdom and everything that is human. Lars was handsome and that was enough to guarantee him love for the duration of his life.

I looked at Margreta for a long time. She wasn't a particularly good-looking woman, or else five pregnancies had worn out the glow that sets men on fire.

"Is that when you started to use magic, in order to get him?" I asked. I knew I had offended her, and I hated myself for it, but in some unexplainable way she too had offended me.

"I also had others who courted me. I liked him best." Margreta said.

"You aren't a witch then?" The repulsive smell of cabbage soup came through the door; it was dinner time, as the prisoner had said.

"No, I'm not," she answered.

"What would you say if I helped you get free?" I asked.

She didn't say anything, but turned to look at the sea shore where she no longer saw anyone.

"Well?" I insisted.

She shook her head; the medium-brown braid of hair swayed against her shoulder blades.

"You won't want to free me in any case," she answered.

"What would you give me if I helped you?" I asked.

Margreta turned to me full of amazement.

"I don't have anything you could possibly want!"

At that moment I had had enough of myself. I struck the door in anger and the guard who stood behind it immediately put the key in the lock and opened it. At the door I turned to say something to the prisoner, but I couldn't think of anything that made sense. I nodded to the guard as a sign that the cell could now be locked.

I didn't go home, but instead went to the beach I had looked at from the prison window. It was deserted. Under my boots the sand was soft and wet. The gulls were screeching further out to sea; it looked as if there was going to be fog. I'll save her, I thought. There was an open shell full of sand at the toe of my boot. Beside it, a closed one; I picked it up out of habit. As a child I used to open them hoping to find a pearl.

But the shell remained closed; inside, there was a tough-muscled mollusk whose slippery foot was visible between the edges. I pulled at the edges with both thumbs, trying to separate them, but nothing happened. In the end I managed to break the other edge, that's all. Reminds me of a woman's organ, I thought and flung it onto the sand.

I continued tramping in the soft sand, and I no longer watched where I put my feet. I knew if I wanted my self-respect back, I would have to see to it that this girl not be burnt. I'll help her, I thought. Since there was nothing for me to gain in it, I would simply be saving her life.

When I came to the edge of the woods, I noticed spring was already further advanced than usual at this time of year. But the May sea groaned behind me like a sick dog.

CHAPTER

TWENTY-EIGHT
༄

*Chapter Twenty-Eight, in which the Judge decides to
push Kjellinus to the wall, but realizes instead
that he is a mere apprentice.*

WHEN I REFUSED Kjellinus permission to interrogate the
prisoner, he managed somehow to mask his disappointment.
But when I said I considered Margreta innocent, he became
furious.

"You're crazy; after all, the husband has already partially
confirmed her guilt."

I said perhaps it was time for us to talk about something
else, for example about young boys who were apparently visiting him.

He wasn't interested in answering my impudence; he
wanted to make a speech.

He said my attitude towards the legal process concerning
witches had demonstrated that an unfortunate change had
taken place in me generally as far as the Christian view of
demons and *magiam divinatoriam* was concerned. Very

unfortunate. Almost heretical. Obviously I wasn't aware of it myself otherwise I would of course have found help for my problem. And surely I, as a judge, ought to have known that the life of a heretic was not a happy one, that heretical beliefs had to be paid for dearly. Who knows, someone might even begin to speculate that perhaps I was in league with the witches; there were, after all, all kinds of worrisome signs this might be so.

"Are you threatening me?" I asked, astonished.

"No. I'm a minister of the Church, and as caretaker of souls, my duty is to direct those who have gone astray back to the circle of true faith," Kjellinus answered.

"It's been said that even Martin Luther himself in his old age had to be forced back to the Lutheran faith," he added with a strange smile on his face.

I didn't laugh; he didn't amuse me in the least. An old man has a different attitude towards the world than a young idealist. When Luther's favourite daughter died in the best years of her youth, the father no longer had the strength to take any joy in the fact that the child was now reborn in Christ's dominion. Perhaps he couldn't thank a merciful death for freeing her from threats of the flesh, the world, the Devil, and the Turks. What about the farmers of Schwaben? Having witnessed their miserable fate, the reformer of faith could very well wonder whether he was a pawn in a political game, in the battle for power between rulers, the people, the Cardinals and the Emperor.

"Why shouldn't Luther have had a chance to examine his beliefs? Can't the true faith be renewable, changeable, capable of refinement, forever more right and human?" I asked, contradicting his idea.

Couldn't I understand that Kjellinus was getting more intense, that every new ideology demanded its guards? People who dreamed up models for better worlds had the strength to fight for their dreams, but they didn't have the strength to see them put into practice, since reality could never match the beauty of dreams. Martin Luther made only one mistake, but it was all the greater for the reason that he didn't die for his idea.

People want to see the fire here and now, they want to witness the flow of blood and hear the last words born of pain. After that, people believe. Only the truth born of suffering lasts; all else is from the anti-Christ.

"I don't think you're quite in control of your senses," I remarked.

Kjellinus shook his head. "I'm not the only one who is worried about you," he said.

"Whom, in particular, do you mean?" I asked, pretending to be unconcerned.

"There is the so-called 'circle of the wise' here on the island; we meet now and then. A number of us have noticed your strange behaviour."

"Name at least one!"

"Well, for example, Major Berg; he has told us that."

"Go to Hell with your worries," I said. "You yourself are whoring with young boys and you have the nerve to lecture me about my morality," I added bitterly.

They didn't scare me, I told myself. They couldn't do anything to me, because I had justice on my side. Suddenly a frightening thought came to me.

"Does Parson Olof Beckius belong to your secret circle as well?"

"It's not a secret circle, we only discuss questions of faith and ..."

"Does he belong to it?"

"I don't understand what you would do with that knowledge."

"Well, if it isn't a secret society, then surely you can give an answer."

"All right, then. Yes he does. What of it?"

So, even Beckius! Perhaps also the Prosecutor, and the landowners, and everybody who held power on this island. Is that why Beckius had got off without indictment or suspicion? They were all involved!

I was silent. Never mind! The situation was under control as long as I didn't allow my imagination a free rein. It was no use thinking about the Bishop's letter, or involving them in the witch case. And they were not against me, only worried about me, as Kjellinus had said. I ought not imagine their power to be too great; they were, after all, ordinary men like me; they were bothered by gout, stomach ailments, hemorrhoids and loneliness. They wouldn't wish me ill.

"We all agree that Margreta H. must be sentenced," Kjellinus said.

"Why is it so important to you?" I asked.

"God has announced to me these islands will not please Him until all the witches have been burned," he answered.

He was so calm, so at peace with himself and sure of his stand. How could one crazy man's mindless dream have become the proclamation of the All Powerful? I ought not to have drunk before coming here; I began to imagine all kinds of things that made no sense. For instance, had Kjellinus dictated the names of his chosen victims to Karin P. while she waited for her execution in the dungeon?

"Well, that was the best available means; the old witch was happy to do a last service for this poor island," Kjellinus said.

"How was it possible? How did you get her to agree?" I asked.

What can one promise someone sentenced to die, a woman who didn't even have a family? With what could one threaten her at that point?

"After all, she didn't have anything," I said.

The Parson smiled, relaxed. "She did have a body and an ability to suffer. Suffering, you see, doesn't demand intelligence or skill; it's the easiest of all abilities."

"What about when she was taken to be beheaded? How did you know she wouldn't deny everything in her bitterness before death while the onlookers — thirsting for surprises — were there to hear her?"

"Everyone has his or her weak point!" Kjellinus answered. His smile didn't reflect brutality so much as professional pride. He was a reader of souls, and he read them well.

"And what was her weak point?" I asked.

"The cat," Kjellinus answered, "hers was the cat."

Yes, there was no reason to doubt his words. Six women had died because of a cat, and the seventh would do the same, but there was nothing to be wondered at in that. A man like Bryniel Kjellinus understood life enough to know everyone was someone's friend. No one could stand complete loneliness. And he knew better than others how to listen to those he interrogated; what to me was nonsense and insignificant had turned out to be the most important news to him.

"I simply let it drop that if she didn't keep our agreement, I would torture the cat to death. If she did her Christian duty, I would keep the cat in food and warmth to the end of its days," Kjellinus explained.

"And she believed you?"

"She had no choice," Parson answered.

Nonsensical is the air we breathe; I had had to live this long before I understood that. Religion is so close to magic and chance happenings that no one notices when the fragile border between the two breaks down and the creative spirit turns out to be self-destructive. What turned an organized pursuit of good into the harness of brutality the Crusaders wore when they were plunged into a blind pursuit of devastation? And the end result was that grown men brawled like bloodthirsty, thrill-seeking youths in the revered buildings of Church and justice.

And the centuries' wisdom had no effect on these egocentric players because they belonged in these houses.

"Did you keep your word to Karin P.?" I wanted to know.

Kjellinus shrugged. "You know cats. Where would I have found it?"

"But you would have kept your word, had you found the cat?" I asked.

"I like cats; I have nothing against them," he said.

TWENTY-NINE

CƠ

Chapter Twenty-Nine, in which the Judge is not at all himself, and in which he changes his mind about the indispensability of music.

FOR TWO EVENINGS, I stood in the grove opposite the church of Sund. If I had proof of the Parson's misdeeds, I'd have reason for extortion against his extortion. He would cease pursuing witches. He would have to give in.

Nothing happened the first evening, with the exception of an anxious sedge warbler that sang nearby. Again and again it began its warbling climbing up a reed, mixing rough and melodious notes and imitating other birds. Then it would dive into the protective branches of birches. Perhaps I stood right in front of its nest, since it came close enough for me to see its rusty-yellow breast and striped head.

The second night I saw two boys. When they had sneaked into the church, I waited for a while and then went in. I didn't sneak in, nor did I listen behind doors. That low I needn't sink. It would be enough that I walked in without warning.

What did I expect to see? Sickening lewdness, or necrophilic ceremonies? I can't remember exactly what I had in mind when I pushed open the heavy pine door. I simply had to know. I believed nothing would shock me; there couldn't be anything so horrible that I wouldn't have known to expect it.

But I was wrong. Opening that door was the worst thing I could have done.

Through the door came the sound of a choir of clear voices which gave the church a radiant, angelic atmosphere. The boys' voices rang — illuminated by an all-embracing, strong religious feeling — at times clear, at times fragile, but all the time amazingly pure. Boys — there were a large group of them — stood before the choir, the statue of the sorrowful Mary on one side, Bryniel Kjellinus, who stopped the singing when he saw me, on the other.

"Now you've spoiled the surprise!" he said. "I'm very sorry you came in without letting me know."

I nodded.

It had been for my sake the boys had promised not to tell anyone. I would have been astonished when a choral series of familiar music had rung out in the church.

"Why did you get involved in this?" I asked.

He smiled; the boys with their red cheeks looked at each other, perplexed.

"It is so powerful; I was certain you would find it moving, as would everyone who understood something about beauty," he answered.

He didn't say it was for the glory of God. Nor that surely it would be impressive if on our island, in our church, there would ring the sounds of the real Passion. He spoke of beauty. It, particularly, had touched him. The profound beauty of the spark of sorrow and hope.

"When do you think you'll have it ready?" I asked.

Kjellinus walked down the central aisle towards me. Sweat glistened on his forehead; a thick parson's mantle was not the most suitable dress for a choir leader.

"We're practising only a small part of it, and I don't know if that even will ever be ready, but I'm thinking of St. Mary's day," he said.

The boys whispered among themselves, someone dared to laugh a little as if he thought they couldn't be heard.

"The witch will have been taken care of and there'll be peace in the land," Kjellinus said. He wiped his face with the sleeve of his mantle and sighed. "I wish you wouldn't be so suspicious."

He came with me outside. Only then did I notice a row of wooden shoes of varying sizes.

"Does she have to die?" I asked. Did I imagine that this moment when he was sensitive to beauty and harmony could change anything?

The Parson raised his shoulders. "Hasn't the matter been discussed through and through?" he answered.

My eyes were burning. Life shouldn't be like this. It should be logical and sensible like the laws that were there to guide it.

"Why specifically those seven women?" I asked. I reminded him that Karin P. had reported thirteen women.

"Six were targets of her own revenge, they were of no interest to us," he answered.

"But why? I have to know," I said.

Bryniel Kjellinus shook his head. "Perhaps even we don't know," he said.

A tear started to travel down the side of my nose. I turned to look at the graveyard and tried, unseen, to wipe the tear away, but new ones took its place. "Who knows then, if not you?" I asked.

"God," he answered. "God knows," the Parson said.

I didn't understand. Was this some sort of game, some kind of lottery by which they had chosen their victims?

"They all had magic spells on their consciences; doesn't that prove that we're right?" Kjellinus asked. I watched the long, sad shadows the crosses cast on the graves.

"One of them said every woman on this island learns to use incantations at the age of five at the very latest," I said.

"You have sentenced innumerable persons to death; why is this so difficult?" he asked.

"According to law, not because of random choices," I replied.

"God and chance are one and the same thing; all of us depart from here in accordance with His will," the Parson said. "It is senseless and useless to rebel against that."

I bent down to pick up one of the smaller wooden shoes. It was clumsy and touching; the image of the sole of a foot was visible because it was darker.

"She will leave so many children behind; doesn't that sadden you?" I asked. He didn't say anything. I dropped the wooden shoe to the ground. I didn't mind any more that he saw I was weeping. "I don't want to hear the Passion," I said.

"Don't be childish," Kjellinus answered. He walked towards the door to let me know he didn't want to see me making a fool of myself.

"You devils have spoiled everything!" I said.

He pulled the door shut behind him. What joy could there be in harmony and beauty that managed to live only in music?

"Suffering is not beautiful, no beautiful works should be allowed to be created about suffering," I got up to go to the closed door. There was no reply.

Perhaps he had simply rolled dice, I thought. Then divided the number that came up among his friends so that each of them could choose a witch or two among the people they knew. The dice could have been like the ones King Kaarle had rolled when he diced with his courtiers: carved in the shape of a woman in a squatting position. Her arms were pressed to her sides so that the elbows formed the two sides of the dice. Kaarle's dice-woman was thriving, broad-backed and with an abundant behind; her shoulders were like a soldier's, but her stomach was flat and she had a small, ebony face with beautiful, sad features like the Madonna. Most of the players delayed their throw so they had a chance to feel the round form and interesting crevices of the tiny woman. Number six in particular had to be stroked and kissed to bring luck. The face between the knees was number one, left hip two, the magnificent shoulders three, the hands pressed against the buttocks and the back four, the right hip five, the soles of the feet and the lower part of the buttocks six.

Where was chance in a game of dice? There was no such thing! If the dice turned up one instead of five, that was the law. No one could yell to interrupt the game and demand a new turn; the moment the dice had left a sweaty hand, spun a few times in the air, something holy and irrevocable had happened. A fate whose word was unshakable had taken direction of the game and decided on our behalf. *Alea iacta est*, the die is cast, and people have given their fates to the toss of a small cube. And not one of them had talked about how senseless a game it was, not even if the game had had a bloody ending, not even those who hadn't participated in it, but who found out later that they were the stakes in the game.

Only I, who believed the world could be ruled by human intelligence, had never understood. A world that believed in laws couldn't possibly believe in dice; that is what I thought. But I was wrong. There couldn't be a contradiction great enough for a human being not to accept it. Just like the little dice-woman. In the sweaty hand of the player she had to submit to everything; she was the slave of the man that held her.

In the air and on the board she became the mistress whose ebony heart didn't quiver before men's despair or fortune. That's what she was, the little bitch! She was generous to whomever she chose and left the others with nothing.

The method didn't matter so much; the end result was irrevocable in any case. The players believed in it, and that was sufficient. I didn't believe, but my part was to be an idiot and a coward who had to submit to the will of others. I was sick of trying to find clarity and logic in the world; those who were wise accepted even what they didn't understand if acceptance was in their best interest.

When I arrived home I found someone waiting for me. The jailer's wife was sitting in my office. The tortures of conscience had made Margreta H. confide in her. What was the matter?

"The prisoner confessed to having seen the Devil," the woman said.

"Does anyone else know?" I asked.

"No, but the Judge better come at once. The girl is completely out of her mind," she answered.

CHAPTER

THIRTY

ᴄᴧ

Chapter Thirty, in which the Judge will discover what the Devil
looks like and what other ghosts move about in a woman's soul.
The Judge is touched by a stain he considers a badge of honour,
and sees two children at a great distance.

THE PRISONER HAD been crying. There was no doubt about
that. She was a slim, small-boned woman, and since her red-
rimmed eyes had a frightened look, she made a very touching
impression.

"I've seen the Devil," she announced. "I saw the Devil in
the middle of the night and now I'm scared," Margreta H. said.

"Tell me! Tell me every detail!" I told her.

But no! It was too hard; she didn't want to relive in her
mind the horrors she had gone through. Wasn't it enough
she admitted to having met Satan?

"No," I answered. "We must get to know everything."

After tears and evasions, an astonishing truth took shape,
a nightmare about a woman who squats in a strange hut with
her baby and her two year old boy.

· 247 ·

The woman is breastfeeding the youngest, and the boy, whose name is Joachim, is playing with straws. All of a sudden the boy screams and runs into the woman's arms. What's the matter? she tries to find out. But Joachim only cries and cries. Fear grips her body, the baby stops feeding, and milk runs in thin streams on the baby's twisted face exhausted from crying. At last the boy manages to say: "Eyes!"

What in the world! Eyes? What eyes? Just then she herself sees them: eyes staring at them from a dark corner of the hut. "Let's turn away," she says to the children. But when they turn to face another wall, the eyes are already there. Yellow, burning, horrible eyes. Horror takes hold of her, but she bravely presses the children against her. "Let's not look," she says and feels how Joachim squeezes her neck with his small fists so that she can scarcely breathe. But even through her closed lids she sees the eyes and knows that it won't matter where she looks, the eyes will be there.

She decides to save the children by taking them away from the hut. She looks down through a trap door in the floor, and is met with another shock. The hut isn't a few inches from the ground as she had thought, but so high that the pines look like tiny weeds down below. She won't give in to nausea and dizziness, but attempts to get away for the children's sake and because of the eyes that stare at them from the walls.

She holds Joachim by the hand. "Mummy will try the rope-ladder first with the baby, then Joachim can come into Mummy's arms," she encourages the boy. All the while her body keeps the boy from looking down. For a split second, she lets go of the child's hand when she feels the step unsteady under her foot, and the boy cries out in desperation.

There he is, at the edge of the opening, in all his horror, Satan himself! And Joachim, little, scared Joachim is in his arms. In the middle of the shapeless face covered with bloody scabs are eyes that couldn't be more abhorrent. "Give me the child; give Joachim to me," she begs Satan.

He wears a long cape over his misshapen body; when the child struggles in his arms, his kicking bares vein-marked skin. "Give the child to me," the mother whispers as humbly as she can. And Satan leans towards her. "Is this what you want?" he asks, astonished. She nods. "Yes, just him, nothing else, the little boy. He is frightened in a stranger's arms," she explains politely, close to tears. And Joachim holds out his hands towards her, touches the edge of her sleeve with his finger.

"All right," Satan says. He smiles and releases the child from his arms. He lets go and the child falls. Joachim falls past her into a dark void.

At that moment she loses her grip on her baby. She knows she should think of the baby, the youngest one in her arms, the one who is puking milk onto her shoulder, but she takes her hand away anyway. Malicious laughter is the last thing she is conscious of....

"That was a dream!" I said. She shook her head and rubbed her mouth with clenched fists.

"I saw him with my own eyes! The Devil!" she answered.

A swallow flew past the bars. It had made its nest behind the window.

"You are not going to be accused of wrongdoing because of dreams," I tried to comfort her. The wings flickered past again. "Don't you understand that it was a nightmare?" I asked.

She examined the tooth marks on her fingers. "But it was the real Devil, wasn't it?" she insisted.

Margreta H. was sure the dream was an omen. The Devil would destroy her children because of her unworthiness. Even in the dream she had known the eyes in the walls were staring only at her, they sought her out. After this nightmare, she understood that unless she took it upon herself to suffer the punishment she deserved, her loved ones would have to pay.

"What do you mean?" I asked. "What have you done?"

Margreta sobbed. It didn't matter what the man's name was, she would never tell that, however much she was threatened. The important thing was she had been so out of her mind that her whole life was about to come to an end. The mother of four children and with yet another one in her belly! That's what had happened.

"You've committed adultery?" I asked.

"I didn't, but I would have," she answered. "If you hadn't come and taken me here," Margreta said.

She had imagined things. Imagined dark, secret, intimate meetings. Even bitter meetings she had imagined, hopeless, and yet full of lasting significance. In the woods or in the boat shed, in dark saunas or when picking berries; the place didn't matter as long as she could be certain they wouldn't be disturbed.

And all these outrageous dreams because of a few long looks from a man, out of gratitude because he had noticed her in the midst of all that was mundane, noticed especially her instead of young, still unattached girls. She had been given a gift that was inappropriate, a surprise, and therefore it meant so much to her that she had wanted to give a gift in return.

Of course Margreta H. didn't tell it like that.

"I imagined all sorts of things when he seemed to like me so," Margreta said. "And I would have carried it through had you not come and fetched me."

"Had you really been faced with it, you might have changed your mind," I suggested.

"Would I?" she asked as if I knew all the answers.

I was astonished. Was she so ready to sink that low? That

meant one couldn't tell anything about anybody, not even about the most obedient and dedicated keepers of the home-fires. Why couldn't we ever be enough for them, we who had put our faith and trust in them; we who shared our lives with them; we who once had been the fulfillment of their heaven and earth? No one had warned us to expect they would place their own daydreams ahead of ours.

"Didn't you stop to think that the punishment for adultery is death?" I asked.

No, that hadn't worried her. That had seemed insignificant compared with all the suffering a blameless life brought with it. "Yes, I did know, but I didn't worry about it," she answered.

"I don't understand; you have a good husband," I said. We sat quietly watching the light and shadows on the granite walls. She tapped her fingers in time with the church bells on the edge of a wooden bench which was worn to a shine. The bells chimed in the distance because of a funeral. One, two, three; the coffin was carried out already — probably from the vestry door, since no important islander had died in the last few days — four, five, six. Her fingers were thin and transparent around the nails.

"Sometimes one just wants to ... do the wrong thing, or ... ," she tried to explain.

Everyone wants to know his or her own worth, is that all it is? I thought. One evaluation isn't enough, not one man's word, when life is so long and full of uncertainties. One needs — even for a brief moment — to get proof of the fact that one exists.

But what were we left with before this threat? Women could take away from us all the self-respect we had nurtured for decades while we pursued our careers, while we were realizing our passions and interests and looking after our families. Good heavens, mere laws were no longer enough for them; they let things fall through the seams the way an old net let strong fish through. Stronger measures were needed, but from what direction?

"Now I know that all the time it meant the same as giving the Devil an invitation," Margreta admitted humbly. Outside, it had started to rain. Large drops fell slowly behind the bars. Her eyes became more red, then filled with tears.

Yes indeed: the Devil! God knows it didn't take too much imagination to think about him; to a man every tempter who caressed his woman was equal to Satan.

When the Church's punishments and the law were not enough to keep a woman under control, the Devil entered the picture and with him a glimmer of peace. Now the women too were frightened, scared, believing or pretending to have faith. Brilliant, cunning and at the same time simply ingenious.

Who was it who argued that women in particular weren't able to manifest the "will of the Almighty?"

A little common irritation, hurt masculinity, oaths between friends fuelled by the strength of liquor, and soon it wasn't difficult to believe that those who had tortured, hurt, humbled, scorned, betrayed, tempted and taken advantage of us men, these dear human monsters, had sucked their powers straight from the Devil. And nothing else was needed for the makings of a holy fire, the start of a crusade, because, after all, the one who was hurt would contain enough fuel to start a fire.

The rain ended as quickly as it had begun. On the front of Margreta H.'s red dress was a small stain which little by little grew larger like a medusa rising from the depths of the sea to its surface. She saw my look and raised a hand to cover her full breast.

No! I thought, a human being cannot bare her soul's filthiest recesses and at the same time be embarrassed by a drop of milk because it reminds the onlooker of the breast hidden under the clothing.

The church bells had ceased chiming; the bars over the window offered only the emptiness of a gloomy, rainy day. But the stain on the prisoner's dress-front, where previous yellowish circles reminded one of earlier and similar accidents, bothered me.

"You haven't let the milk run dry?" I asked.

She nodded embarrassed.

"You haven't given up hope, after all," I said. She didn't understand, or didn't want to answer.

She was embarrassed by the stain which in my eyes rendered all her foolishness and weakness meaningless, even her potential for betrayal. To me the drop of milk was like a badge of honour on the chest of a deserving soldier, a proof of bravery: One must not accept defeat until the battle has been fought to the end. A person wasn't beaten until she was brought to her end.

"Don't speak to anyone about your dream," I said.

"Why?" Margreta asked.

"I don't know; but it's better that you don't," I answered evasively.

On the way home I chose the road along the beach. The sea was as grey as on the day my father had shown it to me for the first time. The same sea, but one day grey and alienating, the next blue and full of the glitter of gold. Was there some sort of a message hidden in it, a secret whose roots were impossible to discover?

There were two naked children beside the chalk cliffs. They had decided to have a swim although the water was still much too cold. White bodies and thrilled screams bit the air, a sudden flash of life in an otherwise dispirited curtain. The children ran into the water up to their knees, each wondering for a second about the other's bravery and the chill of the sea.

Just as one turned to go back and stand shivering on the sand, hands between knees, the other threw himself into the waves in a long dive. When I had left them behind me, I could still hear shrill screams as they raced each other to their clothes.

There was something familiar in all that, in the smell of the sea at that very moment, the boats in the distance, the sudden changes in the wind's direction. I remembered what it was like trying to pull pants on over wet feet. Had I been brave enough to get wet, or had I stayed on the shore?

I did dive in! At that very moment the water hadn't felt cold, only before and after. As a child I had been brave. Hadn't I once even thrown myself into a bed of nettles just to show I wasn't afraid? What was it that had peeled the daring off me and made me a hapless onlooker? Was it everyday life? Having to live at the mercy of temporal laws? The indifference of one's fellow human beings?

I stopped the horse and got down to walk. Far out on the open sea white triangles bobbed up and down, sails that were not at the wind's mercy, but rather used the wind for their benefit. Even boats are smarter than I am, I thought. Even boats answered a challenge, but I continued to harbour doubts.

We don't hate women, I said to myself. God help me, we adore, love and idolize them more than our children, more than ourselves.

And yet we did not. When did the holy turn evil? When we met, got married, made love, got stuck with each other and wore each other out to the point of becoming wounded but remained, nevertheless, stuck with each other? Living together always exposes the claws of one or both, but living separately is even more brutal. Love is a kind of imprisonment, but a blessed and privileged imprisonment. That's why we aren't too concerned about the thickness of the walls, nor do we ask why the one who had the opportunity hit the other; there were no human beings in the prison, only prisoners.

The horse tried to steal a bite of fresh shoots from under some old dry grass but couldn't reach them.

"Go ahead and eat," I said. The cloud cover had developed a few cracks and let an occasional ray of sun through. And the horse's contented munching triumphed over the murmur of the sea.

THIRTY-ONE

ᴄᴻ

*Chapter Thirty-One, in which the Judge has a night visitor
and finds out that fire doesn't burn everything, nor does
time heal all wounds.*

ONE NIGHT INGEBORG came to see me. I had left the door
unlocked as though I had had an inkling something was
about to happen. She immediately put her hands inside my
shirt, against my chest. "Aren't they cold?" she said.

I couldn't hide the fact that I was moved. Her appearance
was a miracle; it belittled the unquestionable laws of life and
death. How was this possible? "I have missed you so," I said.
I put my arms around her, but I didn't dare to squeeze hard.
"I have missed you," she said. "Very much?" I asked.
Ingeborg put her head on my neck. "Very much," she said. "I
have missed you more," I said. "No, I have," she insisted.

I sat up to study her better. A pale face, some dark shim-
mer in the hair. The shoulders and knees as round as before,
the same pulsating vein in the neck. "You still have blood
running in your veins!" I said, astonished. "Of course, now

that I'm here with you," she answered. The emotion became unbearable; I was forced to embrace her with all my strength even if that were to reduce her to nothing. But she stayed there, all the more alive, all the more real.

"And as badly as I treated you," I said. She brushed her cheek against my chest. "That is forgiven," Ingeborg answered. "Forgiven and forgotten!"

The memory troubled me. Ingeborg sitting on the cell floor, tailor style, head hanging down. And I hadn't gone in. I hadn't. "What are you staring at?" she asked. The tone was gentle with only a hint of impatience. "You cry very often nowadays," she said. I quickly dried my eyes. "Yes, this is already the third time," I answered. Ingeborg took my face between her hands, caught the escaping tear with the tip of her tongue.

She came under the covers. We lay for a long time pressed closely against each other. "Don't you have any sorrows?" I asked. "No sorrows, but I do have dreams," she answered. She put her leg between mine, not to tempt but to find a more comfortable position. "What kind of dreams?" I asked. Her foot was not cold but warm and it radiated heat although it didn't exactly mean to do it. "I dream about being old," Ingeborg said. "An old woman who is fragile and precious like a Christmas decoration at the end of a Christmas dinner table where all the children and grandchildren make a fuss over me," she said. "I stole your old age from you," I moaned. She turned her head to look at my face. "Please, don't go over all that yet again. Who knows, I might have died in any case," she said.

I realized she knew everything, saw everything, heard everything. It was part of her essence now that she was dead. She knew what I did and thought, but I didn't know anything about her. "Have you met people you used to know, there?" I asked. "Where?" she asked absent-mindedly while she stretched herself in my arms like a child waking up. "There, on the other side," I answered. "Oh there, yes, quite a number; after all, there's my mother, my first husband, yes and Niklas Tarkkakäsi," she said. "Does he still shoot at you with flaming arrows?" I asked jealously. "Sometimes, when time seems to go too slowly," Ingeborg answered.

She was very close to me with her dark hair, and her round knees were pressed against my legs. But I didn't dare. An anxious thought came to my mind. "I don't suppose there ... I don't suppose there, after all ... ?" I asked. "Make love?" she helped. I nodded. "It's part of the church service there, the practice of religion," she answered. "Not as liturgy, but as prayer," she said.

It wasn't Heaven then, was it, since they believed in something of that kind? But passion there was from God, not from the Devil. And there was no other suffering except the disappointment of an unheard prayer. For even there you found unfulfilled wishes, one-sided love, and having to be without a mate.

Her calm voice melted away my rigidity and suspicion. She was dead but living. Languid, warm, and teasing. And the small breasts were dimly visible through a white undershirt. "Can we?" I asked. "Yes, we can," she answered.

And I warmed myself on the shadowy smoothness of her body, and she on mine; we visited each other as one visits a friend's house. "My own!" I said. "Yes," she answered. "Yes, yes!" she said.

She knew more than I, because she was dead. Perhaps she knew all that God knew. And more than that no one could dream of knowing. But why had she come back? How could she have come from where nobody was supposed to come back?

"I returned because I became holy," she said. "What do you mean, holy?" I asked, embarrassed. Ingeborg gave my cheek a light kiss; triumph shone in her eyes. "Just like Catherine of Alexandria and Margaret of Antioch who died accused of being heretics," she answered proudly. "They were martyrs and now we know that their murderers were the heretics and not they," she said. "Was your becoming a saint my doing?" I asked. "Yes," Ingeborg answered. "You tried to kindle our fire with an ordinary flame but it only killed us," she said.

I lay quietly for a long time, my head on her chest. She was also silent, but she knew I was listening. It did beat, the heart that had been burnt and buried. I knew now her words hadn't been mere boasting. The fire had not gone out, nor would it, even if we killed a hundred more women. Perhaps we would have to destroy them all before we'd have peace from the fear of burning.

I felt I ought to have shrunk away from her like a criminal, but since Ingeborg was so magnificently forgiving towards her own destroyer, I stayed. "Why aren't you bitter?" I asked. She laughed like a girl. The same way my daughters do when they tell secrets to each other. "Have you ever heard of bitter saints?" she answered. I still didn't understand what was so funny about that. She gave me small kisses to wipe away my expression of annoyance. "I feel a great deal of pity towards you, but I wouldn't be here if I were bitter," Ingeborg said. "I don't want pity," I said. "Yes you do, but it won't help you deal with your deed any better," she answered.

I was angry; got up and walked to the window. You could see a run-down storage shed on the opposite side; sleepy buckthorn bushes grew in front of it. Near the compost was a pile of lumber, which in some ways reminded me of my carriage, but it couldn't have been as broken down and scattered about as that. And when had the mountain ash trees grown to such a lush wall between the house and the sea?

"Why does it look like that?" I asked. "Time can change things, but it can't change your despair," Ingeborg answered. "I'm no saint. Why must I live with no end to it?" I argued. She stretched her eternal body and rubbed her head. "It is possible that even guilt belongs to the things nothing kills. Not even death," she suggested happily, as if she were offering candies around.

I became angrier. "I must feel endless guilt then, and the others nothing?" She let out a quick laugh. "I am the victim, you cannot expect that ..."

"I admit I brought you pain, but there's also the pain of tenderness, and in using it to manipulate us, you are the masters."

"Is this the right moment to dig up — ?"

"And I'm not at all sure the pain I made use of is the most cruel and brutal kind," I shouted.

I wanted to ignore her, her triumphant being, her condescending smile and directorial hand gestures. I looked at the storage-shed, the unkempt ugliness no one had had the sense to dispose of. "Also, I wouldn't be surprised if it could be proven that your tender predacity gave birth to my limitless evil."

Of course I was immediately filled with regret. I guessed the result: when I turned around there was nobody in the room. The bed clothes were partly on the floor, feathers stuck out from one corner of the pillow as if someone had bitten into it. I was in pain; why did she do this to me? "It is easier to die as a martyr than to suffer criticism, or what?" I shouted vengefully after her into the emptiness.

I could still see the impression of Ingeborg's body on the mattress. I pressed my cheek to it and began to cry. I pulled the mattress into my arms, cradled it as if it were Ingeborg, but the pain only got worse.

Was someone laughing? A light bump against my groin and increasing laughter. I realized how ridiculous I must look, my head pushed into the pillows, my backside shaking from crying....

I got a grip on the bare foot that inflamed my groin. Ingeborg gasped from pain. I twisted as hard as I could. A loathsome crack indicated something had broken, either an ankle or toes. She tried to get away, but I pulled her almost to the edge of the bed and pressed a pillow on the spitting mouth. Let's see how long you'll laugh at me! I pressed the pillow down and pulled on her hair so she couldn't twist and turn. A big handful of sand-coloured hair came loose, and I stuffed it into her mouth to be sure of the end result. I sat straddling her chest now, and was pounding it with all my strength and all my weight. I thought I heard ribs crack.

At last she stopped resisting and lay there quietly under me. To be sure, I pressed an ear to the pillow, but couldn't hear anything. Her limp hands rested alongside of her body; she was like someone drowned.

I swung my body off her and curled myself under her arm. Her chest didn't move. "Did you have to torture me?" I mumbled, as if asking for forgiveness. She didn't answer.

I couldn't stand seeing her body. I had to get rid of it. I couldn't stand seeing what I had done to that good person ... how I had crushed her beautiful body....

I took hold of one foot; the other hung in an unnatural position. I pulled the body gently from the bed. The head crashed onto the floor. But then I heard another sound. A very strange one, like laughter!

At that very moment she kicked herself free and jumped back onto the bed. She laughed so much that she couldn't get a word out of her mouth. She pounded the mattress with her small hand and laughed so that tears ran from her eyes. Even her toes curled from this burst of hilarity. There was nothing wrong with them, either.

"How foolish you are!" Ingeborg said when she managed,

at long last, to make her voice audible. "And there you stand like a nestling fallen out of a nest," she continued. "Did you really believe you could punish me?" she asked.

"Did you really believe you ... ?" she asked time after time.

But where she ought to be, where the bed ought to be, are a pile of rocks. Tree saplings, whose names I don't know, grow in between the rocks, clinging stubbornly to life.

And her voice, Ingeborg's voice, vanished hundreds of years ago.

THIRTY-TWO

෭

Chapter Thirty-Two, in which the Judge has to admit that no human being triumphs in cunning over life.

*C*OURT PROCEEDINGS? The very last ones?

Strange, but the most difficult thing is to recall the details. I've had time to think things over. All kinds of thoughts come to mind when one has measured the faces of cliffs and the shores of the sea for years. A rock has made a deep crevice in the cliff, but the rock hasn't accomplished this on its own. Huge, mysterious masses of water have spun it over and over, burrowing it deep into the cliff. Was I any more guilty then than the rock? Did I not also have someone spinning me, my enforcer?

Margreta H.'s case doesn't absolve me of my other deeds. A dishonest merchant doesn't become honourable by making one honest sale.

After such a long time it's easier to remember one's bad deeds than good ones. Undoubtedly I was being poetic; I flogged myself and the entire justice system, exposed my failures, the wrong testimonies, lies obtained through torture, the scheming and the mockery. I was a hero who bared his chest to piercing arrows and welcomed them.

I didn't smear Kjellinus, although he had earned it. I don't know if I wanted to save him, or to keep the performance all to myself.

The jurors were uncomfortable. While I humiliated myself, I also put them down. They had been led to wrong sentencing; they had been made to look like fools who had no judgement. My statements were downplayed in the court records, "omitted because the matter concerned immaterial things."

"I'll write an explanation myself as the conclusion to the records," I said to the Court Clerk. It was obvious he was baffled.

After the session I remembered best:

Margreta H. didn't make a move even though the gavel had struck. Her eyes were red, either from crying or sleeplessness. She was standing, arms tight against her body.

The door behind her was open. Fine, grey dust rose against the light; the wind was gaining strength. A little girl's face was flattened against the window. Probably the child tried in vain to see into the dark courtroom. No one came or went through the door. The jurors waited for the woman to do something, but she acted as if the whole matter had nothing to do with her.

It occurred to me that she may have walked those steps so many times, walked them in her thoughts. Across the room to the door, down the stone steps to the lawn, through the gate to the gravel road. Perhaps she believed they didn't even exist any longer except in her imagination.

"Go now; it's time to go," I said, somewhat disappointed. I had expected something other than this; open joy, or at least a sign of relief.

"It's over; do you understand?" I asked.

"Yes," she answered. "Of course."

Outside, a child began to cry. Probably not hers, but the sound made an impression. She took a couple of steps as if testing, and when she saw no one tried to stop her, she walked quickly to the door.

Then, after that, nothing. The case was closed, except for the clean white pages that waited to be filled. The reconcilers of mistakes, immaculate arms that would, at long last, release me from evil. I would become empty, they full. The sacrifice, amends, and redemption! I thought.

I didn't take the shortest way home. I wasn't in that much of a hurry to get to my desk. The horse could stand under the cliffs where it smelled of fish nets and yews.

Seeing it from above, the sea at the foot of the cliffs looked like a large velvet blanket with silver bands glistening in its folds. Further down on the shore something moved. In the early spring Torsten had killed a black wolf. He said it was a cross between a dog and a wolf. More vicious than an ordinary wild beast, he said. The dog in it wasn't afraid to approach a human being, and the wolf in it wasn't averse to killing. And perhaps it had difficulties reconciling the two aspects within itself. The conflict of wills made it a monster, or so Torsten thought.

Something moved down there while I was sitting on the cliff, and I remembered the wolf the field-hand had killed. It had had hoarfrost on its snout, transparent ice pellets in its fur that had chimed when the carcass was carried home. Where would such an animal have come from to these islands? Over the ice, or had it been born here? Why hadn't the dog been too frightened of the wolf to mate with it?

"I hope you don't mind if I join you without an invitation!" Kjellinus called out and came from behind the hawthorns. His face was sweaty after the climb.

"Of course not," I answered, "only a dog comes when called...."

There was nothing within sight out on the sea, no boats, no men, not even birds.

"Did you come to push me off?" I asked.

Kjellinus took off his shoe and shook it without haste. The wind took the sand and needles and carried them over the cliff.

"Of course I don't understand that kind of hysterical outburst born out of regret," he said. "I don't understand why you insisted on embarrassing yourself."

"I have decided to write a full explanation of the whole legal process concerning witches no matter how much you threaten me," I said.

Kjellinus put his shoe back on the foot which, without it, had looked as orphaned as a snail without its shell. "You ought to cut down on your drinking," he answered laconically.

I looked out to the sea, he towards the valley. I waited for him to mention it: all this is yours if ... Or at least make nasty references to what would happen to my family if I didn't ...

"The choir practice has come to an end," he announced after fumbling with his shoe for a while. "Because of a couple of boys; their voices are starting to change, it can't be helped, they're at that age," he explained.

"That's too bad," I said, perplexed.

I didn't regret of course what had happened. What else is music but the means to lie beautifully? It has nothing to do with life, which is confusing, unexplainable, and boring. By what right do composers search and find implied meanings in useless works? With what special license do they gild painful existence?

"What do we need moving chorales for?" I asked.

Kjellinus smiled. "To move us," he answered.

"I don't want to be moved," I said.

"Yes you do," he insisted, "you just happen to have chosen drinking."

"I'm not a drunk," I said, hurt. Kjellinus stood up.

"People long so intensely to be moved that they do all kinds of laughable things because of it," he said.

"Such as?"

"Such as falling in love!" he answered.

The dusk got thicker very quickly. With it, soil would become ash, hay the hair of the dead, pebbles turn to nail fragments. I longed for the winecellar door's comforting squeak.

"If you want to destroy your reputation and your position by making ridiculous confessions, I guess it's time for me to do you a favour in return by destroying the pages," Kjellinus said.

"Return what favour?" I asked.

We started to go down the slope. He wanted to sanctify our lies so that we lived long and prospered on this island. He probably believed he was only protecting his fold, creating discipline and order for it. Mistakes, dreams and visions were like a broken-down fence that led the poor creatures gone wild to their destruction.

"You did destroy Ingeborg O.'s notes, did you not?" he asked.

"What notes?" I asked, and let out an arrogant laugh.

"Those pitiful pages where she confessed she had fallen in love with me," Kjellinus answered.

Butterflies were fluttering around the horse, white, restless, blind dancers. It was spring, one mustn't forget that. Just as one mustn't forget pain or death.

"I value that as the deed of a friend, although the legality of what you did is debatable," he said.

"What do you mean?"

He, for his part, couldn't grasp what there was to understand in any of it. Surely I hadn't for a moment been so naive as to imagine that the torturer the woman mentioned in her notes was actually the Devil? Surely I ought to have understood that it had been a plot to make the foolish woman lose her head. How would the witch otherwise have found pen and paper? For what other reason would such paraphernalia have found their way into the cell of a hardened criminal, but for her to sign her death sentence with? "A man will fall for anything when a woman starts unbuttoning her blouse; a woman when a man pretends to be baring his soul."

"She and you! Is that true?" I asked. There were butterflies everywhere around us. I tried to get hold of them, but they cleverly got out of the way. Somewhere in the distance a dog on a leash barked.

"When you didn't arrange an investigation into the matter of the writing material, but went into the cell yourself to destroy it, I realized you were on my side. Why did you start making a mess of things later on? You will surely still need an interrogator who has a sense of the criminal's weaker points. I insist that with the aid of only the Provost and the thumbscrews we won't get very far," Kjellinus answered.

I got into the carriage. I no longer asked or said anything. Perhaps it was his way of punishing me, taking revenge by inventing lies. One thing was certain, I would never find out the truth about him. Not even with thumbscrews.

"You'll destroy what you've already written yourself, isn't that so?" he called after me.

I thought of Margreta H. How, exhibiting astonishing self-discipline, she had walked out of the courtroom as if out of her own home to her chores outdoors. How she would take the baby into her arms the same way, the youngest and the next youngest, as if after any ordinary separation. I didn't believe she would even cry.

The horse ran fast; it knew it was on its way home. Darkness fell. For the first time I wasn't afraid of the dark; light is most visible when it's really dark.

And I had no reason to complain. Only a moment ago I had possessed nothing. Now I had hatred. It filled me the way love had, and equally as well as longing.

I took a deep breath of the spring air. How could I have thought I might, by writing, by making a confession, cleanse the human being from me, the slave?

Only another human being could do that by holding you down to remove the skin and, having done that, caring and being tender towards you until a new slave skin had grown, a skin that must be torn off again.

If you accepted suffering as the building material of the world, you had to learn to know it.

That is how I have been paying back my debt. Day by day, year by year. Lived on behalf of those who were not allowed to live. Guilt is not yet wiped away, but a day will come when it has shrunk and is as small and light as a feather.

Then I will take it on the palm of my hand and blow it away. It will disappear with the wind and I will be no more.

All this I, the Circuit Court Judge, Nils Psilander, swear happened the way I have told it, without any additions to or omissions from the truth. May it be so enshrined.

ॐ

*J*UST A MOMENT, JUDGE! You haven't told everything. Who tore the pages out of the court records?

— You can't disappear just like that, do you hear? You have possessed me for months, got me up in the middle of the night, confused my thinking, tortured my innocent family.

— Judge?

— First of all, the intention was not that you would start drinking and explaining the imaginings of a paranoiac. Why didn't you bear your guilt like a man? The innocent already have innumerable saints to protect them, a long, boring row of martyrs, but the guilty don't have a single one. Why wouldn't you take that crown to bear?

— Why do you disappear just now when we have started to get along comfortably? Your dry humour, that cleared the way for you to reach me, pleased me. I'm not without humour myself, though perhaps you thought I might be.

What is this haze in the middle of which we've been made to walk, walk and meet shapes whose familiarity we can never be certain of? In moments of dawn like these, I am painfully aware that life flows slowly towards its exit, and I've understood nothing about the scenery and people that have flashed by me.

Am I a time game that functions according to predetermined and already known rules? Is my soul filled with the sad desolation of events calculated beforehand? Is it that, specifically, that I see when standing on the seashore?

— Judge, I'm looking for an answer! You were supposed to give me an answer.

(I can hear music from downstairs. How strange, in the middle of the night. I listen carefully. It's a child crying, not music. I have to go downstairs now, for a moment, but Judge, if you're still around, don't go quite yet!

This time it's the oldest one, my four-year-old. He isn't thirsty, nor does he need to go to the bathroom. He can't say why he feels like crying. Perhaps he had a bad dream? He can't say, but he wants me to hold his hand till he's asleep again....)

There's someone walking along the beach. The sea is neither stormy nor calm. The scenery is a state of the soul and this view has to be somewhat dark without being depressing. It's dawn, the sun might rise at any moment. There's a light wind from the sea.

— What is your judgement? Is he but a trifle without a will created by someone nameless? (It is possible ... a child's hand in the hand of an adult can make you think all sorts of things.) Had I given him a life for no good reason, do you suppose? ... it's possible....

It's possible that the sea wouldn't exist without someone on the shore. That it would surge, rise, fall, ripple, tear at its underwater plants millions of years unnecessarily, without being seen or heard in the night of nonexistence.

Standing on the shore he looks ridiculous because of his small size, particularly if he imagines himself able to defy the endless masses of water. But precisely for that reason, he is their creator.

It is possible there's room in him for hundreds more contradictions than in the bastardized mixture of hound and wolf.

— Murderer and victim, Judge. A peculiar reconcilia-
tion, seen from your point of view. But in addition,
there are thousands of others. Or ten, fifteen, twenty to
the thousandth power.

— Does it not evoke in you a will to return? So many
things remained unclear, without answers.

— In cruelty you were excessive, and you lacked tenderness. You couldn't find more suitable sentiments for
your epitaph. If you thought your story would change
something, you were wrong. I guess you tried to show
that the existence of evil doesn't mean the absence of
goodness, that it is precisely the moral pursuit to elimi-
nate evil that gives birth to goodness. But all that does-
n't quite manage to touch me, it no longer seems
important....

To be wise like a snake and kind like a dove, but to be
a human being, nevertheless!

— Judge?

There is, before me, a semi-cloudy inlet of the sea. It
is neither stormy nor calm. This is not one of those days
when the sea is on the attack, but neither is it one when
it timidly approaches the shore. No, scenery is a state of
the soul and this view must be grey and somewhat
gloomy, but not entirely without hope.

$\backsim$